LIFE BEGINS AT THE CORNISH COTTAGE

KIM NASH

Boldwood

First published in Great Britain in 2025 by Boldwood Books Ltd.

Copyright © Kim Nash, 2025

Cover Design by JD Smith Design Ltd.

Cover Images: Shutterstock

A CIP catalogue record for this book is available from the British Library.

Paperback ISBN 978-1-83561-390-0

Large Print ISBN 978-1-83561-389-4

Hardback ISBN 978-1-83561-388-7

Trade Paperback ISBN 978-1-80656-052-3

Ebook ISBN 978-1-83561-391-7

Kindle ISBN 978-1-83561-392-4

Audio CD ISBN 978-1-83561-383-2

MP3 CD ISBN 978-1-83561-384-9

Digital audio download ISBN 978-1-83561-385-6

This book is printed on certified sustainable paper. Boldwood Books is dedicated to putting sustainability at the heart of our business. For more information please visit https://www.boldwoodbooks.com/about-us/sustainability/

Boldwood Books Ltd, 23 Bowerdean Street, London, SW6 3TN

www.boldwoodbooks.com

To all of my friends who have lost the other half of your heart.
To Lisa B, to Jane P, to Lynne R, to Sara D, to Rebecca C. You've all
been through things that you never thought you'd have to endure and
you've shown such unbelievable strength and resilience. Your
husbands would be so incredibly proud of all that you have achieved.
You are amazing!
This one is for you!
Xxx

1

Two years ago I lost two things. One was my husband. The other was myself. I must be really careless because as if that wasn't enough, while out for lunch one day with my friends, I also lost my dignity.

Time stood still and a chill ran down my spine when I came out of the ladies' toilets of The Fisherman's Haunt and saw who Michelle and Jo were talking to. Someone that without a shadow of a doubt I would have recognised anywhere despite it being donkeys' years since I saw him last. His stature hadn't changed one bit. Those broad shoulders and muscular forearms, his tall, athletic frame upright and formal. Sometimes a particular memory of a person who was so deeply embedded in your head never goes away. Of all the days in the year, why did he have to pick this particular one to visit the same restaurant as me?

His head turned in my direction and he pointed towards the toilets. Oh, my! Surely he wasn't coming this way. This couldn't be happening. My heart started to pump like mad and I furtively ducked behind the nearest pillar to try to work out my next course of action. As I glanced round, I noticed that the doors to the kitchen were right behind me and might possibly be my only escape route. I risked the chance and peeked out from behind the pillar and took another look. He was still talking to Jo and Michelle and I could hear them both giggling, far higher pitched than normal. Bloody traitors. Give them a good-looking man, and they were putty in his hands.

Jo spotted me, caught my eye and waved me over, raising her voice.

'Emma. Are you OK?'

I darted even further behind the pillar, commando-style. My back flat against the wall, I realised that I had two choices. I could either put on my big-girl pants, take a deep breath, be brave and go out there and face the music, pretending I was totally holding it together. Or I could push open the kitchen doors and make an excuse as to why I was there, hoping that they had a back entrance I could leave through. Then I could text the girls to let them know I'd had to leave suddenly, hoping that I'd had a lucky escape without him knowing anything about it. After all, these escapades work in the films so I couldn't imagine why this wasn't a perfectly viable option.

While I dithered about my decision, I heard footsteps coming my way from the main restaurant floor. I panicked. As I burst through the kitchen door, which to my horror was one of those swing-both-ways doors, there was an almighty crash and I walked directly into the path of a poor unsuspecting waiter who was reversing through.

I'm sure that the pained yowl he made could have been heard from outer space. The two plates that he'd been carrying in his hands, along with the one that had been balancing on his arm, dropped and smashed on the floor. I apologised profusely to the poor lad, who looked like he was going to burst into tears. As I completely lost my balance, I felt myself heading south and promptly hit the deck too. We both watched in slow-motion alarm as roast beef, upside-down Yorkshire puddings, roast pota-toes, carrots and parsnips landed half on me and half on him and bright green garden peas were jet-propelled across the floor. Dark brown gravy was dribbling down my white linen trousers and his startled little teenage face glared at me, I wasn't sure whether in surprise, disgust or just plain horror.

'Woah! What the hell is going on here and more's the point, what the hell are you doing in my kitchen? Back to work, every-one. Show's over.' A tall, imposing man in chef's whites stood over me. 'Did you not see the sign on the wall which said staff only?' This must have been the head chef whose authoritative voice was getting louder the nearer he got to me. I looked over my shoulder quickly towards the door which, thank heavens, had closed behind us both and gave a rather loud sigh at the same time as the teenager piped up.

'Clearly not. She's a flipping mad woman. A proper mentalist!'

'That's enough, Harvey. Go and get a dustpan and brush and the mop and bucket from the store cupboard and we'll plate some more food up.'

I shook out my normally perfectly coiffured hair. As I reached up to smooth it down, I realised that I'd just wiped the mashed potato which I didn't realise was on my hand through it. Was the day able to get any worse? I took a deep breath as I realised that I needed to style it out and offered my hand to the chef.

'Hello... Do you think you could help me up, please?' I didn't know whether to laugh or cry. This would probably have been quite hilarious had it been happening to someone else.

The corner of his mouth twitched as he reached down and pulled me up to standing.

'Are you hurt?' he asked.

'Only my pride! I'm honestly so very sorry,' I replied.

'Bad day?' He took a tea towel from the work surface to his left and handed it to me. He looked younger than I originally thought he was now I was closer to him.

'Thank you.' I wiped at the rich gravy that was seeping into my trousers, making it look even worse and like I'd had a bout of diarrhoea. 'You wouldn't believe me if I tried to explain.'

'Suppose you want to get let out the fire escape then? I presume this *was* an escape plan. Bad date, maybe?' He grinned.

'Something like that. Can I help you clear up first? Pay for the damage? I really am sorry.' I reached down for my bag and realised that I'd left it at the dining table. A deflated sigh left my body and a tear rolled down my face.

'Don't worry about it, my love. Let's just call it training. Poor lad has only just started today and his nerves were in tatters anyway, so it's always good to get something thrown at him this early. He might think twice before walking through the wrong side of the door now. Good practice, really. So maybe I should be thanking you.'

I looked towards the restaurant area as another member of staff came through into the kitchen. He was very intuitive, for a man.

'Is your bag in there?' He nodded towards the door.

'Yeah, with my friends.'

'Want to go and get it?'

Frantically I shook my head. 'Christ, no! I can't go back out there.'

'Want me to get it for you?' he asked.

'I couldn't ask you to do that.'

'You didn't. I offered.' This man might just have been my guardian angel.

'You're very kind. I'm not sure if this had happened in reverse that I'd have been so... well, you know... understanding.'

'You have a nice face. Besides, my mum always taught me that you have no idea of what is going on in someone's mind, so you should always be nice. Kindness costs nothing. Now tell me where your friends are sitting. Do you want me to give them a message?'

'They're sat at the table in the bay window that looks over the sea. Could you tell them that I'm going to go home, please? Oh, and I'm Emma, by the way. Emma Montgomery.' I reached out my hand again and this time he shook it.

'Martin. One sec, Emma.' He headed out the door. The left door, not the right one. He winked at Harvey, who was now cleaning up the mess. The poor lad. I felt so guilty at what I'd put him through.

A minute later the opposite door swung open and Martin walked back through swinging my pale blue Michael Kors handbag and handed it to me.

'I told them you weren't feeling well and were having a sit down in here before going home. Offered them their meals for free and they're just having a pudding.'

'Oh, wow! Will you not get into trouble with the owner?'

'Ah, well, I'm married to the co-owner, and I'm the other one so I think we'll be OK. Do you want a minute while you gather yourself?'

I nodded. 'Yes, please, if that's OK. Was there anyone with them? A man, maybe?'

'There was. Grey-haired; beardy; sporty type. Sun-tanned too. Good-looking, I suppose, if you like that sort of thing. Tom, I think I heard them call him. He was sitting at their table.' I couldn't work out whether his face was about to break into a grin, or whether he just had a naturally smiley face. But the thing that was puzzling me more than anything was why on earth was Tom Sullivan sitting at the same table as my friends?

At least I'd done the right thing by disappearing into the kitchen even if it didn't work out quite as well as I'd planned. He would still have been there when I came out of the loo and I really wasn't ready to face him.

'Is there anything I can do to thank you, Martin?' I felt like I owed this man something for his kindness.

'You can put us a great review on Tripadvisor if you like. That's worth its weight in gold to be honest. And a review on social media too if you have time. We're new in the area and need all the help that we can get.'

'I can definitely do that and I can tell everyone how fabulous you are. The meal was divine, by the way. Thank you, Martin. I won't forget how kind you've been.'

He mock-bowed to me. 'You're welcome, Emma. Door at the back takes you out to the car park. Take care now and do come back and eat with us again soon.'

As I walked towards the rear of the kitchen, I slipped a folded twenty-pound note into Harvey's hand and he stared at me in amazement as I apologised again and left the building.

Martin walked back to the kitchen counter and shouted over, laughing, 'Emma! I hope the nasty man you were hiding from never finds you.'

I hoped the same thing very much. I couldn't actually believe that after all this time, *he* had ended up in Sandpiper Shore.

'So come on then. Why did you mysteriously disappear when you saw that the lovely Tom was at our table? Dish the dirt!' Michelle handed me a mojito as we sat on the terrace to where she'd summoned me on their return. At times, she could be incredibly impatient and when I first met her it grated on me a little, but I realised that we all have quirks and people who truly loved you accepted them instead of trying to change them. I did love these girls dearly, even though I hadn't known them for a very long period of time.

Michelle and I both lived in properties on Jo's land and the terrace outside of Jo's gorgeous recently refurbished cottage was where we came together every Friday for cocktails, otherwise known as 'cocks on Friday'. The sun was just setting over Sandpiper Shore and we sat looking out over the sand dunes to the beach beyond where the sea twinkled in the distance. Our once-weekly early evenings had become a sacred ritual, and a therapy session for the soul. I always felt like I could take on the world when I spent time with these two inspiring women.

I looked out to sea. Since I'd got back, I'd got so many

thoughts swirling around my head. Tom was someone who, along with all the feelings and emotions that were stirred up if I did think about him, I'd shut in a box, never to surface again. That's the trouble with boxes though. The lids can always be prised open.

'You're making it all so mysterious that you will have to spill the beans now.' Jo put her hand on my arm. 'Surely you know by now that you can trust us both?'

Maybe these feelings that were churning inside me now *would* be better if they were out in the open. They always said a problem shared was a problem halved. But once the Tom box was open, could I close it again?

I hid my face behind my hands.

'Promise you won't laugh.'

'Of course we won't laugh. Well, we'll try not to, won't we, Chelle?' Jo giggled. 'I'm only joking, Em. We won't. We promise.'

When I took my hands away from my face, I noticed that Michelle had her fingers crossed. She laughed and uncrossed them as soon as she saw me clock this.

Blurting it out seemed to be the only way to stop me dithering. 'We were in a play together.'

This time it was Jo's eyes that showed surprise.

'*A play*? What sort of play?'

'*Romeo and Juliet*, if you must know.' I put my glass down on the table in front of me and folded my arms defensively.

'When was this?' Jo asked, her eyebrows slowly returning to normal.

'When we were at college.' There, I'd said it now. 'That's it. Nothing more to tell.'

Jo and Michelle shared a look and Jo raised her eyebrows.

'Why the big fuss then? Why did you hide from him?'

'Oh, God, this is like the Spanish inquisition. You can stop interrogating me, you know.' I laughed. I loved them both dearly, but they were so persistent at times.

'Absolutely not until you tell us the truth. Come on, Emma, we do know you and we also know that you wouldn't have done what you did today for someone you were just,' she made air quotes, 'in a play with.' Michelle was right, they did know me and could see straight through me.

'What are you not telling us?' Jo asked.

I shrugged my shoulders and took a deep breath.

'We were together.'

Michelle's eyes widened. '*Together*, together?'

I sighed again. 'Well, so I thought.'

My mind drifted back to my time at college. I was a naïve seventeen-year-old who had met Tom and fallen head over heels.

'I thought we were in love. He clearly didn't. That's the end of the story really.' Reaching for my glass, I took a big swig and gulped as it caught the back of my throat, making me cough.

'And...'

'That's it,' I replied.

Jo raised her eyebrows at me, knowingly.

'OK. Will you stop asking about it if I tell you the whole truth? And again, you need to promise not to laugh.'

'Maybe...' replied Michelle, grinning.

'I can't promise...'

I batted Jo with the nearest cushion. While I knew they were jesting, it was through kindness. They wanted sharing to feel lighter for me. They had been such good friends. So I decided to tell them the truth.

I took another deep breath and ploughed straight back in.

'I was an army child, as I'm sure I mentioned before, and didn't make friends easily. We moved around from one place to another and never really put down any firm roots. I was always the new kid and I didn't put any effort into making friends because as soon as I did, we'd move again, so there wasn't much point. It just hurt too much if I formed attachments.' I swallowed as there was a lump looming in my throat which was in danger of going either way, while talking about these memories. Luckily, it went away.

'Mum and Dad were both strict parents. It wasn't the greatest childhood, to be honest, even though I know they loved me in their own way. But the one thing I adored doing more than anything in the world was amateur dramatics so after school I went to drama college to study performing arts. I loved acting because I could be someone else, someone completely different. I didn't really like myself at that time of my life, to be honest.'

'Gosh, that must have been tough. I've never really thought about how it might be for the child of an army family.' Jo's expression was sad.

Michelle looked surprised. 'I can't even think about you like that, Emma. You always seem so full of confidence with your shit together. You've gobsmacked me.'

This was one of the reasons why I never really told anyone. I didn't want their pitying looks.

'Tom and I were chosen to do the lead roles in *Romeo and Juliet*. We practised together outside of college. He came to my house when Mum and Dad were away and I went to his. His parents were very different to mine. They were lovely.' I smiled as I remembered Mrs Sullivan and how she always used to bake the most delicious cakes and send me home with food parcels. And Mr Sullivan used to either make sure that Tom walked me home, or he would give me a lift.

'Tom and I became close. I really liked him. He was the only real friend I'd ever had. After weeks of spending tons of time together as friends, we became even closer still; we kissed and it was wonderful.' I stared out to sea, remembering my very first kiss. It was dreamy; his tender lips; the feeling that it gave me in my heart.

'So, you snogged his face off and then what?' Michelle sat forward in her chair, eagerly waiting for more. 'Give us the juicy part of the story.'

I smiled, my mind drifting to another place, another time.

'We spent a whole summer together and I thought he liked me as much as I liked him. That we were boyfriend and girlfriend. I was a seventeen-year-old girl with a body full of raging hormones and a jumble of emotions. The night before the play we were rehearsing and when he kissed me, I told him I loved him. He told me he loved me back. We planned to do the play and because my parents were away on the night of the play and couldn't come, he was going to stop over at mine for the first time and we were going to, you know...'

'Oooh, nice!' Michelle grinned.

'On the day of the play I overheard someone at school, a girl called Julie Cartwright, talking about me. She had been a bully all the way through school, and even though I was only there a year she made mine and lots of other girls' lives a misery. She continued to behave the same way through college and that day she walked onto the stage set and told everyone that he only spent time with me because he felt sorry for me. Said everyone called me "Fatty", including him, and that they laughed at me because I had no friends. Then she said that he'd been seeing her behind my back. She and all her friends ridiculed me. They said I was a total fool to believe that he actually liked me. Told me I made myself look stupid in front of everyone. It was mortifying.'

'The bitchbag!' Michelle spat.

'I bloody hate Julie Cartwright already. Does she still live around here? Let's go and find her and duff her up! And her friends too,' Jo scoffed.

I laughed despite how I was feeling. It was good to know that these two had my back even though they never knew the person they were slagging off.

'So, what did you do?' Michelle asked. 'I hope you got in a scrap and beat the shit out of her.'

I gave a short, sharp laugh.

'I asked Tom if it was true. He'd said he loved me so I asked him again – in front of everyone in the play. He was dumbstruck; just stood and looked at me with his mouth hanging open. I was mortified that he couldn't answer and I ran off.' Even just thinking about this all these years later was reminding me of what a terrible time it had been for me. 'After licking my wounds for a couple of days, I ducked out of the lead role position. Julie took it over, in fact.'

'Yeah, I bet she did.' I laughed at the bitter way Jo said this.

'They were obviously an item, and I just hadn't seen it. From that day on, they were inseparable. Instead of doing the lead role, I became the stage director and distanced myself from both of them and ignored him if he tried to talk to me. I suddenly gained loads of new friends, probably because I divvied up all the parts out and found that I was better at that side of things anyway. The play was a huge success and I was always the person who organised the college plays after that, until I left. Anyway, it was all such a very long time ago. I'm well over it now,' I explained.

'Clearly! And that's why you hid in the kitchen at the restaurant and didn't want Tom to see you.' Michelle frowned. 'You can't spend your life hiding when times get tough, you know.'

She leaned across and rubbed my arm. 'You're too bloody fabulous to hide away!'

'That's very kind of you to say. I was just surprised to see him, that's all. Last I heard he'd got married to Julie and they'd had a daughter. I just wasn't prepared to see him. Anyway, how do you even know him?' I asked, needing to divert the conversation from me for a while.

'I don't but I met him in the mini market recently. We both went for the last loaf of fresh bread in the bakery aisle and he let me have it. When he saw us in the restaurant, he came over to say hello on his way to the loo. I thought he was a right dish. If I didn't have Demetri, I might have even had a go myself,' Michelle explained.

'Had a go?' Jo laughed. 'You are funny, Chelle. I'm surprised you recognised him after all those years, Emma. I thought he was rather lovely, to be honest.' Jo hugged her arms to her chest. 'Dreamy, in fact. Totally charming.'

'I'd recognise him anywhere. He hasn't changed at all apart from the grey hair and a few more wrinkles. Not that I looked that much, obviously.'

Michelle and Jo shared a look that I'm sure they thought I hadn't noticed.

'Anyway, it all worked out for the best in the end. I went on to meet Ben and realised that what I thought was love that I felt for Tom was just a stupid teenage crush and didn't mean a thing. True love was what Ben and I had. So, don't be fooled by his charm. A leopard never changes their spots. Anyway. Like I said, I don't want to give him the time of day.'

Another look passed between my friends.

'Anyway, I wanted your thoughts on some of the Lonely Hearts Club events I'd been thinking about. Can we chat about that instead, please?'

I'd had the idea to set up the Lonely Hearts Club, knowing how difficult it was to make friends. The three of us had all found ourselves single for differing reasons and it's blooming hard to do stuff when you're on your own. If it wasn't for meeting Michelle and Jo, I think I would have hibernated for the rest of my life. We'd formed a club locally and there'd been a few events so far, including coffee mornings, lunches and evening meals out, a theatre trip and we'd even muted the idea of a holiday. It was very early days and I had so many plans to make it bigger and better and not let people who were really lonely feel even worse because they hadn't got someone to do things with.

Michelle suddenly jumped up out of her seat, startling us.

'Let's talk about those tomorrow over coffee. Go and get yourselves spruced up again. We're going back out. I've got a surprise for you!'

'Oh, Michelle, surely you know by now that I hate surprises.'

'Yeah, I know, Emma, but you need to lighten up a little and trust your friends. You're going to love this one. It'll cheer you right up and make you forget all about Tom.'

3

I groaned loudly as we approached The Smuggler's Rest and saw the sign outside the entrance.

'Ah, no! You do realise that this is my worst nightmare and not fun for me, don't you? I'm pretty sure we've had this conversation before.'

'Oh, give over. I thought you also said you loved a performance. If you can perform, then surely you must be able to sing and dance too.' It felt like Michelle didn't know me at all. This was one of my all-time fears.

'Michelle, I am not getting up to sing in the karaoke. It's just not for me.'

'All right, Em, keep your knickers on.' Jo grinned at me and then realised when she saw my straight face that I wasn't finding this at all funny. 'Emma, love. You need to shake off your inhibitions and live a little. Nobody cares if you're fabulous or awful. It's all about the taking part.'

This was bringing back all my worst memories. All my life, and probably since I'd been publicly humiliated by Julie and her mates, I had worried about what people thought of me. Despite being able to hold a tune, I had never sung karaoke and wouldn't be starting now.

'Come on in anyway, you can watch us instead. Let's go and get a G&T. It's all for a good cause.' Jo grabbed my arm and guided me towards the door.

'You go, girls, I'll go home. I just don't fancy it.'

'It's for the local air ambulance, Emma. I know it's a charity that you support.' Michelle stood with her hands on her hips, knowing that she'd played her trump card although she wouldn't have known the impact that her words would have had on me, because she never knew me then.

My mind drifted back to the worst day of my life. When my husband Ben had his heart attack, we'd been at home eating sausage and mash for tea and Ben started gasping for breath, holding his arm and turning a very funny shade of red. When I ran out into the street screaming, one of the neighbours called for an ambulance. My nearest neighbour Kelly, who we'd lived next door to for over twenty years and was a midwife, had tried to resuscitate him before a paramedic car swiftly arrived and took over. An air ambulance arrived in what was probably just a few minutes but at the time felt like hours.

I remembered tightly clutching the arm of the kind female paramedic. 'Save my husband; please save my husband.' She released my arm from hers and took my hands, looking directly in my eyes to ensure I understood what she was saying. She said that they were doing all that they could, that they had a tube down his throat to breathe for him and would come back and update me as soon as they knew any more.

When the paramedic returned, informing me that they were incredibly sorry, Kelly held me in her arms as I slumped. There was nothing more they could do for him, they said. He'd gone.

I remembered that a ridiculous thought went through my head and the poor air ambulance paramedic must have thought me a complete lunatic when I became completely fixated on the fact that I'd insisted we had sausages for dinner. I explained to her in great detail that he wanted us to have liver despite the fact I never liked it. Said it was good for me. I was hysterical about the fact that I shouldn't have dug my feet in. If I'd known it would be his last-ever meal, I would have cooked the liver. They said that I was in shock and Kelly in her soft Irish accent told me to sit down, drink the hot sweet tea she'd made me and 'for Pete's sake stop worrying about the fecking sausages!'

Michelle's voice jolted me back to the present.

'Emma! Are you coming in or not?' she asked, her hands on her hips. Jo had already gone ahead.

I let out a loud exasperated gasp and held up my index finger.

'One drink. And then I'm going home.'

* * *

The Smuggler's Rest was in full swing and as there were hardly any tables left we had to sit by the makeshift stage. Michelle and Jo were like two excitable teenagers, and put their name down on the sing sheet, not revealing what they'd chosen. It didn't matter. I was only stopping for one anyway.

Our local vicar and his wife, Graham and Tina Lockheart, were on the table next to us and there really must have been something in the local water because they were also in full-on hyper-enthusiastic mode. They had been in the village for over five years and had managed to increase the size of the congregation dramatically since they arrived with their acceptance of anyone and everyone. There was also an understanding that you could come and go to their church as often or as little as you pleased with no pressure whatsoever.

The most amazing couple – kind, compassionate, gentle, and approachable – they both had a knack of making you feel that you were the most special person in the world and gave their time in abundance. I had been so grateful when Graham had agreed to give the Lonely Hearts Club the church hall free of charge one night a month as their gesture of goodwill, in the hopes of getting the community to bond even further. They hoped it would be a good way to pull people in from the surrounding villages.

Graham had conducted the most life-affirming and intimate funeral service for Ben after his sudden death and his grave in the small churchyard was a place that I often visited when I needed to get some clarity in my life. Neither Graham nor Tina ever commented about how they'd see me sitting by my husband's grave talking out loud. Mostly I was berating him for leaving me so early in life. A life in which we had so much more to do together. We thought we had so much more time.

Sometimes, on the days at his graveside when I gave in to the tears, when grief hit me smack in the face, as if by magic Tina would emerge. She would rest a gentle hand on my shoulder, warmth flooding throughout my body, neither of us needing to share a single word, before she double tapped and left me as quietly as she appeared. Every single time this happened I felt better from her healing hands. She seemed to know exactly what I needed in that very moment. There were other times when I was in a funk, that Graham would tell me a joke, something silly and childlike, but it always made me laugh and lifted my spirits. Just being in their calming presence made me feel like not only a valued member of their parish but also a very good friend.

Between them, they had helped me more times than they would ever know.

However, when Graham, who I'd only then noticed was wearing jeans, a band T-shirt and a leather jacket, stood up and gave the most amazing rendition of Meatloaf's 'Bat Out of Hell', really going for it, headbanging away, I had never been so flabbergasted. When Tina joined him in a long and high bouffant wig, handed him a cowboy hat and they belted out their version of 'Islands in the Stream', they had the audience eating out of their hands. The coins and notes which were being thrown into the air ambulance collection buckets were filling up nicely.

'Right, we're on! You coming to join us, Em?' Michelle jumped up and grabbed Jo's hand and I shook my head vigorously.

'Ah, come on! It'll be a laugh,' Jo shouted back and I literally crawled back within myself at the thought of being up there, me singing in front of everyone. The fear of people laughing at me was the reason I'd never involved myself in this bonkers pastime that people seemed to absolutely love. Why would anyone put themselves through that?

They literally sounded like a cat's chorus with their very 'special' version of 'I Will Survive'. They were truly awful but it seemed that the worse the singers were, the more the audience loved it. They were given a rapturous round of applause before returning to our table.

Michelle flung herself back in her seat, laughing.

'I enjoyed that so much! You don't know what you're missing out on, Emma.'

'I honestly do! It's just not for me. I wish I could be more carefree sometimes but I just can't bring myself to look daft in front of anyone.'

'Maybe you need therapy for that,' Jo replied, grabbing her gin glass and taking a large gulp. 'I bet you've missed out on loads of amazing stuff in your life because you didn't want to look foolish.'

When I thought back to the times that I had said no to things, because I wasn't sure what people would think, there was a list as long as my arm. Ben always liked me to be calm and collected, not to make a fool of myself. Opportunities to have fun had passed me by several times. Like when his family had invited us to a water park and I didn't want my hair to look a mess and didn't want to be sitting around in wet clothes so I had sat on the sidelines and watched with him instead, missing out on all the enjoyment.

'Coming to dance, Em?' Michelle held out her hand to me as she and Jo got up on the dance floor.

I shook my head. I loved to dance too, but only when I was at home, alone. No one needed to see me strut my stuff in public. Someone had once told me I looked ridiculous when I danced and it had never left me.

It hadn't really struck me until now and made me sad to think that I cared so much about what people thought; that my friends were right and that I had missed out. People don't realise the impact that words make. A throwaway comment can stick in your mind for a lifetime and permanently hinder your confidence.

Trouble was, when over half of my life was already behind me, I didn't think that I could ever change. Once more, here I was, sitting alone, while everyone else had shaken off their inhibitions and were having fun.

I was busy contemplating this while staring into my third gin and tonic of the night, despite me saying I was only stopping for one, when the vicar flung himself into the seat next to me. He'd suddenly gone from being a grinning bundle of fun on stage, to a frowning face of misery.

'Are you OK, Graham?' I asked.

'I'd love to say yes but I'm not. I hate to admit that I have a huge problem,' he replied.

4

Michelle and Jo returned from the dance floor, laughing and grabbing their drinks. Tina joined her husband and immediately batted him on the arm.

'I hope you're not bothering this lovely lady with our problems, Graham. I told you that the headbanging was too much. You need to get your breath back too and rest like the doctor told you to. Then we'll talk and try to get things sorted out.'

'Are you poorly?' I asked. He had gone rather a bright shade of puce.

'Oh, she's fussing for no reason. I'll be fine in a minute.'

'I most certainly am not, Graham Lockheart! If you don't listen to me and our GP, you're going to be dead and buried before we know it.' She looked at me, realising what she said with a grimace. 'Sorry, Emma. No offence intended.'

'None taken. We're your friends though and you've helped me enough times when I've been having a bad day, especially when Ben first died. If something is stressing you out, we might be able to help.'

Tina jumped in and answered on his behalf before he had chance to get a word in.

'I keep telling him to stop stressing about it. That if we let it percolate for long enough, there's an answer to every problem. He, of all people, should know this. He teaches this to others every day.'

'Yes, well, there's no answer coming to me on this. It's like this you see, girls.' I smiled, loving the way that he called us girls even though we were all in our fifties. 'We had a local amateur dramatics company coming in to do a production for Christmas. It was to raise funds for the air ambulance again. That's why we've put on this impromptu karaoke session tonight. If we don't raise more money, there's a very good chance that we can't fund the local air ambulance and we all know that in this little corner of Cornwall, it's very much needed.'

Michelle jumped in. 'Oh, yes, I saw that advertised on a poster outside the church hall. So, what's the problem?'

It was Tina's turn to complete the puzzle. 'They've pulled out with less than eight weeks to go. The company has folded so it can't go ahead. We're completely devastated. We'll have to refund the money for the tickets we've already sold. We'll have to let down all the little children who were looking forward to us having a local pantomime. And we'll not be able to raise the funds that we so much need.' She wiped away a stray tear.

Graham reached out to his wife and she wrapped her hand around his before he spoke.

'And I suppose you should probably also know that I'm having to see the GP regularly because he says I've got a heart issue. Says that I must eradicate as much stress in my life as I can. Or I might be very ill. Or worse.'

'Gosh, that's awful. I'm so sorry this has happened to you.' I hated seeing this wonderful couple look so worried. Only a few minutes ago, they looked like they were having a whale of a time. It just goes to show that you never know what people are going through and what myriad of burdens a brave face can disguise.

'Well, there's absolutely no need for you to worry! I reckon we have the perfect solution.' Michelle was swaying a little as all eyes landed on her. She couldn't hold her drink very well and was definitely a little bit tiddly. 'Emma can do it.'

I spat my drink out.

'What?'

'She was only saying earlier that she used to be the stage director at several productions and how much she loved doing it, weren't you, Em? It's the perfect solution.'

'Gosh, that? It was over thirty-five years ago at least. I could never do something like that these days.'

'Oh, Emma. Really?' Tina clutched her hand to her chest, ignoring the last few words I'd spoken entirely. 'That would be amazing. The answer to all our prayers. Literally. Graham, it's a miracle, don't you think?'

At that very moment, I was wishing that I wasn't such a people pleaser. Years ago, someone had given me the advice that no was a complete sentence. If someone asked you to do something and you didn't want to do it, the answer was just no. No explanation needed. Just no. Sadly, I had spent my life altering my own boundaries for others, ending up with me doing the things they wanted, rather than the things I wanted. I had tried to get better since I'd been on my own, but I still hadn't mastered the art completely.

Graham knelt by the chair next to me. 'Honestly, Emma, it would be amazing. I can imagine the faces on those little school children now when the curtains go up and they get their Christmas pantomime after all. Please say yes. It would mean the world to us all. You'd be saving Sandpiper Shore.'

Wow! No pressure whatsoever. A little voice in my head was pecking away at me.

Just say no, Emma. You've got this. It's just a tiny two-letter word. So easy to get out. Come on, girl. Say no! No! No! No!

I was ready to refuse. I just needed to take a deep breath and say the words, that I wasn't capable of it and didn't want to do it when Jo piped up.

'I mean! How can you possibly say no to a vicar with a dicky ticker?'

5

The next morning when I woke, my head was totally scrambled. I had been brave the night before and plucked up some courage. Not quite to say no, but I did say that I would have to think about it, in the hope that I might be able to come up with an excuse. I would try and help Graham and Tina find an alternative plan but nothing was coming to me. I lay and looked at the ceiling, racking my brain. Whenever I had an issue in the past, I'd always had Ben to talk it through with, but now, lying here in my king-sized bed alone, with a huge space next to me, I felt lonelier than ever. How had my life changed so much in the space of a couple of years?

When I moved out of the beautiful home where Ben and I had lived together, I wondered how I would feel? Would I regret leaving the place where we made all those memories?

However, I had decided that it was time for me to make memories of my own. If I could change anything, I would have him here by my side, but I couldn't. It was what it was and nothing could turn back the clock. The day of his heart attack was such a shock to me at the time that I don't think I absorbed what had happened and it was only recently that it had finally started to sink in.

I went through the first year of widowhood in an absolute daze, mostly numb and in total disbelief as to what had happened. The second year of grief had started off being even more brutal. Realisation hit on a day I sat wearing his dressing gown for the umpteenth time after spraying it with his after-shave and breathing in the scent of him, because I was petrified that I might forget what he smelt like. He was finally gone. I was alone and I had to make a new life for myself. I didn't have a choice in the matter. That was the day I started to box up his things and make in-roads into kick-starting a new life for myself. If I didn't, there would have been no one else to do it for me. I was angry at the world but didn't have anyone in particular to blame for taking away what I thought would be forever. Grief was raw and real.

Grief; such a small word for such a huge thing. Something that doesn't just change you. It shatters the life you had as well as the life you thought you were going to live. You have to rewrite your own story. Your dreams. Your priorities. Discover and create a whole new identity. You don't even know who you are any more without that hugely important person by your side.

All my life I had been plagued by things that I couldn't control. My parents moved from base to base, and I followed them around. At one point during my hormonal teenage years, I remember having a huge row with my mother and I yelled at her, raging that people in the forces shouldn't have children. I knew that it was a totally irrational statement even at the time, but sometimes it was the way I felt. While other people at school were in friendship groups – which were hard to infiltrate – I'd never felt more alone.

When I moved to college and Mum and Dad both retired, we

finally set down roots in Cornwall. And that was when I found a love for drama. All because of Mrs Dawes, my college teacher. A teacher like no other. Her passion was not only for her subject, drama, but also for the support and love that she poured into her students. She made me feel like I mattered. She was someone who finally believed in me and made me feel like I could take on the world.

When she asked me to take on the role of stage manager I had never taken anything more seriously. We cast the roles together and even the cool girls at school started to befriend me. It was only when Mrs Dawes pointed out that I should just be a little cautious, that my new friendships could influence my decision as to who would play the best lead part, that I realised I should maybe keep the cool girls at arm's length. That way I would not be disappointed when they didn't include me in things. She told me that you didn't need to earn friends. At the time, I didn't really believe her and over the years had questioned her thinking.

After throwing open the curtains of my bedroom and allowing the sun to stream in through the window, I quickly dressed in my running clothes. Then I leaned against the wall as I squashed my feet into my already laced-up trainers. Every time I did this I laughed to myself. An act of defiance against my father as he always told me that I had to unlace them. Because I was always so wary of him, I used to follow all his rules.

'Morning, Jo. Beautiful day.' I jogged on the spot and waved to Jo as she was pegging out bedclothes on the washing line. She lifted a hand in a return gesture and made a muffled sound, not able to speak properly as she had pegs wedged between her lips. 'Catch you later,' I called before heading towards the beach at the end of our garden.

As I ran along the sand, the salt spray in the air, I felt blessed to have this beautiful place literally on my doorstep.

Some would say it was by chance that Jo and I met. I believe that there's no such thing as coincidence and that you will always meet the people you are meant to meet.

When divorcee Jo inherited the house and needed to raise some cash, she was looking to sell some jewellery and furniture. I was helping Ben's brother Joseph out in their valuation business and I was able to guide her in the right direction. We both became friends with Michelle too, who was scoping out the area with a view to relocating. We all got on like a house on fire and when she mooted the idea of converting two of the properties in the grounds of her beautiful Cornish cottage and renting them out, I bit her hand off. It was time I had a fresh start. Michelle took the other property and the rest, as they say, is history. The three of us became the firmest of friends and I'd never felt closer to two people. These inspiring women came into my life when I needed them the most.

As I ran along the beach, my mind wandered to the pantomime production. Maybe it wouldn't hurt to pop into the church hall and speak to the vicar and try and talk him out of it. See if we could find another solution to his problems.

The only thing that was niggling at me was that churning feeling was back in my tummy. Excitement. I couldn't remember the last time I'd felt excited about anything. The last couple of years had been tough in so many ways and just the thought of finally having a project, something to get stuck into, was really starting to become a possibility. Lots of ideas swished around in my mind and when I returned home, I laughed as I saw Michelle snogging her boyfriend Demetri on the doorstep.

'Floozy!' I yelled across the garden.

'You're just jealous,' Michelle yelled back, grinning like the Cheshire Cat.

'Too bloody right I am. Jammy cow! Have you got a brother, Demetri?'

Demetri was a doctor at a hospital and we'd met him on a recent visit when Jo was convinced she was having a cardiac arrest and luckily it turned out that it was just a panic attack. Not that panic attacks aren't a real thing and serious too, but luckily it was nothing more serious. I didn't think I could cope with another person I loved being taken away so suddenly. He blushed as he waved and made a swift exit towards his shiny red sporty Audi and slammed the door. Michelle leant her head up against the door frame and she was frowning as she watched him drive away. She had clearly drifted off into a little world of her own. When she realised I was observing her, she gave a nervous little laugh.

'Fancy a coffee, Em?'

Coffee wasn't really what I usually had when I came back from a run, but I felt like the invitation was nothing to do with the drink, but about needing a little support from a friend.

'Would love one, mate, but I could really do with a quick shower first. Can you give me ten minutes?'

'Perfect, see you then.'

6

'So, it looks like it's all going well with Demetri then?' I asked Michelle as she poured coffee into three mugs and we sat in the chairs that overlooked the dunes.

'Well, it is... And he's totally and utterly lovely! Everything I should want in a man. But...'

'But what?' I couldn't help thinking that she looked a little forlorn and unsure of what she was going to say, but my hunch had been right and she did feel the need to talk.

'I don't know. I've been on my own for so long, I'm just not sure about throwing myself into a relationship, to be honest. What if I do all of that and get used to having him around and he dumps me anyway?' Michelle sighed and gave a weak smile. I squeezed her hand.

There was a gentle knock and Jo poked her head around the door.

'Everything OK? When you asked me for a cuppa I did wonder.'

'Michelle was just telling me that she's not sure about being in a relationship with Demetri.'

'I thought you liked him. He is the Hot Doctor, after all.' Michelle smiled back at Jo.

'I do, and he is. He's bloody lovely but that's the trouble, isn't it? Someone wheedles their way into your heart and then wham! They let you down and you're back at square one.' Michelle heaved a great big sigh. 'So, what's the point?'

Jo looked at me and I held her gaze. Michelle had these moments from time to time and we talked her down. It all went back to how she was treated by a previous partner who ran a mile when the going got tough.

'Love. Companionship. Belonging. Connection. Support. Those are just some of the points that spring to mind immediately,' Jo replied. 'And the joy that you get from being with him. He makes you smile so much too. And laugh.'

'Yeah, he does make me happy, but...'

'No one can predict the future, Chelle. I would never have thought I'd be without my Ben, but I am. You have to live for the now,' I added, hoping our wise words would help.

Michelle smiled. 'You see, I knew that I just needed a chat with you two. You always make me see sense.'

'I couldn't imagine ever being in a relationship with anyone else after Ben. But I think I *am* ready for a flirt. I have to admit that I do miss it. I'd crap myself if someone ever reciprocated and run a mile, which is probably why I sometimes target my flirting towards people who are unobtainable.' I chewed the inside of my cheek, only just realising that I did this, and it made me ponder.

'And after twenty-five years of marriage to Michael,' Jo said, 'the thought of ever being involved with anyone else scared the living daylights out of me, but then I met Seamus. It was exactly at the wrong time. I wasn't looking for someone to be involved with but sometimes people come along when you are least expecting it. You don't have to rush into anything major, Michelle. Look at me and Seamus. We're just taking it slowly and learning along the way. That's the wonder of it. Just enjoying getting to know each other.'

'I know you're right. It's just these random mad wobbles from time to time, they invade my every thought. Thank God for you two to talk sense to me. Thank you for being my therapists.'

I wished Michelle saw what we saw. She was amazing.

'I just don't want to see you throw away something special, Michelle. If you don't love, you potentially miss out on so much. And you deserve love just as much as the rest of us. It's fundamental to our core. Wasn't it the Dalai Lama who said the human species were created to be loved?' I was sure I remembered someone telling me that.

'Was he that bloke in the pub last night?' She winked at me and we all laughed.

However, it broke my heart that Michelle was so effervescent and full of life on the outside, but deep down was vulnerable and had low self-esteem. It was clear from the few times we'd met up with her and Demetri that he absolutely thought the world of her. He was always buying her little gifts and showering her with affection in front of us, doing everything he could to show how he felt about her. She just needed to work at trusting him.

In my humble opinion, she needed to let go a little but I understood that it was easy for me to say this and that for some people it's a really hard thing to do. I was no dating expert, after all.

Just a widow who would probably be on her own for the rest of her life.

'Anyway, I can't believe you said that you wouldn't help the vicar last night. Are you regretting it today? Have you had any other brainwaves?' Jo asked, tilting her head to one side.

'I've thought of a couple of smaller events that the Lonely Hearts Club might be able to help out with. A sponsored walk, a car wash and a book sale maybe?' None of these ideas were making me excited though.

Michelle filled up our cups. 'You could always rethink the panto idea. There were times yesterday when you talked about the amateur dramatics you used to do when your face lit up.'

I actually hadn't been able to stop thinking about it. My run earlier had been full of my memories and my thoughts about whether I could actually pull it together. I'd decided that I'd pop out to see Graham later and have a chat. It couldn't hurt.

7

As I got back to mine, patting down my pockets to find my key, pondering what I was going to do with myself for the day, my mobile started to ring. I fished it from my back pocket and could see that it was Joseph, Ben's brother.

'Don't tell me you want me in today after all?' I laughed.

'Hi, darling! How are you? How's the beautiful Sandpiper Shore this morning? Been for a run yet?'

'I was out hours ago. You can't beat an early-morning run to start your day off.'

I remembered back to the time when I'd first taken up running just after Ben died. Instead of lying in bed wallowing, I decided to experiment with pounding the pavements and concentrating on just my breathing and my feet; it was like meditation for my soul. For the time I ran, it made me forget what had happened. Before I remembered again.

I found that it had really helped me and wondered whether there were other people who might like to join me in a weekly run. There wasn't a park run event anywhere near here as we were quite in the sticks in Sandpiper Shore. Maybe this could be a great community event and something that the Lonely Hearts Club members might be interested in.

I'd started to make some notes about an event and how I could develop the idea. Maybe we could have a beginner and an intermediate group. Some might be running for the first time and some hardened runners who might not want to be held back. The more I thought about it, my brain was working overtime, coming up with a plan to move the idea forward.

'Anyway, darling. I don't need you in today at all. In fact, I'm calling with good news. The receptionist we interviewed last week has just called to say she'd love to accept the job and she starts on Monday. We can manage without you today but if you could come in on Monday to do a handover, that would be amazing. The new valuer starts on Monday too, so it'll be all systems go. I can't tell you how much I appreciate you helping us out over the last year or so. Once you've shown Rebecca the systems side of things, you can start doing all the things that you ladies that lunch do. You know, get on with your own life...'

I exhaled loudly. I knew that this day would finally arrive, but it still packed a punch. I'd been working in Ben and his brother's business temporarily, but to be honest, it had helped me immensely. Probably more than it had helped them but it had never been a permanent arrangement.

'Are you there, Emma?'

The thought of me having long days ahead with no real plans was quite scary to me and I was starting to feel quite emotional. In an effort to get him off the phone before I burst into tears, I needed to think of an excuse to end the call.

'Sorry. Yes, I'm here. The signal went a bit funny then. That's great news, Joseph. I've got to go now as my friend has just arrived and is waiting for me. Thanks for letting me know. See you Monday morning.'

'Bye, darling.'

I hoped he didn't see through my sudden lie. As I went into my kitchen, I thought about how this was another stage of my life I was moving on from. Working for the business filled my time, but being around Joseph, who was so like Ben in his mannerisms some days, made me just feel sad. He was right and it was time to move on. But what did I move on to?

Having too much time on my hands was something that drove me mad and one of the reasons why I'd recently started up the Lonely Hearts Club. It had been one of the best decisions I had ever made, both for me and for others.

Jo was recently divorced and her grown-up daughters didn't need her 'mothering' them any more, having busy high-flying careers of their own. Inheriting and renovating the cottage meant that she could fulfil a life-long dream of living by the sea and starting over. She'd taken a leap of faith and all was working out well for her. She'd thrown herself wholeheartedly into the project. I didn't mind confessing that I was envious as she seemed fulfilled and happy in her life, especially when the handsome Seamus was around. She deserved happiness.

Michelle was a bit of a contradiction; working in a high-powered job and the social media face of her company – an internet sensation her boss called her. But with her parents long gone and her brother in a different country, when she arrived home at night she had no one and had never felt lonelier.

Greatly inspired by Jo when she met her, after careful consideration, and a miraculous last-minute redundancy offer, Michelle took the plunge to relocate to Cornwall and set up her own freelance PR and marketing business. She had decided to start making her own dreams come true instead of those of the person who owned the company she worked for. She chose her own hours, working as much or as little as she wanted. Her life/work balance was definitely something she was totally in control of.

We had all experienced life-changing circumstances which were thrust upon us and because I realised that there must be loads of people in the world like us, I decided that I wanted to form a group where people could make new friends and have some company and that's how the Lonely Hearts Club had begun.

It was so hard in later life to do this but I discovered, after talking to many people, that it was much needed and so I was delighted with the success we'd had so far with plenty of people turning up, which was amazing to see.

It really did give me a sense of pride to do this for others. Connecting others in this way felt like it was giving me a purpose, which was exactly what I'd been searching for. If I was being truly honest with myself, even before Ben died.

I'd loved him dearly, still did, but it was only in the short time I'd been alone that I realised how much of my life I'd put on hold for him. He was a perfectionist and knew exactly what he liked and how he liked it. The places we went to on holiday were the places he wanted to visit. The things we did on a weekend were those that he decided we should do. And I went along with everything to keep him happy, losing myself along the way. I wasn't the first woman to do this for her husband and I certainly wouldn't be the last.

I wasn't unhappy. Not at all. We were very lucky. Still loved each other after so many years, but I realised now I was alone that life was short and you had to find the things that gave you a little fire in your belly. I'd been on a couple of foreign holidays since I'd moved to Sandpiper Shore. I'd always wanted to visit Croatia and the Italian lakes but neither were places that Ben fancied so I decided it was time I got over myself, put on my big-girl pants and went on my own. I had a perfectly lovely time but I wished I hadn't had to do it alone. It made me more determined to try to organise friendship holidays too. If you didn't have a partner, at least you could still do it with a friend. This definitely gave me more of a purpose and more than that, something to fill my time with. Sometimes the days went on forever.

But every time I thought back to the vicar's dilemma and my time organising productions and wondering whether I could do it all over again, a flame lit within me. I felt like I owed it to myself to explore it further. Surely just having a chat about it wouldn't hurt. It didn't mean that I had to commit to anything.

Before I thought about it too much and talked myself out of the idea, I decided that I would try to catch Graham at the church hall. I thought it might be nice to pop into the corner shop and get something to take with me, maybe some flowers or a plant. I knew both Graham and Tina were fond of gardening.

In a little world of my own, I shouted a greeting to Mary who was behind the counter. It wasn't until I got to the end of the first aisle that an image of the back of the person that she was serving at the till came to me and a shiver ran down my spine. I had only glanced the side profile but wondered if my mind was playing tricks on me again, at a vision of a man with grey hair and a neatly trimmed beard. I tried to peer around the end of the aisle, but the only person I could see Mary serving was Scott, who had recently moved to the village with his wife Aggie and their family. Maybe I'd just got them muddled up. They were of a similar height and as a former sportsman, he definitely had an athletic build, although he had dark, wavy hair.

Scott was a very handsome ex-premiership goalkeeper who had recently retired from the game.

I shook my head in an effort to clear it and bring about some clarity. I was being ridiculous. I'd got Tom Sullivan on the brain.

8

'You were only saying recently to Tina and me that you don't know what to fill your time with,' Graham said with a warm smile. 'Have you thought about more Lonely Hearts events? Don't forget I said you could have the church hall once a month for free.'

He poured tea from the pot and handed me a china cup and saucer. I loved that they never had mugs. I normally made tea in a mug with a teabag, rarely using a pot. How lovely it was to actually make an effort, I thought, and I vowed to do this from now on. Everything we did these days was for convenience and to cut time. Sometimes it was nice to take the time to do something nice. Especially when time was not of the essence.

'I know it sounds ridiculous, Graham, but I've felt so lost since I lost Ben that I don't know what makes me happy these days. His business took centre stage in my life for so many years and then his success took so much of my time and energy that I forgot about myself. How sad is that?'

'Not sad per se, but normal. I'm sure there are a lot of people in the same position,' he replied. 'What did you love doing when you were younger?' he asked as he stirred his tea, the spoon chinking against the china cup.

'I can't really remember. I shut away so much of my childhood because we moved around so much.' Thinking back to my upbringing always made me a little reflective.

'There must have been something though. Something that used to give you that fizzy feeling in your tummy. What would your inner child say?'

Graham would probably never realise how close to the jackpot he'd hit. I grinned now at the teenage memories that came flooding back. Did I have the nerve to say it out loud? Was I brave enough?

'It *was* the amateur dramatics that we talked about briefly last night. I liked to act, sing and dance originally but then I worked out that my strengths lay in the organisational side of things instead. I *loved* that.'

'Aha! So that's where this magnificent idea of Michelle's came from. Actually, I *can* see you doing the acting, singing and dancing side of things too. You glide everywhere you go; you don't walk. Like a dancer.'

'Do I?' It was not something I'd noticed about myself.

'Do you think you can help us then? It really would mean the world to us both.'

'I'm concerned because I haven't done anything like that for years. I do love the idea of raising funds for the air ambulance though. They were so amazing on the day I lost Ben.' I gave a loud sigh, my mind briefly flitting back to the day Ben had had his heart attack, but I pushed away the thought. 'I'd love to raise some funds for them, give something back. They're such an incredible charity. And I did love the organisational side of things. It's a lot to take on though. The responsibility is huge.

There are so many roles to fill too. And eight weeks really isn't long, you know.'

Tina joined us at this moment and smiled sweetly as she sat in the armchair opposite.

'It would be amazing and raise a great deal of money – very much-needed funds for the charity. What about your friendship group? I bet there are loads of people in there that would love to be part of something like this. And it would be something for you to throw yourself into. Wouldn't teenage Emma love to show the world what she could do?'

'I'm very grateful for your confidence in me, I really am. But...' I looked from Graham to Tina and then down at my hands. 'Do you really think I'm the right person for the job?'

'I couldn't think of anyone more perfect, Emma. I think we were meant to have that conversation last night and you were born to do this. I just know you'll be amazing.'

Despite me being extremely apprehensive, that fluttery feeling was happening in my belly again.

Two hours, three cups of tea and four chocolate Hobnobs later, the performance date was etched in my diary, the vicar's wife had agreed to be my stagehand and I had a vicar who said he'd love to be in the production but only if he could play a pantomime dame. What could possibly go wrong?

9

'It's not going to be spectacularly large. It's only going to be a small production.' To listen to Michelle and Jo oohing and aahing at the next Friday evening get-together, you'd think I was the stage director of a West End musical. Graham and Tina had also joined us for an hour too which was most unusual for a Friday night but we didn't have time to waste.

'Oh, Em, this is way too exciting to think small. You could easily do this. There'd be so much help around. Me and Michelle could be the ugly sisters.'

An olive flew across the front of me and smacked Jo straight in the face.

'Speak for yourself, Joanna. I'm way too beautiful to have a part like that.' Michelle preened spectacularly and we all fell apart as it was so far from how naturally down to earth she always was. 'Anyway, the ugly sisters must be men. It's tradition.'

But as I got that buzz of excitement feeling in my tummy that we talked about earlier, my brain was working overtime. I was looking at Jo and Michelle but wasn't really listening to what they were saying. All I could think about was how it used to light me up inside when the curtains went up on the first evening of our plays; how full of joy my heart was when I looked at the audiences when they were on their feet and clapping loudly at the cast who were taking a bow.

I remembered that everyone wanted me to help them learn their lines, so I literally knew every word of every play off by heart. Me. The army girl who had no friends suddenly became the person that everyone reached out to. And it was the first time in my life that I ever felt like I belonged anywhere.

Graham clapped his hands together, grinning in excitement. 'This is going to be so wonderful. How jolly exciting! First and foremost, we need to choose what we are going to perform.'

I chewed the inside of my cheek. I did have an idea but wondered what they were thinking. Graham shot up out of his chair, clearly elated, making me jump.

'We hadn't got as far as putting the title on the poster outside the church hall, so the world is our oyster. If we did *Aladdin*, I could be Widow Twanky. Oh, please, Emma.'

Tina laughed out loud. 'This is a life-long dream of his, you know, Emma. You'd make a vicar very happy.'

'While I think you'd make an amazing Widow Twanky, my initial thoughts were around *Cinderella*.'

'Oh, now you're talking my kind of language.' Tina's face lit up. 'I know that story inside out too.'

'Me too and I think that's an important factor taking into account that we don't have tons of time.'

'On the other side of that, you could say that people know it too well. Unless you come up with a unique idea around the story so you can bend the script a little.' Graham pressed his lips into a fine line. 'I suppose I could also be one of the ugly sisters, we'd just have to be careful about who we cast as the other one. I would need to be the prettier and funnier one. *Obviously!*'

At that moment, an idea popped into my head, although I wasn't sure if it was ridiculous or genius.

'We could make her a middle-aged menopausal woman called Cindy, pissed off with life. Is that completely bonkers?'

Tina clasped her hands to her chest.

'Bonkers is our middle name! Imagine the fun we could have with that angle.'

Tina and I giggled. Along with Michelle and Jo, I felt that we were insiders united in a world that only people in the mid-life women's club understood.

'Let me get my notebook.'

When I had agreed to take on this major project which was now occupying every waking thought and some of my sleeping ones too, I had started to make a list of everything that would need to be done to put on a pantomime before I met up with the Lockhearts again. There was so much to think about that I was starting to wonder about the magnitude of the project and whether I'd taken on more than I could chew. Up until I had agreed, it had just been an idea, but Graham and Tina had forced my hand and said they'd help with everything and we already had a date which we had to stick to because Christmas was a busy time for a vicar and his wife. The pressure was on but as I sat now, flicking through the pages which fluttered in the gentle breeze, I consulted my notes and read aloud my action points.

'We will need to form a team of people to help, hold auditions, think about costumes, set design, props. That's before we've thought about sound and lighting and practical things like selling tickets and producing a programme.'

I'd have to start work on the script as soon as possible, and on top of the panto itself, I'd also committed to the Lonely Hearts group and made a promise that I'd organise more events over the next few months too. I wanted to make sure that I was totally organised and had some systems in place to ensure I didn't drop any of the plates that I was sure to be spinning.

'This is going to be the best thing that's ever happened in Sandpiper Shore,' Graham declared loudly.

'Oh, no, it isn't.' We heard Seamus's voice as he joined us from around the side of the cottage, slinging his arm around Jo's shoulder and giving her a brief but lingering kiss on the lips. She blushed as their eyes connected, and I saw so much love and admiration in just one glance. I gulped at the realisation that I would probably never have another chance at a love like that. But I was grateful that I had something to get my teeth into, instead of sitting knowing there was more out there for me but not knowing what or where it was or how to find it.

Even though I was going to be run ragged by these two huge projects, I hadn't felt this alive for years. I noticed that I could feel a smile on my face. For the first time in a long time my heart felt happy. I felt as if I was connecting with life again. I felt like a flower that had been planted from a bulb and was finally starting to grow with the possibility of even blooming at some point. Slow but definite progress.

10

I could hear people whispering, wondering why I'd called an emergency meeting of the Lonely Hearts Club, and only hoped that I'd done the right thing as I took my place at the front of the church hall. The chairs were all laid out in what I suppose you'd call theatre style, which seemed quite appropriate.

I clapped loudly to stop the chatter and get everyone's attention, taking a deep breath before I started to speak. Standing up and talking in front of a group wasn't really something I was used to doing.

'Good evening, everyone. Thanks so much for coming along tonight at such short notice. It's really nothing to worry about, I know some of you are speculating. Basically, I need your help.'

Eager faces stared back at me from the thirty or so people who had turned up. The group was predominantly women but there were also two middle-aged men, which was so great to see. In this day and age, and at our stage of life, it's hard to make friends whether you are male or female, although I do think women are better at doing something about it. It's important for all our mental health to have contact with the outside world and already I had seen how much the group was starting to change people's lives. It was also nice to see some separate friendships forming between the people who came along. To say I was proud of what had already been achieved was a bit of an under-statement.

'Sandpiper Shore will be holding a Christmas pantomime.'

A combined oooh came from the audience followed by a group ahhh at my next words.

'In eight weeks' time. And this is where you come in.' A nervous little laugh escaped me before I continued. 'I need people to act, help with the set, help with costumes, people to design tickets and posters, people to sell tickets, get some PR coverage, put the posters up around town, help with lights, sound. The list goes on and on. I was rather hoping... that within this group, there might be some of you who would be interested in being involved.'

Silence and blank faces greeted me and I realised that I may have made a huge mistake. How on earth was I going to be able to pull this together in eight weeks when no one was willing to help me?

A hand raised slowly from the back row.

'Hi, I'm Denise and I'm a graphic designer, and I'm sure I could help out with the posters and tickets if that helps.'

'Denise, you are an absolute gem. Thank you so much.'

Another hand raised, and I was surprised to see that it was Aggie, one of our neighbours who has a brilliant business helping people find their own style. I was a little unsure of why she was even at the meeting of the Lonely Hearts Club. She must have hundreds of friends. 'I might be able to help with costumes/wardrobe,' she said.

Jo added, 'I know my way around a sewing machine too, so maybe I could help Aggie.'

Michelle smiled from the front row. 'Obviously working in PR and marketing means that I can get in touch with the local press and make some pre-show noise and see if we can maybe give away a couple of free tickets as a giveaway prize to get some coverage too. I'll have a think to see what other angles we can look at too. Maybe we could even set up a Facebook page.'

Tina's hand shot in the air. 'The church has a Facebook and an Instagram page. We could give you access to that and you can maybe post from there too.'

Michelle looked stunned. 'Are churches allowed to have social media?'

Tina responded with a smile. 'No idea, but we thought that we'd try it and see if anyone tells us we can't, rather than not try it at all. We have to get with it too, you know. And it's the way of the world these days.'

Stephanie, one of the younger girls who I'd not properly met before, but had seen her face around, raised her hand next; at a guess I would say she was in her mid-to-late twenties and she was heavily pregnant.

'My dad has just come back from living in Australia and has moved back into the area. He was involved in amateur dramatics out there. He did a bit of acting and is a brilliant artist too. I'm sure I could ask him if he might be interested and he might also help with the set design. He was going to come along tonight but was a little bit apprehensive and I couldn't seem to persuade him, so I've come along on his behalf. Hope that's OK. He'll say yes though, I'm sure of it. It'll do him good to get out. He'd be great at sets.'

Tessa shouted up from the back and I noticed that her eyes

were wide. 'Great at sex? I thought this was going to be a pantomime, not a sex show. Disgusting!'

Everyone laughed.

'Sets with a "ts", not an "x", Tessa. Have you got your hearing aid in?' Jo asked and pointed to her ear. Tessa had really come out of her shell recently. When Jo moved to Cornwall and discovered that the cottage she inherited came from her birth mother Tessa, she couldn't have been more surprised. They'd been getting to know each other since their secret had come to light, and a lovely relationship had formed between them, all totally encouraged by Jo's adoptive mother, and Tessa and she had become incredibly close friends. Tessa had insisted on coming along to the Lonely Hearts Club, she said to support Jo, which was delightful to see but we all had a sneaky suspicion it was because she also wanted to make some new friends and get out and about since her best friend, Jo's Aunty June, had died.

It never ceased to amaze me who had come along to the group. All these people feeling that they needed to make friends. What would they have done if we hadn't formed the group?

My heart started to fill with hope. Maybe putting on a production in eight weeks' time wouldn't be so bad after all. There were many more raised hands over the next fifteen minutes and I was trying to keep up with writing the names down for the tasks we had on my clipboard, hoping that Tina was catching those that I didn't. There was one lady called Sarah whose brother worked for an audio-visual company and she said she'd ask if he could help. There was Mary from the store who said she'd be happy to sell tickets and have a poster up on her noticeboard and said that she'd ask at the local business owners' fortnightly meeting to see if anyone else would do the same. Sarah also said she wasn't averse to taking a small role if we were struggling although she'd rather someone else do that side of the stage. Lots of other volunteers came forward for selling tickets which was so encouraging.

We all agreed to meet up again in two evenings' time and if people couldn't make it, they were going to report back in a WhatsApp group that one of them would set up with an update on progress. We hadn't got time to waste.

Once they all left, I slumped down into one of the chairs and Tina handed me her list, sitting down next to me. The relief I felt was immense.

'What an amazing community you've created, Emma.' She looked as proud as punch.

'Thank you. All I've done is bring people together though. They're the ones who are pulling together to make this happen. Not me.'

'Nonsense. Every group needs a leader and you have just proved that you are the right person for the job. They listened to you, volunteered for the tasks you wanted them to, and have now gone over and above to say they'll ask others to get involved. That's community spirit at its best. Well done, my dear.' She patted my arm.

'It hasn't happened yet.' I forced a laugh.

'It will. Have faith and all will work out well. Shall we combine lists and make sure we've covered everything so far and then we can work out what's next?'

'Thank you for believing in me, Tina. I truly appreciate it.'

'You don't know how happy you've made Graham. He was worried sick and I was very concerned about him. He seems less stressed since you agreed to do this and a little more like his old self. Even the GP says that his blood pressure is dropping and becoming a little more normal. Whatever normal is these days. Life is quite stressful, even for a vicar and his wife, you know.'

'You do so much for everyone else, Tina. I hope you are

taking some time to do something nice for yourself too. Self-care is so important.'

'I'll be OK, my love, but thank you for thinking of me. So, grab your list then and let's get this show on the road, shall we?'

11

Two days later and – ridiculously as I was the organiser – I was also the one who turned up to the church hall five minutes late because Graham had stopped me for a chat at the vicarage. I threw my bag down on the chair behind me and started to assemble the sheets of whiteboard paper Michelle had lent me. Graham had agreed that we could stick them to the walls of the hall. Once they were assembled, I turned to face the audience briefly before referring to my clipboard.

'OK, so firstly, Denise, did you manage to have a think about the ticket and poster design?'

'I did and they're ready for you to look at. I've printed a couple of examples off for your initial thoughts and I just need to drop the name onto the design. Here you go.' She passed them to Tina and me.

'Oh, shit. We need a name too! That needs to go on the list. Sorry, Tina, didn't mean to swear.'

'Don't mind me, Emma. I'm quite used to it. You should hear Graham when he gets going.' She winked at me and I knew she'd only said that to make me feel better. I couldn't imagine a swear word coming out of his mouth.

'OK, maybe at the end of the evening, we could do a brainstorm on a name for the show then. How does that sound, ladies? Tina has very kindly brought some wine along so that might help to get our creative juices flowing.' Nods all around suggested that this was a good idea, although they were probably just happy with the offer of wine. I looked down at the designs Denise had put together which were way more than I could have ever wished for. 'We'll have a vote on the designs too. Thanks, Denise, these are fantastic.' Denise grinned as she went back to her seat.

'So, Stephanie.' I scanned the seats but couldn't see her. 'Is Stephanie here yet?'

'No, but she's sent me a message to say she'll be here any minute. She had to stop by and pick her dad up on the way.' Tina smiled. 'What's next?'

'Script,' I replied.

'So, how's that coming along?' she asked.

'Yeah, I'm definitely getting there,' I responded. 'I'd love a couple of volunteers to read through that with me one night if possible and just see whether I've hit the right beats. I should be finished by the weekend.'

A couple of hands went up and Tina made a note of Sandy and Maggie's names and I said I'd be in touch as soon as I was finished with the script. I'd been up till 3 a.m. the past couple of nights working on it and could honestly say that I'd thoroughly enjoyed doing it. I just hoped that everyone else would like it too.

'So, once the script is finalised, we'll have the cast list and then we can start to do auditions and think about costumes! Have you had any thoughts about that, Aggie?'

'Indeed I have. Jo and I have been talking and we thought

that once we have the cast list from you, and who is going to be doing those roles and that's all confirmed, then we can decide what we think that character should wear. We can put that on the wall chart and ask everyone in the village to let us know if they have anything suitable. If not, Jo and I are both pretty useful with a sewing machine. I've spoken to the local haberdashery and they've said that we can go through all their material stock and see if there's anything suitable. They even offered the materials for free as part of their contribution towards the event.'

Tina clapped her hands together. 'This is so wonderful. You know what else we could do with, Emma?' I hoped she wasn't going to throw anything too unexpected at me. 'Or even *who* we could do with? To take part, I mean.' She slowly turned to Aggie. 'Do you think Scott might be a closet thespian at all? We're desperate for more men to be involved. And he would definitely get the ladies swooning. That would tick a big box for us.' Aggie had told us confidentially that Scott was struggling a little with his mental health since retiring, not knowing what to do with himself now he was living a normal life and was hoping that she might talk him into joining the Lonely Hearts Club.

She laughed. 'Definitely not. But he is a good husband and after the years I've spent following his career around the world, I think the one thing he can do now for his wife to make up for it is do everything I tell him to. Don't mention it to him yet if you see him, because I'll have to pick the right time to ask him... I mean persuade him.' Her eyes twinkled. 'Oh, hell yes! He'd love to take part. He just doesn't realise it yet. Put him on the list.'

We all laughed but I hoped he wouldn't mind. Having a name that everyone knew would be a huge pull for the locals and they'd really appreciate him being part of the community. He'd not been seen out and about much, even though Aggie and the children were always around town.

Sarah passed on the message that her brother who had the audio-visual company said he was going to pop over to see us the next time we met up to see what our requirements were but that he was extremely confident he'd be able to help us. Not only had he offered to help with the hire of equipment but also with the running of the lights, which was wonderful news. This led to a discussion about ticket sales and using the money that we generated to pay for the things that would incur a cost. Another person in the community called Gill who was an accountant offered to look after the finances, which was a huge help and another thing that I was dreading sorting. Finance was not my strongest point.

The side door of the church hall flung open and Stephanie came rushing through, shouting behind her, 'Come on, Dad. Hurry up.'

'OK, folks, why don't you all grab yourself a tea or a coffee, or even a glass of wine and I'll just pop to the ladies' and then we'll be back to hear from Stephanie.'

There was a real buzz in the room when I returned and for a moment I just stood and watched as everyone mingled, seeming to blend together in a joint purpose. It was a wonderful thing to see and I felt a well of pride bubbling up inside of me.

A tap on my shoulder brought me back to the present and I turned to find Stephanie behind me, someone beside her with his back to us. She turned to the man and pulled him towards her.

'Emma, I'd like to introduce you to my dad. Dad, this is Emma that I was telling you about.'

'Emma,' he said in a voice that sounded like the richest golden honey ever as he turned and smiled, bright blue eyes crinkling up and showing laughter lines in a tanned face.

Ever since I'd been to the restaurant with Jo and Michelle, I'd had a feeling that something was going to happen yet I couldn't predict what. I just put it down to my nervous apprehension about doing the panto. But I hadn't prepared myself for coming face to face with the boy with whom I once thought I was madly in love. The boy who broke my heart.

12

'You two already know each other? How?' Stephanie's furrowed brow matched her puzzled expression. My eyes had locked onto Tom's and I couldn't tear them away and even worse, to my horror, I couldn't seem to form any words.

'Emma and I are...' his eyes never left mine as he continued after a little cough, 'old friends. From college. We were all set to be in a play together. She was the Juliet to my Romeo. My leading lady!' His face lit up and he beamed at me.

Stephanie clutched at her chest. 'How romantic! Did you get to kiss on stage?'

All I could remember was the first time that Tom ever kissed me, when he ran his hands through my hair and tilted my chin towards him. How we awkwardly bumped noses and laughed nervously. But then how when his soft, gentle lips touched mine, I had melted against him and our lips perfectly moulded together. The memory was still so strong in my mind that it almost took my breath away, the emotions all rushing back.

I wondered if I'd made more of it over the years. Whether it really felt like that, or whether it was a false memory, but I didn't think I'd ever forget how it really felt.

It was her father's turn to frown. 'No. She ran out on me and broke my heart.' He laughed nervously. 'We never did get round to the stage kiss, did we?'

I shook my head, not trusting myself to speak, remembering the off-stage kisses instead.

'She decided to do all the behind-the-scenes stuff instead. And very good at it she was too. It was your mum who stepped into the Juliet role and the rest is history as they say. How the devil are you, Emma? It's so nice to see you. How have you been? Gosh, it's been, what? Over thirty years? Thirty-five? More, maybe?'

Horrified that he reached out as if to touch my arm, I took a step backwards before we made contact. How dare he joke and say that I'd broken his heart and make light of it, when all the while it had been he who had broken mine?

My mouth felt dry, my lips felt welded together. It took a while before I was able to speak. I pulled my shoulders up, lifted my head and gave a tight-lipped smile.

'Tom. How nice to see you.' Nodding in acknowledgement, I didn't know where my unusually cool, clipped tone had come from. 'I'm not sure how long it's been. A while though.'

'Wow, Steph. When you said that the lady who was doing the group was called Emma, I never thought for one minute that it would be *my* Emma. What an amazing coincidence. We were such good friends, weren't we, Em?'

Him saying my name that way made me remember how it used to make me swoon. He was a proper dreamy teenager and looking into those big blue eyes now was a reminder of how much I enjoyed spending time with him. How we laughed and how kind he was to me. Until he wasn't.

Until the day that Julie told me what he really thought of me, when he wasn't brave enough to admit it himself. The day I sobbed behind closed doors, no friends to help me, my parents not knowing anything about it. And I had to pick myself up, dust myself down and go back to school the very next day. That's why when Mrs Dawes asked me to take on the role of stage director, I accepted. Then at least I no longer had to act alongside the boy who broke my heart.

And now, over thirty-five years later, he was once more standing in front of me.

Tom suddenly reached out and took both of my hands in his, taking me by surprise.

'Look at you, Em. You're all grown up...' I lowered my eyes, not trusting myself to look into his, 'yet still the same.'

The first opportunity I got, I dropped his hands and took a step back.

Stephanie didn't even seem to notice how quiet I was when she explained why she'd brought her dad along.

'Mum and Dad moved out to Australia ten years ago. I'd moved to France to work as an au pair with a wonderful family who lived in an amazing chateau and Mum had always wanted to go. Not sure Dad was so keen, were you?' She laughed. 'But then he always did do as he was told. A proper hen-pecked husband, weren't you?'

He cleared his throat. 'Well, I wouldn't say that exactly, Stephanie, thank you very much.'

Stephanie's voice cracked when she went on. 'Mum died two years ago. Cancer.'

This made me soften, despite everything. I knew how it felt to lose your life partner.

'I'm sorry to hear that. That must have been tough on you both.'

'But we must think about the future and not dwell on the past, right, Dad? And he's come back to live in the UK because,' she patted her heavily pregnant stomach which looked like she could give birth any day, 'he's going to be a granddaddy.'

This time I reached out to Stephanie and touched her arm. 'I'm sorry, I can't remember if I've already congratulated you. A new baby is always such lovely news. When are you due?'

'New Year's Eve. It's bittersweet not having Mum here for what will be one of the most important things that's ever happened to me but we can't change anything, can we?' She looked at her father and the love that these two shared shone like a blinding light. What a beautiful relationship they had and it was nice that he would be able to enjoy having a grandchild. And even though I had hated Julie Cartwright for over thirty-five years, I now regretted hanging on to an emotion that didn't serve either of us. I just felt sadness. For Tom, for Stephanie and for Julie, in fact. And for Ben. For those that got left behind and those that hadn't. Life really was unfair at times.

'Anyway, Dad said that he'd love to be part of the show if he could, and he's very happy to be involved with the set design and all that malarkey too. He's such a great painter and I know he'll be able to come up with some great ideas.' Her face suddenly became incredibly animated as she shouted out, 'Oh! My! God!'

Tom and I both grabbed her arms and in unison asked if she was OK. Pregnant women shouting out suddenly was quite a scary thing.

She laughed. 'Yes, of course I'm OK, but I've just had a brilliant idea. The panto is a skit on *Cinderella*, isn't it?'

'It doesn't have a name yet but yes, that's right,' I replied. 'Why do you ask?'

'This was absolutely meant to be, you know. You and Dad. You can play Cinderella and Prince Charming. It'll be like *Romeo and Juliet* all over again.' She practically jumped up and down and clapped her hands together excitedly. 'You might get your stage kiss after all these years. How much fun would that be?'

I looked at Tom and saw a fleeting look of horror which disappeared as quickly as it appeared, leaving just an embarrassed smile behind. It literally took my breath away, because it was exactly the same look I'd seen on that stage all those years ago when Mrs Dawes told us to kiss and that was when Julie had laughed out loud. Then when I'd run off to the side, that's when she'd told me that she and Tom were an item and that he felt sorry for me. Mortified was not a strong enough word for how I felt back then and it had affected how I'd lived my life ever since.

'Sadly, Stephanie, while that's a lovely idea, it's not one that will come to fruition. I'm needed as the director of the play.' I turned to her father and nodded. 'Thank you for your offer of support, Tom. We'd gladly accept your help with the set and if you'd like to audition for the part of Prince Charming, I'm sure we'll find a perfectly acceptable Cinderella as your leading lady. Now if you'll excuse me, I have a whole list of other jobs that won't do themselves.'

As I walked away from the first friend I ever had, who had also turned out to be the boy I fell utterly and madly in love with many moons ago, I wiped a tear from my cheek. My heart hurt. It seemed that lots of people in my life left me. Maybe Michelle was right. If you didn't put yourself into vulnerable positions, you never had to experience the gut-wrenching pain that life threw at you.

13

When Melanie sashayed into the church hall the following morning, I knew that she was my Cindy. She was half an hour early so I was on my own in her audition but it was a done deal before she'd even stepped on stage. Middle-aged with beautiful, poker-straight long blonde hair that swished behind her, she commanded the room. Her voice was melodious and I knew our audience would be rooting for her from the moment they met her on stage. She had also volunteered to help with the organisational side of things which I thought was a little presumptuous but brushed it aside.

I also knew in my heart that Tom would be the perfect Prince Charming but I was determined that I would find someone else. More auditions were taking place but from those who had already put their names forward, they were either too young, too old, too short, or too tall. Maybe just not 'Tom' enough.

When I gave Melanie the good news, she just took it in her stride as though she already knew that the part was hers. I'd love to have that much confidence but we were just very different people and that, I supposed, was what made the world go round.

She insisted on being involved in the future auditions for Prince Charming, saying that she'd like to have a say if she was working alongside someone.

Tina waltzed in, looking as fresh as a daisy, which was the opposite of how I was feeling. 'Morning, Emma. Reporting for duty bright and early. Is the script ready for me to look at yet?'

I'd been up till 3 a.m. finishing it off and when I did go to sleep I dreamt about Tom, so sleep was a distant memory for me and I'm sure I looked dreadful.

'It is, I've printed off copies for you, me, and have dropped off Sandy and Maggie's copies to their houses on the way here. I've also printed off some of the parts I'd like the people coming for auditions to read. I literally haven't stopped for days. I'm exhausted!'

'My dear, you need to make sure that this doesn't take over your life. You must rest sometimes too. You know that old saying, put your own oxygen mask on first, so you can help others. A day or two of rest here and there will do you the world of good!'

I smiled, knowing she was right. Maybe later, I'd do a weekly plan so I could make sure I wasn't totally consumed by the panto. And of course, there was the Lonely Hearts Club too. There were lots of people relying on me there, although many of them were involved in the panto and wouldn't have time to even think about being lonely.

We set up a long table on the main floor in front of the stage, ready for the full day ahead of us.

'Are you sure you're OK, Emma?' Tina asked. 'You look a little peaky.'

'Long story. But yes, I will be, thank you. Shall we call the first one in?'

Auditions were fun but exhausting. By the end of that day, we had got Graham the vicar as one of the ugly sisters, with Bill,

Seamus's father, as the other one. Somehow, Aggie had managed to get Scott, her husband, to agree to be Press Stud, which we thought would be a good alternative name instead of Buttons. Michelle was delighted to be cast as the Fairy Godmother. We were trying to persuade Jo to take on the role of Dandini and the role of Prince Charming was still yet to be filled, though we had another full day of auditions tomorrow. It was full-on but it needed to be at this stage. Once the cast was assigned their roles, we could move on with everything else.

Watching Melanie during the rehearsals was interesting. She made lots of notes in a notepad that she produced from her handbag and seemed to go through the script crossing things out and writing in the side margins. As she was sitting the furthest from me it was impossible to see what it said, but I would hope that she wasn't changing the script after all the hard work I'd put in. Certainly not before I'd had feedback from Sandy and Maggie too. I may have been worrying for nothing. There was a possibility that she was making notes for her own role. I hoped so very much. She excused herself at around 4 p.m. as she had an appointment that she had to get to.

Tina sighed.

'Do you mind if I just sit here and read through the script, Emma? I know that once I get back to the vicarage there'll be so much to do, I won't get chance. I may as well make the most of the peace and quiet before I return to the mad house.' She put her fingers to her lips. 'Ssshhhh! Don't tell Graham I said that.'

I laughed. 'Your secret is safe with me. That's fine, I'll stay a bit before heading home then and do the same. I have no plans tonight and it's nice to have company even if we're just reading next to each other.'

We sat in companionable silence, going through our notes and reading through the script again.

'Hi, Emma.'

When I heard Tom's voice behind me, I closed my eyes and took in a deep breath, only to find Tina peering at me inquisitively when I opened my eyes again.

'OK, love?' She put her hand on my arm.

'Yes, thanks. Long story for another time,' I whispered close to her ear and then pasted on a sweet smile before I turned to face Tom, trying to remember not to look too deep into his eyes.

'Tom. How can I help?' When he held my gaze, I knew it was going to be impossible not to become mesmerised once more.

'More about how I can help you and I rather hoped that we can... you know... be friends. Maybe even grab a drink... a coffee, I meant, not like a drink-drink. Chat about old times.'

I could feel that my brows had furrowed.

'Ah, I don't think I'll have time, to be honest.'

'We'll need to talk about what stage scenery you were thinking about too so I can help you from that side of things.'

Tina took in the situation before her, as if she were sitting alongside the net at a tennis match watching a ball move from one player to another.

'I'm busy at the moment. Sorry!'

'Nonsense!' Tina interrupted. 'You were only just saying you didn't know what to do with yourself tonight. You can go now.' I narrowed my eyes at her and she grinned back at me. 'I need to lock up and get back to the vicarage anyway. My vicar needs me.' She started to tidy her papers together. 'Go on, Emma, off you go with Tom.'

It would appear that not only did you not say no to the vicar with the dicky ticker, you also didn't refuse the vicar's wife. She shooed us towards the door.

I huffed and started to gather my stuff together when the front door flung open and Melanie wafted in.

'I think I left my purse here. Oh, yes, there it is.' It had fallen down the side of the chair she'd been sitting at. She grabbed it and turned, physically bumping into Tom.

'Oh... err... helloooo.' She held out her hand. I wasn't entirely sure whether she was expecting him to kiss it or shake it. After they shook, she put her index finger to her lip and tapped it gently before swinging round to Tina and exclaiming, 'He's the one.'

Tina and I exchanged a glance, not knowing what she was talking about. Tom hadn't a clue what was going on. She nodded profusely as she circled him like a shark homing in on its prey. 'Yes. He's the perfect middle-aged Prince Charming.'

'But Tom is just here to help out with the set design. He's not taking part in the play.' I felt defensive and answered on his behalf, but there was clearly no need as he spoke immediately after me, with his own thoughts.

'Well, I wouldn't say no if there was a minor part going, but it's been years since I acted really.'

'Ah, well, now I know you've done it before, there's absolutely no way that I'm going to take no for an answer. There you go, Emma; there's another cast member for you.' She reached out and touched Tom's cheek. 'Oh, you and I are going to have so, much fun.'

I'm not sure how she managed to make it sound both sleazy and sexy at the same time, but Tom's eyes nearly popped out of his head. She grabbed her bag from the table, popped her purse inside and sashayed out of the door with a little wave.

14

I wasn't sure how long I could sit opposite Tom in the pub without a gin and tonic in my system for a little Dutch courage. Conversation flowed reasonably easily under the circumstances. Years ago, someone told me that if you were ever nervous, just ask someone about themselves and they'd normally love to open up. It seemed to do the trick with him.

'So, tell me about Stephanie. She seems like a lovely girl.' I knew we'd be on safe ground if we talked about his daughter.

'She's an absolute star. She was an easy kid to be a parent to. A lovely temperament.' He winked. 'She must get that from me. Her mother, as you might remember, was a hot-headed redhead with a very fiery temper.'

I laughed. 'Stephanie said you were a hen-pecked husband. Is that why?'

He looked quite dejected when he replied. 'Sometimes it was just easier to comply. Ever felt like that in your life?'

If only he knew. My life with Ben was like that most of the time. I loved him deeply and was happy to go along with his suggestions, but I did feel like a lot of me, my wants and desires were quashed so that he could achieve his dreams. Now I just needed to dig deep within me and find out what I truly wanted from life. I still felt at times like I was surviving rather than thriving. I'd heard a lot of people felt like this in their mid-life phase and it had never been truer.

Now that Julie had been brought up, he talked about her a lot – how they'd emigrated and that she'd fitted into life out there, but that he'd really struggled to find his way; his purpose.

'If truth be told, Em, I hadn't realised how much I missed the UK until we came home for a visit. It felt strange to leave that life behind, but I was glad to come back to the UK when she passed away.'

'That must have been tough for you.' Much as my negative feelings about Julie had clouded my opinion over the years, I couldn't help but be empathic, knowing how it felt to go through the loss of a partner.

'It was, but to be honest with you, Emma, Stephanie doesn't really know this but our marriage had been over a long time before. When we went out to Australia it was make or break time. Julie said she was going with me or without me. I couldn't bear to break up our family at the time but then Stephanie decided that she was going to go travelling and there wasn't really anything else keeping us here. My parents had already passed away and Julie's had never really been that bothered with her. I no longer had a reason to stay. She sold it to me by saying that it would give us an opportunity to reboot our lives and our love for each other. I thought that maybe in a different place things might be different. But I was a fool. They weren't.'

'I'm sorry to hear that.'

'Thanks, Em. You're still so easy to talk to. You've not changed one bit, you know.' He smiled, turning to me and looking deeply into my eyes. I gulped.

'So, you couldn't fix your marriage by going to live in the sunshine then?'

'Nah. I'd finally plucked up the courage to tell Julie I was going to come back to the UK but on the same night that I was going to tell her, she told me that she had been diagnosed with lung cancer. I couldn't leave her then, could I? I'm not someone who could have let her deal with that on her own. We muddled through together for the next year or so in our own way. In fact, when the pressure of not being able to do anything about it had gone away, it felt a little easier to deal with. We pretended to Stephanie that everything was OK when she came to visit and to this day, she doesn't know. No one does.'

'Did Julie know?' I couldn't help but ask.

'I think she had an inkling. She thanked me just before she died for sticking by her side, particularly at the end when I could have made other choices. She never came right out with it and said she knew but it was implied without having to say the words. Probably for the best really and my conscience knows that I did all I could to help the mother of my daughter and woman I married, literally till death did us part.' He hesitated and for a moment had a wistful look in his eyes. He seemed to snap back to the present then, took a swig of his pint and turned back to me. 'So how about you, Em? Are you married? Got kids? Tell me what's been going on in your life?'

It should have felt wrong sitting and pouring my heart out to someone who had meant so much to me at a certain point in my life; however, it felt so right when it all came out. Maybe it was because he had also been widowed. Different circumstances. Same result. Or maybe it was the gin.

'Anyway, less about what a sad old pair of widows we are.' I was always good at changing the direction of a conversation. 'You need to tell me about your experience in painting set designs.'

'Well, I was in an am-dram group of ex-pats out in Aus.'

'There are far too many abbreviations for me in that sentence, Tom.' He laughed and I loved that he still found me funny. He used to tell me that I was the funniest person he knew.

Realising what was happening here, I suddenly caught my thoughts and realised that I was going to have to be very careful around this man. Nostalgia and emotions were both running strong. The teenage smell of musk and cheap aftershave, replaced now by, if I wasn't mistaken, Hugo Boss for Men. Over-sized T-shirts and baggy jeans swapped for smart designer jeans and an open-necked shirt, sharing a glimpse of sun-kissed bronze skin. But those big bright blue eyes were exactly the same apart from the crinkly laughter lines around them now. He'd aged beautifully, that boyish cuteness replaced by manly good looks, a short, well-groomed beard bearing tinges of greyness that matched his hair.

'You don't have to play the part of Prince Charming, you know.' My mind still hadn't been made up as to whether I wanted him to or not. 'You could just get involved in the set building and painting. Don't let Melanie bully you into doing something you don't want to do.'

'Ah, she hasn't. I think she's given me the push I need. Stephanie has been telling me that I need to make a life for myself now I'm back. That I can't sit around moping. I've tried to tell her that I'm not moping, that I'm just comfortable in my own surroundings with my own company, but I'd be lying if I didn't say I missed having someone to do something with.'

I sighed. 'Agree wholeheartedly. I miss cooking for someone. Someone needing me, I suppose. I haven't felt needed since I lost Ben. It's one of the reasons why I agreed to set up the Lonely Hearts Club and got involved with the panto. Makes me feel useful. And saved me talking to myself at home.'

'Well, if you'll have me, I'd love to be involved in both. I wasn't thinking of playing such a big part, to be honest, maybe just be someone in the background, but if it's up to Melanie I'm not sure there'll be much choice in it. She seems to be very determined about that.'

I laughed. 'She's not someone I know very well, she certainly was very dismissive when I asked her about joining the Lonely Hearts Club. Said she wasn't "the type" but was quite interested in finding out what it was all about.' I put those words in speech marks with my fingers. 'God knows what she must think of us lonely old widows in the group. Probably thinks we're just old saddos who are past our prime.'

'Less of the old. People *in* our prime I'd say. Someone called me an older gentleman the other day. I was horrified. I don't feel old. Do you?'

'I really don't.' I sighed. 'I still feel like I've got so much more of life to live.'

'God, me too. So, what are your hopes and dreams for the future?'

I gave a forced laugh, feeling tears welling up. 'I'm not sure I know any more. I thought I knew but then when Ben died, I feel like my dreams died with him. This might sound totally daft but I'm not sure who I am without him.'

I didn't want to dwell on these feelings. They weren't even thoughts that I'd shared with Jo and Michelle and I wasn't sure why they were coming out while I was talking to Tom. Maybe it was because he was easy to talk to. Maybe it was because he was in a similar position to me. Maybe it was because we seemed to fit back together, just like we had when we were teenagers.

'It's weird, isn't it? Just when you think your life is mapped out for you, then it all changes again. I suppose it keeps us on our toes though.' He nudged me with his shoulder and teen memories came flooding back into my head and my heart. I remembered now that he used to do that to me all the time.

'Yeah, that's life, I guess.'

Grabbing my jacket from the seat next to me, I stood suddenly, with a need to get out of there and away from him. It all felt a bit too much. All this opening up was messing with my head.

'I'm going to have to go now, Tom. It's been... nice. Thank you.'

He raised himself from his chair. 'More than nice. I'll walk you home.' Still a charmer, I noticed.

'No need, I'll be fine.' I was a strong, independent woman, and didn't need a man to make sure I got home safely. Also, I wasn't sure I wanted him to know where I lived. Can't even say why. I just didn't.

'I insist.'

It didn't seem like I'd have a choice in the matter and he took my jacket from my hand and held it open for me to step into. I could feel his warm breath on my neck and as our hands brushed, a little spark of static electricity made us both jump. I hoped it wasn't a sign of things to come.

15

When I closed the front door to leave the house for my run the following morning, the first thing that made me smile was that the sun was shining gloriously. It was that time of year when a day full of sunshine was an absolute bonus before autumn set in fully, followed swiftly by winter. The sun always lifted my heart. I couldn't imagine not living by the coast, it was always beautiful, whatever the season, but spring was always my favourite. A month full of hope and possibility with the days getting longer and more light, making you want to do more.

Summer by the sea was always a delight as long as we weren't too overrun with tourists. There was a fine balance between that and it being good for the local economy. Autumn was not too bad, as there was still some good weather around at times, but winter was definitely not my season. Days when you got up in the dark and the light went early, made me feel gloomy and low. I hadn't realised how much until I spent my first winter alone, after Ben died.

I tried to live a life purposely full of gratitude and each morning I'd try to find three things I was grateful for. It was too easy to wake up and feel sorry for myself. For the cards that life had dealt me. Doing that felt like a more positive start to the day.

My morning run on the beach had involved deciphering a head full of memories, while the gentle lapping of the waves tried to soothe my soul. Getting muddled between the past and the present, I turned my attention to thinking about my three things for the day.

The first came to me easily. I was thankful for my friends. Jo and Michelle had become the family I never really had. Two women that I knew cared for me deeply despite the short space of time we had known each other.

The second was my surroundings. I'd felt like Lady Luck was on my side when Jo said that she was looking to rent out a property; it hit me just at the right time. I wanted to start afresh in my life, putting the memories of my marriage to one side, and to grasp life with both hands and make new memories of my own. To live this close to the sea, where I just walked out through a natural pathway through the dunes, was purely magical. To be on the beach within seconds of my front door and to see the waves ebb and flow through my lounge window was food for the soul. Spending time on the communal terrace overlooking the beach beyond was a pure treat and our Friday night social events were a total joy.

The third thing I was grateful for on that particular day was for finally finding a purpose. Both the Lonely Hearts Club and the panto were giving me a feeling of being needed. Being wanted. It seemed to fill something within me that I hadn't known how to fill.

My thoughts drifted to the evening before and how very different Ben was to Tom. They were very unalike in looks as well as temperament.

Ben liked everything to be perfect. He knew what he liked

and wanted and would do everything to make it happen. He was quite intense at times over certain things. So much so that I felt like he might have a condition like OCD. He even lined up products in our cupboards in a 'sleeping-with-the-enemy' style. Nothing out of line. And that included me too, I supposed. I hadn't realised until I wasn't in it any more. I felt freer now to explore things that I hadn't felt I needed to before and even though this was something new that had been forced upon me, it wasn't something I was averse to delving into further.

In contrast, and I know I didn't know Tom that well, but he seemed so relaxed and chilled about life. Maybe he hadn't always been that way. Perhaps Australia and its laid-back way of life had influenced his demeanour.

When I arrived at the church hall, Melanie was already waiting for me. It felt like an ambush from the moment she opened her mouth.

'Morning, Emma. Beautiful day. So... I've been thinking...'

'Morning, Melanie. Can we just get in first and put the kettle on before the auditions start? If we don't grab a drink now, we might not get a chance for a while.'

While I pottered about in the kitchen making drinks, she bent my ear constantly, questioning things that were in the script, the music choices, the costume suggestions and even the cast. It was quite overwhelming. I had promised to consider all her suggestions and she agreed to send them over to me in a message so I had a record of them all. I was a little irked that she wanted to change things I'd already put in place and it felt a little personal, like she was criticising me and what I'd done. All the hard work and the late nights that I'd put into this panto already and then she comes steamrollering in trying to change things.

When Tina arrived, Melanie then went on to bend her ear as well. I believe she hoped that she'd find an ally, although I wasn't so sure that Tina would feel the same. When Melanie popped to the loo, Tina and I just stared at each other. I felt quite exhausted.

'Blimey, she's a bit full-on, isn't she?' I blew out air between my lips. 'Seems that she knows better. I found out this morning that she'd already told Aggie she wasn't happy with the costume choice for Scott's role and had made some alternative suggestions.'

'She means well,' Tina replied, 'and to be honest, there's a couple of suggestions she's made which I think could work and might make life easier for us all.'

This surprised me somewhat.

'Oh, right... I'm sure she does. It might just be nice if she discussed them with me first rather than just go ahead. I didn't imagine that you would have been on her side, Tina.'

'Emma, my love. This is not about taking sides. It's about doing what's right for the panto. And making life easier for the rest of us. Taking some of the pressure off you and me is surely a good thing.'

While I did think that Tina was trying to give us the least amount of stress possible, it dawned on me then that this was just a *part* of Tina's very busy and full life. I could probably say the same about Melanie. Whereas this *was* my life. I didn't really have much else to fill my time, especially since Ben's brother didn't need me any more in the business. I should pull myself together, take the emotion out of the situation, and think about what was best for the production and not about how her suggestions were aimed at me and my failings. Working with Joseph had helped a little, given me some of my confidence back, but there was a huge part of me that still needed a boost.

I made a promise to myself not to make this panto the only thing I had to focus on in my life. That I still needed to research and discover other things that I could throw myself into, as well as the Lonely Hearts Club. Maybe I needed to investigate whether there were any business opportunities I could look into further. While Ben and I had paid off our mortgage and his life insurance enabled me to have money in the bank, I couldn't just do nothing. I could look to train in a new field. Try to find these other things that people talk about all the time. Their passion and their purpose. I needed to find mine.

16

Friday night soon came around and it was time for cocktails on the terrace again. Sometimes Seamus and Demetri joined us, never for more than a quick drink, but on this particular occasion it was just us girls, for which I was glad. I was shattered. It had been a busy old week and I was looking forward to chatting things through. Both Michelle and Jo were great at giving it to me straight but also sympathising at the same time. However, there was surprise in their faces when I told them what had been happening.

'So, this woman who you don't know from Adam has come in and started changing things around already?' Jo enquired. 'I'm not sure I like the sound of her, to be honest.'

'Oh, she's lovely and she's only suggesting things that are good for the show,' I replied.

'Yeah, those types are the worst,' Michelle said. 'The sort that smile sweetly at the same time as stabbing you in the back. So, you don't notice that it's happened. I've worked with a few people like that over the years. There was a time at my old company where a new girl started and everyone thought that the sun shone out of her arse. She poked her nose into everything and ended up taking over some of the roles that I had been managing. And then she made suggestions that I'd been making for a while, some of which, most in fact, she knew about, and instigated them and everyone thought that she was the Messiah.'

'Gosh, that must have been tricky for you. How did you handle that?' I asked.

'Honestly, I couldn't bear working with her. However, we finally found a way to work together and I did stand up to her and tell her exactly what I thought. It made for some fiery meetings and a couple of times I picked her up on it in front of other people, to show that I knew exactly what I was doing. My boss had a word with me at one point, because this woman had gone crying to him that I'd been cruel and she felt like I was bullying her. It wasn't me bullying her though, she was like a bulldozer, coming in and taking over.'

'No, she's not like that,' I said, wondering if I'd overexaggerated things. 'Her suggestions have been really helpful. It started to rub me up the wrong way but I think I'm starting to accept her ideas are good and back off a bit.'

Jo held her hand up to stop Michelle speaking.

'*Back off?* This is *your* play, Emma. You've put so much hard work into it over the last few weeks. Don't let someone else come in and take all the credit. Even if her ideas are good, there are ways that you go about this sort of thing. I can see that you're starting to doubt yourself. You make sure you are standing up for yourself, my girl. You are way too amazing at this to be walked all over. Anyhow, tell us all the things that have been going well in the play and I also want to know when we get to do our words with other people. We've rehearsed our words separately, but it'll be great to see it all come together with the other characters. We can't wait.'

It was even great for me to hear everything that we'd accomplished in that week. Townsfolk, palace officials, ball attendees had been appointed, some with minor speaking parts, but mostly those who would be on stage, joining in with the singing and a couple of very basic dance numbers that I'd thrown in. Also according to Graham, the director was not only the organiser of everything but also the choreographer too. Tina was frantically learning the songs that she didn't already know on the piano and brushing up on those that she did while I was working out the dance moves.

We'd even finally agreed, after much deliberation at our most recent meeting, that the panto would be called Cindy Rella, so it was still recognisable but gave us some leeway to make it our own.

'Oh, and I'm meeting Tom tomorrow evening to go through the scenery.' I threw in at the end as I remembered that we'd planned to meet in the pub.

Michelle jumped up. 'Oh. My. God! Are you going on a date with Tom on a Saturday night?'

'No, it's not a date.' I frowned at her.

Michelle and Jo shared a look, which did not go unnoticed.

'It's *not*,' I protested. 'We have to go through the set designs so he can make a start on them and we just simply haven't had the chance to do that yet, because he's been working all week.'

'Has he got a job now then?' Jo asked.

'He's doing some consultancy work. He used to be in HR and set up his own company while he was in Australia so he could pick and choose his hours. He's been doing some networking over here and has some freelance work that he's been doing.'

Michelle grinned. 'You seem to know an awful lot about the handsome Mr Sullivan.'

'Don't be daft. He was telling me when we were texting the other night.'

'So, you text each other at night, do you?' Jo enquired, and I couldn't help notice her smirk.

'Stop it, you pair. It's nothing more than two old friends who had to get in touch with each other about a joint project. Stop making it something more than it is, please. I've only just lost my husband. The last thing I want is another man in my life. We're just friends.'

'What's that old Shakespeare line? "The lady doth protest too much, methinks", is it?'

Grabbing the nearest cushion from the garden seating, I whacked Michelle on the arm, nearly sending her mojito flying. Luckily, when she spilt some on her dress when it sloshed over the side of her glass, she found it funny.

'We're only playing with you, Emma. We just want you to be happy. And you do get rather a glazed look in your eye when you talk about Tom,' Jo explained.

'That'll be the vodka in the mojito, I think,' I winked at her and she and Michelle giggled.

'You can laugh, Chelle. You have a little glint of something when you look at Demetri too.'

Michelle looked wistful for a moment.

'Ah, well, I'm still not sure about that. Not sure about any of it really. I still get a funny little feeling when his phone goes and he goes off all mysteriously and answers it. He always says it's work or family stuff but I'm not entirely sure I'm getting the whole picture.'

'Maybe he's a spy and not a doctor after all and that's just a cover-up,' Jo suggested with a big grin.

We all laughed at that.

I loved the good-natured banter between us. I knew that they were only jesting to make light of the situation. They really were the best friends I could wish for, thinking of my happiness.

That evening when I went to bed I thought back to several times in my life when I had let other people take over something that I was passionate about. I wasn't sure what was within me that made me let this happen, but it was almost like what I was trying to do wasn't worth standing up for. I immediately backed off when overpowering people came into my life and shrank myself to fit. I was such a people pleaser that as long as I didn't upset anyone else, I'd back down on what I wanted. And then the one night that I did the opposite, when I insisted that we had sausages for tea instead of the liver that Ben wanted, he went and died. That'll teach me to stand up for myself.

17

When I gingerly peered my head around the entrance door at The Smuggler's Rest, I spotted Tom waving at me from the bar. I'd told him in our message exchange that I'd never been a fan of walking into a pub on my own so he said he'd look out for me. He was just paying for drinks and had a pint of Guinness in one hand and a glass of wine in the other. I was surprised that he'd already chosen my drink for me. Especially when he would have seen me drinking gin and tonic the other day. As he passed me, he shouted over his shoulder.

'Follow me. I've grabbed a table over in the corner.'

It was a busy Saturday night and the bar was busy, so we squeezed our way through the throng. To my surprise, sitting at that table, and who I now realised was clearly the drinker of the glass of wine, was Melanie. She smiled and I knew I was looking puzzled because I could feel my brow furrowing. She seemed quite pleased that she'd put me on the back foot.

'Grab yourself a seat, Em, and I'll go and grab you a drink from the bar? Gin and tonic? Or is there something else you'd prefer?'

'Gin and tonic would be lovely, thanks, Tom.'

I sat at the table, opposite them both as it was the only seat available, because Tom's drink was at the other vacant spot.

'Emma, darling, how lovely that you could join us.'

I was actually under the impression that *she* was the one joining *us*, but I didn't want to be picky so just let it go. As Tom returned to the table and when she put her hand on his arm, she seemed to smirk at me but the facial movement was so quick, I wondered whether I'd imagined it. Remembering Tina's words from the other day, I just had to trust that Melanie was here with good intentions.

I got my notebook and pen out, showing that I meant business.

Melanie turned to Tom.

'Tom, darling, I think we should change up a line or two here to show the emotions of the scene more. Maybe you could put your arm around me as we speak. Look into my eyes more. What do you think?'

He tried to pull me into the conversation.

'What do you think, Emma?'

But Melanie jumped straight back in before I got chance to answer.

'We don't need to bother Emma with this. She's got lots of other people she needs to be sorting out. We're the leads. We can deal with things like that ourselves.'

I coughed and asserted myself.

'Well, it would definitely be nice to be consulted. I don't think that actually works in that scene, to be honest. I think...'

Melanie spoke over the top of me.

'Oh, don't worry, Tom, we can definitely do some private rehearsing and work out what's best.'

That wasn't the only time during the conversation where I

felt like I may as well not be there. Feeling very left out, I excused myself to go to the loo, and when I came back, they seemed cosier than ever. However, when I thought about it, why shouldn't they be? He was just a friend and I believed that she was single too even though she was wearing a wedding ring. He was entitled to hang around with whoever he wanted to. In my personal experience, from chatting to several other widows, men seemed to find it easier to move on after the death of a partner. It was almost like they didn't want to be alone, whereas the women who'd been widowed seemed to take it as an opportunity to rediscover themselves.

'So, I was thinking that for the ball at the end, we should go big. Huge, in fact. What do you think, Em?' I was trying to answer Tom's question when Melanie spoke over the top of me.

'I think we should keep it as simple as possible, Tom. I was thinking of very basic scenery with lots of fairy lights and a romantic dance between you and me... I mean Cindy and Prince Charming, of course.' Her shrill little laugh went right through me. I tried to channel my inner Michelle and when Melanie finished giving her opinion, I just stayed silent.

They both looked at me.

'Ah, you're waiting for my opinion? Thank you.' I knew I sounded confident on the outside, but felt very differently internally. 'Well, Tom, as you've already said, the script lends itself to a big grand ball and I'd love for the scenery to be in keeping with that theme? That OK?' I smiled.

He nodded and if I'd blinked I would have missed the curl of her lip at us agreeing. She folded her arms, not needing to say a word to show that she wasn't happy with the fact we had made a decision. While Tom talked me through his thoughts, sketching out some designs on my pad, he said that he'd been really looking forward to doing some painting again. Apparently when he'd been in Australia he'd taken up painting as a hobby and found it most enjoyable but hadn't got back into it.

Melanie huffed and said she was going to the ladies'.

'I'm sorry I didn't get chance to let you know Melanie was joining us, Em. She kind of ambushed me outside. Said that she'd heard us making arrangements and thought she could tag along. You don't mind her joining us, do you?'

I felt like I was caught between the devil and the deep blue sea. If I said yes, I would appear mean and bitchy. If I said no, then it would encourage him to invite her at another time. I hesitated for probably a second too long, before he said, 'Right, OK. Sorry in that case but there wasn't really a lot I could do. I couldn't outright say no, could I?'

I felt a weak smile cross my face. Maybe I was imagining it all.

'No, I suppose not. I just find her a bit... well... full-on, I suppose. And she seems to be taking over the whole show.'

'Course she's not. This is your pantomime and no one could ever take that away. You know you are the best at this type of thing. Just listen to her thoughts and then do it your way if you want to. You're the boss.'

Melanie's shadow fell over the table.

'Who's the boss? *You*, Emma?' Melanie put her hands on her hips, smirked and cocked one eyebrow. 'Really?'

Again, I thought about what Michelle would do in this situation and it gave me some courage.

Before she had chance to sit back in her original seat, I took the space next to Tom. 'Yes, that's right, Melanie. I am.'

18

We all seemed to settle into our roles quite comfortably. Everyone who had been allotted parts had gone away to learn their lines and those helping behind the scenes had started working on their allocated tasks. Jo and Aggie were trying to put costumes together for the whole cast, which was a massive job, but Michelle, who was handling our social media, had put a call out on a local Facebook page, asking people to drop in any clothes that might fit a certain criteria.

Tom was apparently nipping into the church hall at every opportunity he had so that he could crack on with the set design. He was working on the things we'd discussed and said he'd been really enjoying it.

Melanie and I were tolerating each other. I was still very wary of her and she continued to undermine me at every opportunity; however, she was an amazing lead role and, as I knew when I first saw her, would be such a massive part of the performance. She didn't hesitate to mention that she and Tom were getting together at every opportunity to rehearse their parts together and once I'd got over the first pangs of jealousy over this, I had learned to accept it. I had no claim on Tom and he was a grown man and could spend time with whoever he wanted.

We'd finally worn Jo down to do the role of Dandini, even though she wanted to be called Dave, short for Davina. She could be called anything as long as she agreed, to be honest. Seamus had reluctantly agreed to be Baron Hardup; we drew the line when he suggested we tweak the name to the double-barrelled Baron Hard-On, even though it did give us all a laugh.

'Family show, Seamus. Family show!' Tina tutted at his suggestion and Michelle, Jo and I tittered like schoolchildren at her prim and proper scolding. We still needed another man to be our palace official and Tom said that he'd ask one of his work colleagues.

Sandpiper Shore Primary School Choir had been invited to come along to auditions to sing a couple of numbers, which we thought would be a nice touch. This was the first time we'd heard them sing, and we knew it would go down well with the locals and hopefully give a boost to ticket sales. As they were leaving, and we were just about to have a sit down and a cup of tea and a recap on our busy old day, a little girl and her mum walked through the door.

'Hello, can I help?' I smiled at the little girl who hid behind the woman who I presumed was her mother, although these days you never should presume anything. At a guess I'd say she was around six years old. 'Come on in, we won't bite.'

'Oh, yes, we will,' shouted Tina from the kitchen. It was a great way to crack the ice and the woman smiled and pushed her daughter gently forward towards me. 'Go on, Rubes. Say what you've practised.'

The little girl opened her mouth and whispered but we literally couldn't hear a thing.

'Big voice, darling,' her mother encouraged.

The little girl practically shouted and blurted her words out all in one big rush and I saw the corners of her mother's mouth twitch.

'I-want-to-apply-for-the-part-of-a-fairy-in-the-pontamine.'

'Remember what we talked about at home. Make sure you breathe between your words. Take your time, sweetie.'

She nodded back at her mum who winked and mouthed 'well done' at her and the girl turned to us both and stuck her thumb in her mouth. I swung round to look at Tina who replied to the little girl who had a very hopeful face.

'Oh, gosh. A fairy? I'm not sure we have any fairy parts to fill. The only one we did have was for the Fairy Godmother, which Michelle is cast in. I'm sorry, was your name Ruby?' She nodded and I thought she was about to burst into tears.

I had an idea and wanted to broach it before Tina crushed her dreams completely.

'Can you sing, Ruby?' Her mum moved slightly so that the little girl couldn't see her and vigorously shook her head and then mimed slashing her throat.

'Yes!' Ruby boomed. 'My daddy says I have a beautiful voice. My daddy nearly died and the air ambulance saved him.'

I could feel my eyes widen. Despite the fact that she'd said it all in one big rush without taking a breath, the words packed a powerful punch.

'Wow. Your daddy is very lucky then, isn't he?'

This time it was the turn of the little girl's mum to look tearful, as she explained.

'My husband, Ruby's dad, fell off some scaffolding at work. He broke his back and he's mending slowly but that's why Ruby is desperate for a part in the panto. She wanted to help to raise some money for the air ambulance as her way of saying thank you.'

Tina was the other side of the room and I saw her hand fly to her chest. I could feel tears welling up inside me too.

I bent down to Ruby's level. 'How do you fancy doing a song for me? If you could pick something, what would you choose?'

She looked pensive, pursing her mouth tightly and squeezing her eyes shut.

'"Shake It Off" by Taylor Swift. My most favourite song *ever*.'

'OK, Tina, can you give us some notes on the piano and Ruby can audition for a singing part?'

'Is the part a fairy? I *really* want to be a fairy.' The excitement had made her speed up her words again. She also let out a big smile as she clearly remembered her manners. '*Please!*'

'Well, we already have Michelle who is the Fairy Godmother but... maybe...' I blew out a long stream of air. 'What do you think, Tina? I reckon Ruby would make a fabulous fairy assistant.'

Tina clapped her hands together. 'It's exactly what we've been missing from the show. How fabulous. Come on, Ruby, let's go and find some music and you can give us a demo.' Ruby's little face lit up like a sunbeam and I could see that her mum melted in a pool of emotion.

Tina held her hand out to Ruby and when she took it, they walked hand in hand to the piano where Tina shuffled through some music sheets. She settled on one, naturally placing her hands on the keys, like a touch-typist places their hands on a keyboard.

I turned to her mother.

'She's adorable.'

'Thank you, but I'm not sure you'll think the same when you hear her sing. She's adorable as a kid but she's no singer, and I'm her mum.'

I laughed. 'Ah, she can't be that bad.' Her mum was probably doing her a major injustice. I was expecting her voice to be soft and angelic like her speaking voice.

The ear-splitting, blood-curdling, out-of-tune sound that came out of Ruby's mouth could not even be described as singing. She even got the words muddled and sang the chorus line as 'shake it up' rather than 'off'. Her mum looked at me with raised eyebrows and an *I-told-you-so* face.

Ruby came running back over. 'What did you think? Was I bwilliant?'

Tina followed, rubbing her ears.

'I think you were absolutely fabulous, Ruby.' I put on a mock-serious face. 'We'd like to offer you the part.'

Ruby burst into tears of what I presumed were total over-whelm and the grown-ups all smiled at each other in solidarity.

'I have to check something first.'

Ruby stopped crying immediately and perked up at my question.

'Do you have an agent? Do I need to get in touch with anyone?'

Ruby giggled. 'You're silly. Of course I don't have an agent. I'm a child!' She held up her hands and struggled to count her fingers, eventually holding up six.

'Ah, that's good. We won't have to pay fees then.'

'Do I get paid? If I do, I'd like to donit it to the air ambulance.'

My own heart melted. What a sweet little soul.

'I'm afraid we don't pay money, but we do pay in biscuits. Would that be acceptable?' I held out my hand for her to shake.

She narrowed her eyes.

'Custard creams, Hobnobs or party rings?'

I blew out another long breath.

'You drive a hard bargain, little lady. You don't need an agent. How about all three?'

She punched the air. 'Deal!'

We all laughed but then quickly her face changed and a big frown appeared.

'Mummy! Do you think Daddy will be able to come to watch me?'

'If he's out of hospital I'm sure he will, darling.' She gave a big sigh and looked at both Tina and me, slightly shaking her head and mouthing, 'Probably not.'

It would be such a shame if he wasn't able to watch this adorable little girl in her star role, but maybe we could see about getting the panto streamed live and he could watch it online. I'd check with the guy who was doing the audio-visual and lighting. We could even ask for donations from those who watched. That way we could reach people in other parts of the country too. Maybe the cast would have family and friends who might donate.

'Well, Ruby, how do you feel about having some homework?'

This sweet little girl nodded profusely and I only hoped that I was doing the right thing.

'Do you think that you can rehearse that song until you know all the words off by heart?' She nodded so hard I thought her head might nod off her shoulders. 'And one more thing?' Her big wide eyes stared up at me. 'Fairies speak really slowly. Do you think you could practise doing that for me too? What do you think?'

'I... Think... That... Would... Be... Most... Acc-sip-table.'

'Now that, my friend, is perfect! You are going to make a wonderful fairy assistant and we'll find you a wonderful dress to wear.'

'Oh... Don't... Worry... I... Already... Have... My... Own... It's... The... Most... Beautiful... Fairy... Dress... Ever...'

'Well, *you*, my little poppet, are going to be the star of the show.'

When Ruby flung herself at me and gave me a squeeze which I thought might damage some of my internal organs, I was totally flabbergasted. Yet delighted. It was nice to have made someone's day. Her mother grabbed both of my hands in hers and tears pooled in her eyes.

'I can't thank you both enough.' She glanced over at Tina. 'You've made her dream come true.'

As Ruby skipped out of the door, holding hands with her mum, she was a very different happy little girl to the one that we first met fifteen minutes before. I heard her say to her mum, 'My daddy is going to be so proud of me.'

'As I am, my darling. As am I.'

As they left the church hall, I thought about what a lovely relationship they had. I could hear them both singing the words to 'Shake It Up' as they headed up the street, swinging hands and laughing loudly. I didn't very often feel emotional at the fact that I'd never had children. Ben had never wanted them, was adamant about it, so I just accepted that as my lot in life. But just then, it hit me like a stab in the heart, that I'd missed my chance for someone who wasn't even here any more. I didn't want to feel woe is me, but sometimes life just wasn't fair.

19

Rehearsals were completely chaotic and all I was able to think about was whether it would all come together at any point.

'Don't worry so much, Emma. Have faith.' Tina's kind words always soothed my worries but didn't completely take them away.

I tried not to roll my eyes when Melanie came over and said that she'd been thinking. I pasted on a smile instead.

'So, about the costumes. I reckon that people should be responsible for their own outfits. That way they're always going to find something that they want to wear and that will fit them properly. What do you think?'

I glanced sideways and could see that Tina's eyebrow raised even though she was sitting next to me looking down at her notebook. I took a moment before answering.

'Yeah, that's a nice idea, Melanie, but it's not how I want to do it. I know exactly what I want people to be wearing and we've already started the process now too. Thanks for your suggestion, but we're going to continue to do it the way we've started.'

'OK, no biggie. It was just a thought to help everyone out.'

She walked away from our table, and towards the box of donated clothes that we'd got so far. Rooting through it, she picked up a really pretty flowery dress and sniffed at it, turning her nose up.

Tina didn't lift her head when she spoke.

'That was a great idea, you know.'

'Yeah, I know.' Begrudgingly I had to admit it out loud.

This time she did turn towards me.

'What is it that you don't like about her? What has she done to upset you?'

The truth was that she hadn't done anything directly. She reminded me of Julie but that wasn't really Melanie's fault. How could I admit that the reason she wound me up was because it dented my self-esteem, which wasn't all that high to begin with? Having someone's faith in me to run the panto had really lifted my spirits at a time when I needed it most. But if I said that to Tina now, it would make me look petty and small-minded.

I could feel my shoulders slump slightly. 'I suppose I feel that she's criticising me when she comes up with these ideas. As if she thinks that my ideas aren't good enough.'

'The growth mindset thing to do would be to think about what's best for the pantomime and not about how you feel a little perturbed that someone had a good idea that could work. And I'm not saying it's a better idea. It's just a different one. And just imagine if you didn't have to worry about the costumes. It would be a massive thing off your to-do list and buy you some time.' She laid her hand on my arm. I always felt that Tina had magic hands that radiated calm and gave you peace. 'Time is so precious these days, Emma. We all know that and at our age, we don't need any more stress than is completely necessary.'

Her wise words were so true. I really should take on

Melanie's idea but to do that I'd have to swallow my pride and I wasn't sure I was ready to do that.

Melanie wasn't her usual effervescent self for the rest of the day. She was more subdued than normal and didn't seem to have her normal enthusiasm. I felt guilty that I'd played a part in that. I needed to think carefully about how I handled this. I didn't want anyone dropping out at this point. At the moment it felt a little bit like a house of cards, balancing nicely, but could topple at any point if something didn't go quite to plan.

As I saw Melanie grabbing her handbag and saying goodbye to Tina, I stopped her in the hallway and asked if she had a minute.

'I've been thinking,' I said.

'Ooh, that sounds dangerous.' She smiled gently and I could tell that she was trying to put me at my ease. Maybe she wasn't the tyrant I thought she was and it wasn't fair to judge her just because she reminded me of Julie.

'Your idea about the costumes.' I took a deep breath as she looked at me expectantly. 'In hindsight, I do think it's the right thing to do. It's a better idea.'

Her face broke into a bigger smile and this time it reached her eyes.

'I'm glad, Emma. It's obviously entirely up to you, of course. You're the boss of the panto but I just want to help you. It's something that I've really enjoyed being part of and you've all made me feel so welcome even though you didn't really know me from Adam. Or should I say Eve? Why is that phrase based around a man? Anyhoo! I'm happy to help in any way. I'm a bit lost, to be honest. I've never admitted this to anyone before, and I think have only recently admitted it to myself, but since my husband and I split up, I feel incredibly lonely and feel that this has given me a reason to get out and about. I'm really enjoying being involved; part of something special. Thank you.'

Gosh. This confession surprised me and made me feel even more guilty. You never really knew what was going on in some-one's life and it only confirmed my mantra even more, that at all times you should just be kind.

20

Exhaustion overcame me and when there was a hammering at the front door, I lifted my head up from the settee and peered at the clock through sleep-filled eyes, realising that the room was in total darkness.

'Emma, are you in there?' Michelle's voice came through the letter box.

'Hang on a mo!'

I swept my hair back from my forehead and forced my eyes wide open, getting up from the sofa and ambling to the front door.

'Are you ill, love?' she asked.

'No, just knackered,' I said. Glancing at my watch, I noticed that it was nearly eight o'clock. I'd only meant to close my eyes for ten minutes but had nodded off for much longer.

'It's Friday night and there's a cock with your name on it on the terrace.'

I smiled. 'It's not every day you get an offer like that.'

'It certainly isn't. To clarify, I did mean cocktail. Hope you're not too disappointed.' She grinned back at me. 'Do you need a minute?'

'Yes, please. Let me just go and splash some water on my face and I'll be up.'

I was glad that I made the effort. Jo had got the firepit going and the flames were crackling away. She threw a blanket at me to cover my legs.

'These nights are starting to get colder. Autumn is definitely well settled in. It'll soon be Christmas.'

'Don't say that. We're nowhere near ready for the panto and there's a couple of Christmas events I still need to organise for the Lonely Hearts Club too. Maybe I have taken on too much after all. I'm no spring chicken and I'm bloody knackered. Ben always used to say that I thought I could do more than I was capable of. Maybe I should just stick to retirement. Have long walks on the beach and just potter around the village every day.'

'Nonsense,' snapped Michelle. 'You are and can be anything you want to be. If you tell yourself you're knackered and have taken on too much you'll start to believe it. You need to believe in yourself the way we do. I don't want to speak ill of the dead,' she looked upwards and mouthed *sorry Ben*, 'but your husband should have said the same thing. He should have supported you the way that we do.'

'Ah, it wasn't his fault. He was a perfectionist. He knew exactly what he wanted and was determined to get it. I wish you'd met him. Sometimes I make him out to sound like a monster when he really wasn't.'

'I don't think you make him out to be bad, but I do think that at times, he knocked your self-confidence. The Emma that we see isn't the Emma that you describe when you talk about you being together. That Emma was a people-pleasing pushover, I reckon. This Emma is an ass-kicking badass.'

I grinned at them both and raised my cocktail glass. 'Yes. I am!'

'You could always take a lover, you know. Like Bridget Jones did in the fourth movie. Get yourself a toy boy. Or a handsome older man. Just anyone really.'

'Honestly, girls, I can't imagine ever wanting to be naked with another man as long as I live. I just don't think I could face it.' I gazed into the firepit, hypnotised by the flames, and shivered at the thought despite the heat. 'No. I'll be happy on my own for the rest of my life. I'll get a cat. Or three. Become a mad cat lady. That'll do me.'

'Emma, can I say something without you taking offence?' Michelle asked.

'Oh, God! You do realise that when people say that it's because you know that you are going to offend them, don't you?' I laughed. She didn't laugh back. I looked to Jo, who was biting her fingernails. It was as if they'd both been talking about me behind my back.

'Go on...' I had no idea where she was heading.

'You're fifty-two years old, Emma. Not seventy-two or even eighty-two. I know it's been hard and that you miss Ben and we don't know what that feels like. But you still have a lifetime ahead of you and that could be a really good one. There are people here who want to see you thriving, not just surviving.' That was the second time in a month that expression had been used. The last time it was me that said it so I knew exactly what she meant. 'I'm going to say something now which will sound harsh but isn't meant to. It's just that I don't know how to how to say it any other way.'

'Go for it. You've obviously got something on your mind.' Irritability was something I was prone to when I was tired and even though I'd napped earlier, I was still absolutely shattered. Again,

Ben was also quick to point this out. As this thought popped into my mind, I clocked again that I'd noticed that these thoughts were becoming more frequent. I was starting to see the cracks that had been happening in our marriage. Maybe it hadn't always been as perfect as I remembered.

Michelle pushed her shoulders back and took a deep breath.

'It was Ben that died. Not you.'

'Jesus, Michelle! You weren't wrong when you said it was going to sound harsh.'

Jo came and sat by me, taking my hand. 'We're just thinking of you, Emma. You're so bloody fabulous and we love you so much, we just want you to be happy.'

'I lost my husband, Jo. I'm not meant to be having a blast. My whole life has fallen apart.'

Michelle sat the other side of me and took my other hand in hers. 'We really do love you, Emma. You deserve someone wonderful to treat you to lovely things and to care about you.'

'Girls, I really appreciate the sentiment and your lovely words, but finding someone else really is the furthest thing from my mind right now. I love you both too. Very much but please, let this drop. I'm well aware of the fact that my husband died. And with him, a little bit of me died too and I'm just trying to readjust to life and navigate my way around the good days and the bad. I'm not going to find the solution by jumping into bed with anyone at all. Even if they look like that fine young boy Leo Woodhall. I mean, who was Bridget trying to kid, when they went out on a date and she told him she was thirty-five? She's a similar age to me and the thought of dating a twenty-eight-year-old makes my insides squirm, and not in the way you are thinking.'

I looked down at our joined hands, then back up again and smiled at Michelle and then turned to smile at Jo too.

'Thank you for thinking of me but I'm fine on my own. Truly. Now if you'll excuse me, I'm going to head off home. I really need my bed.' I stood and waved my hand in the air as I pottered across the lawn back to my apartment. But I could feel two sets of eyes boring into my back with every step.

21

What Michelle and Jo had been saying to me the evening before had been playing on my mind all night and I woke late after a restless night's sleep. Overtiredness wasn't helping but I couldn't stop thinking about their words. It also made me wonder what people would think of me if I did decide to do more with my life. Would they think I didn't care about Ben any more? If I did ever start to see anyone else, would they think that I'd forgotten him? Gosh, navigating widowhood was hard.

When the phone rang it startled me. Michelle's name flashed up on the caller display.

'Are you up? I need to see you.'

'It's a bit early. I've not long woken.'

'Blimey, it's eight o'clock. You've normally been out for a run and been back by now. It's important, love. I wouldn't ring otherwise. It's also really good news too.'

'OK, give me five minutes to have my first cup of tea and come round. I'll put a pot on.' I smiled to myself remembering how when my own mum used to say that she couldn't wake up until she had two cups of tea, I couldn't understand it. Now I could totally relate.

When Michelle burst through the door a few minutes later, she was beaming from ear to ear and practically hopping from foot to foot.

'Come on then. What's got you all in a tizzy?' I took my time and poured her a cup of tea from the pot, stirring gently, the complete antithesis of her own excitable state.

'The county magazine wants to do a feature on you. They've asked if they can come round to the church hall this afternoon to take some photos and do an interview. Or they can come here if you'd rather. We'd just have to let them know of the change of location.'

'What?' I very nearly spat my tea out. 'They want to feature me? What on earth for?'

'Because you are so inspirational and you are helping the people who live in the county of Cornwall both with the Lonely Hearts Club and the panto.'

'I'd rather not if you don't mind, Michelle. I know this is the field you work in, but it's not for me. Please tell them thank you. I'm flattered, but it's a no.'

She rolled her eyes and huffed before continuing.

'Well, it's a bit like this, Em. I can't.'

'Why ever not?'

She shrugged her shoulders at me. 'Because... I've already said yes, you'll do it.'

'You did what? You had no right to do that without having my answer first.'

'Mmmmm.' She stared at me, shaking her head.

'Are you... OK there, Chelle?'

'I knew you'd say no. I wish I'd bet Jo that fiver now.'

'You've both been betting on me?'

'Yeah, Jo said you would do it, but I said you wouldn't. That's why I accepted on your behalf. Before you had the opportunity to turn them down.'

'You really did too, didn't you? This isn't a joke?'

Michelle shook her head.

'Think of it like this, Emma. It's free publicity for both of the things you are involved in. You will sell tons of tickets for the panto near and far and there'll be loads of people that'll read about what you're doing for lonely people too and that will probably mean you'll get more people wanting to join. It's a win-win.'

I could feel a headache coming on.

'Sorry, Chelle, but it's still a no. You know how much I hate having my photo taken and I've got nothing to wear that's suitable.'

'What a shocking excuse. You've got more clothes than me and Jo put together and they're all really lovely. You always look amazing.'

I reached up to my hair.

'I'm sure if we rang Aggie she'd come round and give you a quick blow dry. You had your roots done a week ago, so you can't use that as an excuse. Aggie could probably help you to pick outfits too. You already know she's great at that sort of stuff.'

I stood staring at her with my hands on my hips. I was annoyed with her for saying yes on my behalf. She really should have asked me first.

'Please say yes, Emma. Think about the exposure the charity will get because of the feature. This sort of publicity is priceless. I thought for that reason alone you'd want to do it. I know you don't want to put yourself out there right now, but maybe you could do it for the air ambulance.'

Michelle really knew where my weak spot was and I could see the corners of her mouth turn up when she realised she'd rattled me. Maybe the vicar and his wife would be more inter-ested in doing it. It was their idea initially anyway and I'm sure he'd love a bit of free publicity for his Sunday sermon.

'I'll think about it.' I agreed just to buy me some time.

'Well, don't think about it for too long because they're coming to the church hall at 3 p.m.' I folded my arms and Michelle tapped her lip repeatedly with her index finger. 'Unless...'

'Unless what?'

'There is someone else who could possibly do the interview. We could always ask Melanie. She's incredibly stylish and photo-genic. I bet she'd do it.'

'Yes, I bet she bloody would.'

Michelle knew that she'd played her trump card.

'Well then. It's up to you to not let her have that opportunity, isn't it? If you want me to come round and hold your hand while they're there, I'd be very happy to. I'll give Aggie a quick bell and get her round here at lunchtime. Maybe we could ask Graham and Tina to be in the photos. How exciting this is going to be. People pay lots of money for features like this. What have you got to lose?'

'Only my dignity when my big fat face appears in the local newspaper for the whole world to see.'

'Ah, don't worry, love. It's not the whole world.' I gave what I knew was a tight-lipped smile. 'It's just the whole of Cornwall.' She grinned and slammed the door behind her.

22

Aggie had come round and we had chosen a couple of outfits together which she thought would work well with a camera. She'd said that when she and Scott had done photoshoots in the past, she'd been told to take a change of outfit so it looked like the photos were taken at different times. Michelle, as promised, was also there to hold my hand if needed.

Aggie was always lovely company yet I couldn't help feeling she sometimes seemed a little sad. I didn't know whether to say anything but decided that she could silence me if she wanted to.

'Aggie, I can't help but feel that you're not yourself today. Is everything OK?'

She sighed. 'I shouldn't really say anything, but I can trust you, right?'

'Absolutely.'

'I'm worried about Scott. He's having a really tough time at the moment. He's not got many friends around this way and I think despite having me and the kids in the house he's desperately lonely. He's really lacking male company. He's gone from being surrounded by men all day long to having no one close to chat to.'

'He needs to come along to the Lonely Hearts Club. We've got quite a few men who come and the more that do come, it'll encourage others too.'

'Thanks, Emma, I appreciate that and it's a great idea. I'll broach it when I think it's the right time. Anyway, we can't sit around here. We need to get down to the church hall.'

Despite my initial objections, the afternoon had turned out to be fun and I fully understood that it would be great for the group, the panto and the charity fundraising which was ultimately what the event was about.

The person who came to do the interview turned out to be the editor of the magazine as the normal journalist had called in sick. I immediately warmed to her sparkling personality as she offered me her hand and introduced herself.

'Hi, you must be Emma. I'm Fliss.' She was clearly an expert in her field and guided me with her questions so I knew exactly how to answer.

Khandie, the photographer, had a naturally smiley face, which made me want to smile too. I was totally in awe of her because she was stunning herself and properly cool. She wore dead funky clothes but she was the one who made me feel a million dollars, telling me that I looked gorgeous and that the shots would look really natural. She did get me into some questionable poses but promised that the images would look fabulous. Some had been taken in the church hall and she then dragged me along to the local coffee shop and took some shots there too. I was starting to look forward to seeing the finished feature in print, despite my earlier hesitation.

Graham and Tina joined me in the panto promotional photos, which were taken outside of the church hall next to the poster. I was glad we hadn't explored the option of including the main characters as I couldn't imagine feeling quite that relaxed around Melanie. Fliss said they'd come back a week before the launch date and do another feature which would be great for those final ticket sales.

As Fliss was packing away, we chattered away like we'd known each other for years.

'You don't know any journalists, do you, ladies?' she asked. 'I need to fill some column space in the mag. We're really struggling at the moment.'

Michelle piped up. 'You should get Emma to do a Lonely Hearts column. That'd be great.' We both laughed, me a little more nervously.

Fliss brought her hands to her cheeks. 'Oh my gosh, that would be absolutely fabulous. What a brilliant idea. That would go down a treat with our readers. We have a podcast show too and are always looking for new and interesting angles for our listeners. Always looking for the next best thing. And I really do think that this could be it! What do you think, Emma?'

I forced a laugh this time. 'I'm no writer, Fliss, or broadcaster for that matter. Sorry.'

She was now like a dog with a bone. 'Well, you don't really have to be perfect, we could get one of the editorial team to tart up the wording to make it readable. And with the podcast we don't want someone who is typically broadcasting with what we call a BBC voice. We want someone with a local accent who is dead natural and knows the topic really well. You'd be amazing. My little mind is working overtime now.'

'I don't really think...' I was trying to find a way to let her down gently but she wasn't going down without a really good attempt to convince me.

'We could have an email address that people could write in

to and you could come up with some answers. A bit like an agony aunt for lonely people. This could be brilliant, you know. A real selling point for the mag too. Please do it, Emma. Or at the very least consider it.'

'It's really flattering of you to ask me but to be honest with the group and the panto, I have enough on my plate at the moment.' I knew I wouldn't have the time, even though it was a good idea, but for someone else.

'Look, here's my number.' She handed me her business card. 'Will you promise me you'll think about it at the very least? It could even start in the new year so the panto is done and dusted and you've got more time on your hands.'

I went to speak but she held up her palm to stop me.

'Not listening. Just think about it, that's all I ask.' She curled her hand into the shape of a phone with her thumb and little finger. 'Call me!' She winked at me and Michelle, picked up her bag and left.

Michelle and I stared at each other in stunned silence before she broke it.

'Well, that was a turn-up for the books.'

'It was actually. Nowhere near as bad as I thought it might be.' The flash of Michelle's raised eyebrow combined with her self-satisfied smirk was slightly irritating yet somewhat amusing too as she knew that she didn't have to utter those *I-told-you-so* words. It was a good job I loved her.

'And get you. You should definitely think about that Lonely Hearts column, you know.'

'Oh, I don't have the skills to do something like that.'

'I think you're wrong, Emma. I can't think of anyone I know who would be more perfect. You were saying that you needed something else to focus on. And once the panto is over, you'll be back to square one again, fumbling around trying to fill your time. You'll only have the group then that will need your attention. This could lead to other stuff too. I'm a big believer that the more people in life you meet, the more opportunities come your way. I also think that people are put in your way for a reason. This could be great for you, Em.'

'It is true, but I can't think about it right now. I'm just taking things one step at a time. My middle-aged brain can't cope with too much going on at once. It's already fuddled with the panto and the group.'

She laughed knowingly. The brain of most women I knew at this age in life was slightly slower to function than in our younger years and a fact that we often laughed about on our Friday night put-the-world-to-rights sessions.

As Michelle and I walked back up to the cottage, taking the long way back along the beach and through the dunes, I could tell something was on her mind. I'd known her long enough to know when she was sitting on something, desperate to speak her mind, but not wanting to upset me.

'Go on, Chelle, say whatever you need to.'

She laughed. 'I was just thinking that we're two peas in a pod really.'

'How so?' I enquired.

'Well, there's me not really giving my whole self to Demetri and you're similar with the opportunities that come your way. Do you think there's something wrong with us both?'

I pursed my lips in thought.

'Why don't you give your whole self to Demetri, do you think?'

She stopped and shrugged her shoulders.

'What if he hurts me? What if I land up in the same place as I did when my last boyfriend dumped me? I'm not sure my bruised and battered heart can cope again.'

I reached out and touched her arm.

'But what if he doesn't? What if it all turns out to be wonderful and you've thrown away something special not everyone is lucky enough to get the chance to experience?'

She turned and looked out across the dunes. 'Life is hard sometimes, isn't it?'

'Do you like him? I mean *really* like him?'

She grinned. 'Yeah, I do. Even if half of me is trying not to.'

'Maybe you should let go then and just see what happens?'

'I will if you will, Emma.'

'What do you mean by that?'

'I'll try to let go of my inhibitions more if you do the same. Give yourself the chance to get to know Tom again. He clearly wants to be friends. Maybe even more than friends.'

I gathered my thoughts while watching two seagulls swoop and dive down to the water's edge before Michelle spoke again.

'Maybe there is no right or wrong. What if we just went with how we feel at a particular time? Stop overthinking everything; live in the now.'

'You're not as daft as you look, you know.'

She bumped me with her shoulder.

'I've been known to have my moments. I'm not asking you to marry him. Just have some fun. Some nights out, some male company. And who's to say that doing the podcast and the column in the paper might not be the best thing that ever happened to you. And if it isn't then at least you can say you've tried. What's that saying? It's better to regret the things you did than regret those you never even tried.'

'Yeah, maybe. My old nana used to say, "Happiness will only come when you let go of the hurt that's holding you back." I suppose it's the same thing really.'

She linked her arm into mine as we headed back on the path

to the cottage and as we reached my front door, she kissed my cheek before speaking her parting words.

'I reckon we all deserve a bit of happiness in our lives, don't we, mate? See you tomorrow. Don't work too hard.' I stood and watched her walk back to her own home before lifting my head towards the sky.

Thinking about Tom made me uneasy. As if the whole situation was opening a can of worms. Before he came back into my life, I thought about him from time to time but since I'd seen him recently, he was constantly on my mind. It made me feel a little bit like I was being unfaithful to Ben. What I had to keep reminding myself was what Michelle and Jo had said to me recently. It *was* Ben who had died, not me. And I still had a whole lot of life ahead of me to live. Maybe I was holding back, with no real reason why. Was it because I was worried about what people would think; what they would say? Someone once said to me that what people think of you is their business, not yours. Maybe it wouldn't hurt me to let go a little and stop worrying about everyone else.

I took a deep breath. It was time to start thinking about me. Time to start living life again.

23

It was a few days later when we all met up again as a whole group. Most of the cast were present and it was the first time we were doing read-throughs. Melanie was in the opening scene wearing what she said she classed as her scruffs but they were probably better than some of the rest of the cast's best clothes. She was being bossed about by Graham and Bill as her ugly sisters. As they were going through the scene, I popped out to my car, which was just outside the church hall door, to bring in a box of clothes I had put to one side.

'Here, let me help.' Tom took the box from me and as his arm brushed against mine, I could feel myself blushing.

'Hey.' He smiled and I sighed, resigning myself to the fact that I was just fooling myself if I thought he didn't mean anything to me.

'Hey, yourself.'

'All going well, is it?' He nodded towards the stage.

'So far.'

'Listen, about the other night in the pub. I was rather hoping it was just going to be just you and me, you know. I enjoyed it when it was just the two of us recently and we reminisced. I didn't realise that Mel was stopping as long as she did. I felt a little bit as if you left earlier than you might have done if it was just us two. So, I wondered if you...' His eyes met mine as he seemed to struggle to find the words and I willed him to go on. 'Well... you know...' The next part was garbled as if he thought that the quicker he blurted it out, the less of a deal he was making it. 'Whether you'd like to go out with me some time.' He rolled his eyes and I was sure I heard him mumble the word *idiot* under his breath.

'What? Are you seventeen again, Tom Sullivan?' I asked, and my own face broke into a grin.

'It's you, Em. You make me feel like I'm a teenager all over again.'

'Oh!'

We stood and stared at each other for what seemed like ages before I spoke again.

'Is that good or bad?'

'I have no blooming idea, Emma. Wait there. Please. Don't move. I'll be right back.'

When he returned seconds later without the box, he grabbed my hands in his.

'Emma. Please may I take you out for dinner one night?'

An uncontrollable flush of heat rose up my neck and into my cheeks. I didn't think I could blame this on my age. This was the moment that I had to make a decision. Should I go or not? I knew that I was stalling for time and he probably thought that I was a complete lunatic for not answering him straight away. I was trying not to show the panic in my face that I was feeling in my body.

'And just to make sure there's no confusion as to what I

mean, I'd like to just confirm that I'm asking you out on a date.' He raised a questioning eyebrow.

I thought back to Jo once saying how sometimes you just had to make a decision. It didn't matter if it was the right one or the wrong one. You could fathom that out later but the anxiety that surrounded most things in life was not knowing what to do. I'm not sure where the bravado came from but all I could hear my inner voice saying was, *Go on, Emma, why the hell not? It's just dinner.*

I was just about to answer him when the door beside us flung open and Stephanie reversed through it like a whirlwind, her arms draped with clothes.

'Hi, Dad.' She reached up and somehow, despite her arms being full, managed to give him a peck on the cheek before she noticed me. 'Oh, hi, Emma. Sorry, I didn't see you there. Can you grab these off me, please, Dad. I'm about to drop them.' She looked from Tom to me and back again. 'Sorry.' She narrowed her eyes. 'I wasn't interrupting anything, was I?'

Tom and I connected eyes, and he answered on our behalf. 'It's OK. It can wait,' before heading off to the backstage area, followed closely by his daughter.

Gathering myself together and fanning my warm face with my right hand, I headed back over to the table, determined to throw myself into watching the performance on the stage in front of me. Melanie as Cindy was brilliant, just as I knew she would be. Graham and Bill were hilarious in what could only be described as throwing themselves in the part as much as they could, being as bitchy to their little stepsister Cindy as possible. There was lots of cackling coming from them and I'm sure they were quite enjoying it. Probably a little more than they should have been.

I could feel Tom's eyes on me from across the room and I was trying so hard not to look at him, but a couple of times I couldn't help myself glance over when I thought he wasn't looking. I didn't seem to be able to stop my heart giving a little skip each time he looked back and smiled. I wasn't sure how this was happening, but I was seventeen all over again with a huge crush on the boy with the big blue eyes and the killer grin.

When he sidled over to me during the second scene he nudged me with his shoulder.

'So, are you going to put me out of my misery then? Are you going to let me take you out?' He grinned. Earlier words that Michelle and Jo, came back to me and a little voice almost popped into my head. *You don't have to jump into bed with him. Just get out and enjoy yourself.*

This time it was my turn to grin and I nodded enthusiastically.

'Yes, Tom. I'd love to.'

His whole face lit up and he did a subdued air punch and an excited 'yes!' escaped his lips before he winked at me and then walked away. I saw Michelle and Jo glance at each other over the top of Melanie's head and give each other a thumbs up. I looked away, pretending I hadn't seen, hiding a smile of my own, and spent the rest of the evening trying hard to concentrate on the play and not the impending date.

24

Date night soon rolled around. Michelle and Jo were making me even more nervous than I already was by coming round and trying to help me choose something suitable to wear.

Michelle shook her head when I came out of the bedroom wearing my favourite little black dress, black tights and black kitten heels.

I did a little twirl.

'Better?'

'Emma! No! You look like you are going to a funeral. Sorry! No offence meant and I know both of you have been bereaved recently but I don't think widow's weeds is a suitable date outfit.'

I retreated into my room and came out in a strappy silky short red dress with silver high sandals. 'I've not worn this for years. What does this dress say?'

Jo and Michelle glanced at each other before Michelle blew air through her lips loudly.

'That dress says, "forget dinner, just shag me now!"' Jo howled. I huffed back off into my bedroom, before returning in a pair of navy-blue trousers, a flowery t-shirt and a navy cardigan.

Michelle shook her head at me. 'Remind me again how old you are? You look like you've borrowed that from Tessa. Sorry, Jo. No offence to your mother.'

'None taken,' Jo responded. 'I think Tessa is even more trendy than this, to be honest.'

'You pair are making this worse for me.' I felt a tear prick the back of my throat. 'I'm going to message Tom and just cancel it.'

'You'll do no such thing, lady. Come on. Let's go and see what we can find together.'

Jo and Michelle managed to get nearly every item of clothing that I owned out on the bed before they had a discussion amongst themselves and turned to me, both nodding profusely.

When I put the denim jacket that they'd chosen over the flowery summer dress and teamed it with a pair of designer sparkly trainers and a matching handbag, I had to admit that they knew their stuff. I felt both comfortable, fresh and reasonably fashionable. The blue flowers in the pattern brought out the blue of my eyes and my lipstick matched the pink flowers too.

There was a knock at the door.

'Oh my God, he's here.' They both laughed at the look of fright on my face.

'Aw, look, our baby is going out on her first date. I'm so happy for her.' Michelle clutched her hands to her chest and swooned. Her pretence at being a proud parent was short-lived when Jo asked if I'd put some emergency condoms in my handbag just in case. I threw a cushion off the bed at her, trying not to laugh as I opened the door to Tom.

'You look lovely, Em.'

'You don't scrub up so bad yourself.' He was wearing a pair of dark jeans, a white shirt and a smart navy blazer. He looked gorgeous and as he leant across to give me a kiss on the cheek, his aftershave wafted across me. He smelt divine. My body gave an involuntary shudder as his hand brushed against my arm.

'I've booked a table at The Fisherman's Haunt. Hope that's OK.'

'Perfect.' I smiled and hoped that poor boy Harvey who I'd probably traumatised for life wasn't working that evening and if he was, prayed silently that he didn't recognise me.

'Ready, m'lady?' He crooked his arm for me to hold and I heard Jo and Michelle giggling from inside the house.

'Bye, Mum. You look great. Have a nice time. Love you,' they called out to me.

I laughed, despite the fact that they were trying to do their best to embarrass me. I loved that we all teased each other something rotten. Something only friends can do and understand.

'Ignore the children, Tom. They'll grow up one day. You wouldn't think they were two middle-aged women, would you?'

'I think you three have a wonderful relationship to be honest. I wish I had mates I could have a laugh and a joke with. I've never felt more of a lack of male company since I came back from Aus. That's why Stephanie wanted me to come along to the group. She was hoping that there might be more men there than there are, to be honest.'

This topic had actually been playing on my mind since I chatted with Aggie recently and she mentioned how she was worried about Scott. With men's mental health being such a talking point in the news, I hoped that it might be something that we could address at some point and get more men along.

'Well, now you come to mention it, maybe this is something you could help me with. I was thinking that the more men that join and possibly organise more male-orientated and mixed events too, then it would encourage both sexes to come along.'

We were still talking about this subject twenty minutes later when we pulled up at the restaurant. Collaboratively, we'd inspired each other and had come up with some great suggestions, and Tom had agreed that he'd try to build up the male side of the group by sharing it in some Facebook groups he was in and down at the gym he sometimes went to. Whilst I did have a nosy at Instagram from time to time, I wasn't a big social media user as I hadn't got a clue how to use it really. Ben's business paid a company to handle it for them, so I didn't even get involved when I was helping out there. Michelle handled that side of things for the Lonely Hearts Club activity so it would be a great help if Tom could get involved too.

All the nerves that I'd been feeling that day had dissolved as I realised that the teenage Tom and Emma who used to chatter for hours well into the night were still just as tuned in to each other today as we talked non-stop all the way through three fabulous courses.

The food, as it was the first time I ate here, was stunning. I chose the twice-cooked pork belly with an apple and radish chutney for my starter. I spent ages deliberating between main courses, finally settling on the pie of the day, which was steak and stilton, in a crumbly suet crust, with herby mashed potatoes and roasted root vegetables. Proper comfort food. For pudding, even though I thought I was ridiculously full already, I managed to polish off a sticky toffee pudding and custard.

'I do like a woman who enjoys her food.' Tom smiled as I put in the last mouthful of my pudding.

'I'm making up for it. I've spent years dieting and being careful about what I ate and worrying about whether it was fattening,' I explained. 'Ben liked me skinny.'

'Gosh. I'm the opposite. I love my food. Just for the record, Emma, you can eat what you like when you're out with me. In fact, I insist on it.'

I smiled back, not wanting to dwell on it, but realising that this was just another of the many differences between Tom and Ben. When would I stop comparing?

As one of the lights behind the bar was turned off, we realised that we were the only ones left in the restaurant and we asked the waiter for the bill.

'I'll get this,' Tom insisted and waved my hand away when I offered to split the bill. 'You can get it next time.' He winked at me and my heart gave that little skip again. It was nice to know that he was thinking there might be a next time. He handed his card to the waiter.

'Please do pass our compliments on to the chef. The meal was fabulous.'

A voice I was sure I'd heard before came to me then and it sounded like it was getting closer, until a familiar face peered around the pillar.

'You can do that yourself.' Amusement shone in Martin's eyes when we recognised each other from our previous encounter in his kitchen. 'Ah, the lovely Emma Montgomery.' He reached across and kissed my cheek and then as Tom stood, he gave him a brief hug. 'Tom. Great to see you.'

'So, you two know each other, do you?' I asked a little puzzled, remembering this nice young man who had been so kind to me previously.

'I'd say so. Tom is my father-in-law and he lives in my spare bedroom.'

'Oh, wow. It really is a small world, isn't it?' I frowned as I remembered that when I'd asked Martin if there was someone with my friends, he described the man that was with them but never mentioned that he knew him.

'It sure is. I didn't think you were working tonight, Martin.

Thought you and Stephanie were having a night in.' Tom looked a little shifty.

'Ah, sadly we were, but the chef who should have been covering me rang in sick so I had to come in. Much to your daughter's disgust.'

'Yes, I can only imagine,' Tom answered, grinning.

'So, how do you two know each other then?' Martin asked, plonking himself down on the chair next to Tom, who was very quick to respond and suddenly acting all businesslike.

'We're old college friends. And we had a bit of business to sort out tonight. Probably best not to mention to Stephanie that you've seen me. You know what she's like. Right then, we'd better be going.' Tom held my denim jacket up for me to put on and seemed to keep his distance.

Martin grinned. 'Your secret is safe with me, Tom. Have a good evening now.' He headed back to the kitchen and Tom seemed quite flustered.

'Everything OK, Tom?' I did wonder quite what was going on. He seemed a little upset to have been spotted by Martin. He let out a huge release of air through his lips.

'Yeah, all is good. It's just that I'm not sure that Stephanie would like to think of me out on a date, to be honest. If I'd known Martin was going to be there, I would have chosen somewhere else. I know that probably sounds ridiculous because I'm a fifty-two-year-old man but she's been so upset since her mum passed away that I wouldn't want to upset her. Especially not in her current state. She's already devastated that her mum isn't going to be around for the birth of their first child. She can be quite high maintenance at times. A bit like her mother.' He rolled his eyes and smiled. 'Sorry, Emma. I hope that hasn't spoiled the evening for you.'

'It hasn't and I understand. It's a difficult situation. I think people who haven't been through what we've been through wouldn't get it. Please don't worry. I've had a lovely evening, Tom. I really have.'

As I turned, I hadn't realised the proximity of his body as our bodies pressed up against each other. Tom's eyes flickered to my lips where they lingered longer than I thought they might before meeting my eyes. He leaned forward and pressed his forehead gently against mine, his breath warm against my face.

'Oh, Emma. Do you ever wonder what would have happened if we'd have got together all those years ago?'

I forced a laugh. 'Not really. It is what it is, isn't it? We can't turn back the clock.'

If only he knew how many times over the years I'd thought about him. How his face had invaded my dreams. And how the same had happened since I'd seen him recently. How he'd got me all in a tizzy all over again.

'We can't, but we have now instead, don't we? And I'm glad we've reconnected. I really am.' He dropped a gentle kiss on my forehead.

'Me too, Tom. Me too.'

25

We travelled back in a more pensive mood, both in our own little thought bubbles. Things had been said that we couldn't hide from any more. We'd talked about the past a little but not about what had happened, although again nothing would change the past.

We were soon pulling up outside my place and Tom left the engine running. I dithered about whether to invite him in and thought about those words of Michelle's and Jo's – *it's just dinner*. It was now up to me to make the next decision.

'Would you... erm... like to come in for a cup of coffee?' I asked tentatively.

Tom turned to face me.

'For clarification, I do mean coffee, by the way. That isn't code for anything else,' I felt the need to explain.

'Ah that's a shame; I was rather hoping that it was code for *would you like to come in and shag me senseless.*'

My eyes must have nearly popped out of my head because he laughed and turned off the engine.

'I am joking, by the way. Christ, if someone tried to shag me senseless these days, I honestly don't think I would remember what to do. Sorry, that might just be a bit too much information. I'm a bit nervous, Em. You make me feel like a nervous teenager. You've always done this to me.'

I batted his arm. 'Don't be daft. Come on in and let's get that kettle on.'

I thought that it might feel funny having someone in my home. This was *my* place. The place where I was starting to rebuild my life. Everything seemed to fit into two categories. Life before Ben. Life after Ben. But having Tom here wasn't at all weird. He just seemed to belong. It was nice that he chose to not to sit on the sofa, where we might have that awkward, shall I sit there or not moment. Instead, he chose to sit in the armchair opposite. That meant that I could kick off my shoes and tuck my feet up under me. I felt totally relaxed in his company. He seemed to feel similar, which was lovely and he didn't shy away from talking about grief and bereavement. It was nice to have someone who understood.

'What was Ben like?' he asked. 'Tell me about him. Only if you want to, of course.'

I liked talking about Ben. Sometimes people didn't know whether to ask about him or not. It was almost as if they thought if they mentioned his name they'd remind me that he'd died. I would never forget him so I can only assume that they felt awkward around me, not knowing what to say. In most cases, they just didn't say anything at all, which was worse. That felt as if he'd never existed.

I really appreciated Tom asking about him. It was nice to talk about some of our lovely memories but I also talked about some of his faults too. Not in a bad way but just recognising that he wasn't always perfect.

In turn, we talked about Julie too and about their life out in

Australia. We chatted about their relationship and it was nice to learn more about this woman who was clearly not the girl I once knew but as a wife and a mother.

'So, what are your dreams now then, Tom?'

He huffed out loud.

'Honestly? I don't know any more. I feel like the older I get the more I just want peace in my life.'

'You do realise that you've got a grandchild on the way and that peace is not something you might be getting for a while?'

He laughed. Gosh! He really was handsome and I struggled to take my eyes off him. It all felt a bit surreal. This man was someone who had played such a big part in my early life, yet I hadn't seen for literally donkey's years. And now he was sitting in my lounge, drinking late-night tea with me. This was so bizarre.

'When I say peace, I think I mean calm. And when I say calm, I mean no drama. Does that make sense?'

I gave him a knowing smile. That was exactly how I felt too.

'I'm sure you can imagine what living with Julie was like – at times, it was wonderful, but she did love drama. I just don't want it. I just want to have peace in my life, strolls along the beach, a potter in my garden and a job that I love doing. Something worthwhile. I'm not even bothered about earning loads of money as long as I've got enough to get by with. I've done the big stressful jobs and I just don't want that in my life any more. I do want to earn enough to pay for holidays, of course. I do love a good holiday.'

'Totally agree. There are so many places in the world that I want to visit. But also loads in this country too. It doesn't always have to be the huge things, does it?'

'This is so true, Em. I think I've just learned that it's the little things that bring me joy these days. Eating a potato that I've grown. Cooking a nice meal. Listening to the birds singing while

I'm drinking my morning coffee. And some time with my family. Not too much to ask for, is it, really?'

It was as if he could read my mind.

'It's lovely in here, Em. You've got a really lovely home. I can't wait to move out of Stephanie's and into my new place. Should get the keys in the next week or so. Perfect timing too with a baby on the way. I'll have to get you to give me some advice.'

'Well, this is a combination of Jo, Michelle and me, to be honest. I think I'd forgotten what I liked.'

'Did you not pick your own furnishings when you were with Ben?'

I sighed.

'I think I just gave in for an easy life. We had very different taste. Ben liked quite dark, deep colours which might suit a gentleman's club more. This is more me.' I waved my arm around me. 'The cool calming blues and greens that come from the sea.'

'I do know what you mean. I always gave in to Julie. On most things, to be honest. And the one nice thing about being on my own now is that I can make my own decisions. It's quite liberating really.' He glanced at his watch. 'Goodness me. It's nearly two o'clock. I should be getting going.' He stood, reluctantly.

'Is it really? I'd totally lost track of time.'

'I've had the loveliest evening. It's been so bloody fantastic to catch up with you. We always did talk for hours, didn't we? Put the world to rights? Maybe we haven't changed so much despite all the years in between.' He hesitated at the back door and chewed the inside of his cheek. 'Would you... maybe... fancy doing this again one of these days? Well, maybe not one of these days, but soon, I mean.' His brow was furrowing and he fiddled with his watch strap. It was quite reassuring that he was clearly a little nervous too.

'Yes.'

His face broke into a smile.

'Fantastic. Shall I call you?'

'I'd really like that. Thanks for a lovely evening.'

'No, thank *you*.' He took a step towards me. My heart started to beat faster and I felt a bit panicky. What happened now? I took a big sigh and closed my eyes. I could feel his breath on my face and then a featherlight touch where his lips brushed my cheek. Opening my eyes, I saw him turn to leave. I didn't realise how disappointed I would feel that he hadn't tried to kiss me. Maybe it was just friendship after all. The mixed signals were confusing me. Maybe he was just interested in being my friend, even though he'd been clear originally that it was a date. I was prone to overthinking and my brain was going into overdrive. My heart sank a little as he gave me a wave.

'Goodnight, Em. Sleep well.'

'Night, Tom.'

I pressed my back against the closed door, waiting for the sound of an engine after the car door slammed. Puzzled that I couldn't hear it, I nearly shot out of my skin when there was a light knocking on the door right behind me.

I peered around the door and Tom was leaning up against the door frame.

'Hi,' he whispered.

'Hi,' I replied.

'I came back because I wanted to say something before I chickened out. I love that we've met up again, Emma and I, well... I still think you're fabulous. I'm not sure what this is between us, or where it could even go, but maybe we could find out.'

I'm not sure where the deep throaty voice or my bravado

came from but I asked the question that had been on the tip of my lips all night.

'Does that mean that you're going to kiss me now then?'

Tom grinned and took a step closer, taking my hands in his. As he leaned forward and I tilted my head towards him, his soft lips reached mine. The kiss was brief and gentle and yet just perfect.

It was at that very moment that I realised I might be in a bit of trouble. The teenage girl with a huge crush on a teenage boy had become a middle-aged woman with a huge crush on that same boy who had now become a man.

He winked and walked back to his car again and this time left me standing on the doorstep, my fingers lingering on the spot where his lips met mine, a heart full of joy and maybe even a little bit of hope for the future.

26

'Tom. Tom, darling. Do you think you could help me rehearse tonight? I'm struggling a bit with my lines. It would really help me. Maybe we could go to the pub together after here.'

Not looking at Tom to see his reaction to Melanie's request was killing me. I glanced up from my notes, still trying to hide under my hair, and saw that he was pulling a very odd face; I wasn't sure whether it was a grin or a grimace. I pulled my shoulders up straight and tried to show that it didn't bother me one little bit.

'I'm not sure I can tonight, Melanie. I've got some stuff to do.'

Ha, in your face, Melanie!

Yep, I was not bothered at all.

She walked over to him and put her hand on his arm and stuck out her lip. 'Oh, please, Tom. It would mean the world to me. We have to get our chemistry right, don't we?'

'Oh! My! God! Look at her making a play for my dad, Emma.' I hadn't noticed that Stephanie had crept up behind me and she was angry whispering close to my ear. 'He's not long lost my mum. It's way too early for him to be thinking about another relationship and I don't think he will be ready for a long time. He loved my mum dearly and wouldn't even be thinking about dating out of respect for her.'

As I turned to face her, Stephanie's hands went to her hips, and her eyes narrowed to the scene across from us. If looks could kill, Melanie would have been a goner. She was, however, on a roll and continued.

'I did wonder if she knew he's a widower but when I saw her last week in the corner shop, she did say that she was sorry that he'd lost his wife. Not a word of sorry for me losing my mum too. She doesn't look very bloody sorry to me. Look at her trying to get her claws into him. I'm going over there.'

Stephanie's tone was harsh as she stomped across the church hall towards her dad.

'Hi, Dad. How are you feeling today? Morning, Melanie. Do you mind if I have a word with my dad, please?' Melanie didn't move a muscle. Stephanie crossed her arms and huffed out loud, 'Alone!'

Melanie shrugged and walked off towards the kitchen, muttering to herself. After making herself a cup of tea, she returned to the church hall, looked around and caught my eye. I took a deep breath and smiled at her as she approached.

'Morning, Melanie. How are you?'

'Well, I was OK until Tom's daughter came in. Tom and I, we have this, well... you know... connection, I suppose you call it. I know he lost his wife not that long ago but you can't grieve forever, can you? You have to move on at some point. Life goes on.'

I couldn't believe that she was saying these words to me of all people. She knew that I'd lost Ben in the last couple of years. We'd talked about it before.

Trying to give her the benefit of the doubt, I presumed that she'd just forgotten in that moment. Her next words, however, confirmed that she was just downright insensitive.

'I mean, look at you, Emma. You've got over your husband dying. You're getting on with your life, aren't you? I bet that's why you set up the friendship group. To find yourself a new man.' Her little tinkly laugh grated right through me. 'Hope you don't have designs on Tom. He doesn't realise it yet but he's going to be mine. So, hands off. Haha.'

Rage built within me. She'd proper rattled my cage. How dare she think she knew how I did or didn't feel about the death of my husband? On behalf of widows everywhere, I felt like I needed to stand up to this judgemental opinion that I had read in books that many experienced. I took a deep breath, before speaking, so that I could portray someone who was in control and not a mad woman who wanted to screech at her.

'It's not a case of getting over someone's death, Melanie. You have no idea what people are feeling. Some days you get a wave of grief wash over you in a tsunami, rendering you totally unable to face the day ahead and just wanting to stay in bed all day. Sometimes you wake up and forget it's happened and expect that person to be lying in bed next to you. Please don't assume that because someone isn't talking about it every minute of every day that they've *got over it*. Maybe they've just been able to cope a little better that day. No one knows what goes on behind closed doors.'

Melanie just stared at me, a little surprised, I would say, by the look of her raised eyebrows at my little outburst.

Even though I wasn't sure whether my words were hitting home, I couldn't seem to stop myself from continuing. She was going to get a lecture from me whether she wanted it or not. I wasn't sure whether it was grief or just getting to a certain age that had taught me I needed to stand up for what I believed in more and say my piece.

'Grief doesn't have a time limit. Everyone is different and it also depends on the circumstances. Some people have longer to adjust when there's been a long illness and have time to say all the things they want to and have a chance to say goodbye. Others lose people suddenly and never get that opportunity and have the trauma of all of that to deal with too. And there's no right or wrong to any of it. Everyone deals with it in their own ways.'

'No need to bite my head off. Is everything all right? You seem a little touchy today?'

It was as if the words I'd said hadn't reached her at all. I knew that in time I would learn to live with the death of my husband, that the feelings would be less intense and I would start to forge a new life. One that I hadn't chosen but had no choice in. Grief would always be part of me, who I was, who I am now and who I will be in the future.

I also realised that there were certain people you just couldn't reason with and were wasting your breath on, trying to make them see what they didn't want to.

I sighed.

'I'm perfectly fine, thank you. Shall we make a start?'

Melanie took every chance she could to openly flirt with Tom. There was a hand on an arm here; a finger picking away an invisible hair there. Stephanie had a face like thunder for most of the rehearsal and I couldn't help but mull over what she'd said about her dad finding someone new. She really seemed to think that he wasn't ready, but not only that, that *she* wasn't ready either. There wasn't just Tom to consider, there was Stephanie too. She'd lost her mother and I knew from when I lost my own mother how intensely painful it was, despite the fact that we didn't always have an easy relationship. Stephanie clearly adored hers. With her about to have her own baby, the last thing she needed was stress in her life. She needed to stay calm for the baby's sake. There would probably never be a time when she needed family more.

It wasn't until I was home that evening that I realised how much what Melanie had said had affected me. I couldn't bear the thought of people thinking that I'd 'got over' Ben so quickly.

Before the night out I had with Tom, I would have just said that we were friends with something very personal in common and that we were helping each other through our grief. But that was before he kissed me and got me all in a tizzy. What if he did want something more permanent? What would people think? What did I think? It was all very confusing.

It also occurred to me that the reason why I was letting Melanie wind me up was not only because she tried to undermine me at every opportunity, but I was also jealous of their sizzling on-stage chemistry. Even Michelle and Jo had mentioned it. I'm sure they were testing me to see what my reaction was. I couldn't answer them because I didn't even know myself.

Before I could stop myself, I sent Tom a text.

> Is there any chance that we could meet up tomorrow night. I know I'm probably overthinking things but I'd love to chat through some thoughts I have x

He quickly responded and despite all that was on my mind, my heart did a little skip when I saw his name pop up on my phone.

Sorry Em, can't do tomorrow night. Have already got a commitment that I can't get out of. Would definitely love to meet up with you though and could do the night after if that's any good. After rehearsal maybe x

Yep, I can do that x

Great, I'll text you in the day to see what time is best for you. Look forward to it x

I felt a little better knowing that I would have the opportunity to start an open and honest conversation around what was happening with us. My thoughts were that maybe I should share with him what Stephanie had been saying and get his take on it. If he still thought that we had something, maybe we could take the opportunity to talk to Stephanie together. Share that we were taking it really slow but that we'd like to see more of each other and ask her for her permission. It was only fair. I hoped that because she knew me, she'd give me a chance. Hoped that she'd want her dad to be happy and to have someone to do things with. One less person to worry about.

I wasn't sure what I'd say if she said no, because I'd just realised how much I was looking forward to seeing him.

I'd already started to fall in love with him all over again.

27

Jo and Michelle were apparently so fed up of seeing me dithering about the situation that they decided to take me to the pub. There was a quiz on, and they thought it would take my mind off things. We were laughing at something daft that Jo had said when we fell through the door, making a bit of an entrance, and headed for the bar.

'OK, so, Emma. I don't want to alarm you but I do want to give you a heads up. Don't look now but you'll never guess who's sitting at the booth in the corner,' Michelle whispered under her breath.

Obviously, Jo and I immediately swung round to look and saw Tom and Melanie sitting cosied up in the little booth, their legs touching and their heads together. Tom must have just said something hilarious because Melanie threw back her head and laughed. That shrill sound went through me and her eyes connected with mine across the room. She even had the gall to wink at me. I wanted the ground to open and swallow me up.

'Shall we go and piss on their bonfire and join them?' Michelle suggested.

'God, no! I do have some dignity, you know.'

'Well, pull it together, love, because Tom is heading your way.'

I dragged my hands over my face and then he was right there.

'Hey, Em. How are you?' He reached across to kiss my cheek but I pulled away. Much as I wanted to ask why he'd told me he had a work thing when he was clearly out on a date with Melanie, I held it together and nodded my acknowledgement.

'Tom.'

'Everything OK?' he asked, frowning. 'Want to come and join us? We've been rehearsing.'

'Is that what you call it?' Jo said under her breath. I elbowed her in the ribs, unsure as to whether Tom had heard or not.

'Are you here for the quiz, Tom?' Michelle asked. 'You and Melanie?'

'I didn't even know there was a quiz on till we got here.' He turned to me. 'Are you sure you are OK, Emma? You've gone a little pale, you know. Come and sit down.'

'No, you're OK. You're right. I am feeling a little under the weather. I think I'm going to go home. Sorry, girls.' I dashed out before they could see my chin trembling and even though I could hear Tom calling my name, I was determined that I wasn't going to turn around. He was not going to see the uncontrollable tears that were now coursing down my cheeks.

'Stupid! Stupid! Stupid!' I chastised myself through pinched lips, smacking my fists against my thighs as I stomped back towards my home. A surge of heat had risen up my neck and my face tingled. When my phone started to vibrate in my hand, I looked down to see his name flash up on the screen. I hit the button to bounce the call with force and turned the damn thing off. There was nothing I had to say to him.

I should never have let Tom back into my life. The past is the past for a reason. I should have kept him at a distance. He'd already let me down once in my life, when I was a young woman, with a myriad of emotions and hormones. He'd chosen another woman over me then. Over thirty-five years later I had allowed him to do exactly the same thing all over again.

28

'Open the door, Emma Montgomery. We know you're in there.' I couldn't help but hear Michelle and Jo's voices as they yelled through the letter box. 'We're not going until you open the door.'

'I don't want to see anyone. I know you mean well, but I just want to be left alone. I'll be fine. I just need to be on my own. I'll come and see you both in the morning. Please, girls. Just leave me be.'

I heard the mumble of voices before Jo shouted through. 'Just call us if you need us. OK?'

'I will.'

'We love you, Em,' Michelle shouted and when I heard their footsteps got quieter I heaved a sigh of relief.

I walked to the far window and looked out to the sea which I could see twinkling in the moonlight but even the ebb and flow of the waves didn't soothe me like it normally did. Unease wasn't a feeling I'd had since Ben had died and it brought back so much. Wandering over to the mantelpiece, I picked up our wedding photograph and studied it closely. The photo showed a couple very much in love, much like a wedding photo should be.

But I was young and naïve and while I had strong feelings for Ben, I did get together with him on the rebound from what had happened with Tom. Ben never knew, of course. He never needed to.

We went out with each other for around five years before he proposed. I found out later, when he dropped it out over dinner one evening, that he was told that he would move up the ranks of his company more swiftly if he was married. I also discovered a few months later from one of his colleagues' wives that he'd been told by his boss that it would be even better if we didn't have children so that he was free to travel around the world with his job.

For years after, I wondered whether he would have asked me anyway. I even asked him once, to which he said of course he would have. But I suppose I'd never know if that was the truth. He never admitted it while we were together and I certainly wasn't going to find out now.

Despite this discovery, soon after we married, I realised that I had learned to love him dearly and we muddled along nicely, but life was all about what Ben wanted. Being seven years older than me, and having more life experience, he was a strong character and at the time a couple of people, my father particularly, had pointed out to me that he could see me agreeing to things to keep Ben happy.

Rebelling against my father and the army upbringing was probably another reason why I married Ben but I never realised until a few years into our marriage just how similar Ben and Dad were. They both liked things just so. Every possession Ben had was meticulously lined up in his cupboards and he didn't like anything out of place. His wardrobe was colour coded along with our bookshelves. When he sulked for a whole week once when I hadn't cleaned the shower in the way he liked it done, I realised that it was just easier to do it his way. It was just a shame that I seemed to suppress myself and my own personality to suit him. When he passed away I realised how much of myself I'd lost along the way and I struggled to forge a way forward because I didn't know who I was any more.

This is why I think I'd let Tom in. He reminded me of the person I used to be. When I was friends with Tom, I went from the chubby army kid to a happy, carefree young woman who loved to spend time acting, singing and dancing. But then when I discovered that Julie and he had been seeing each other all along I felt like a total and utter fool. Humiliated beyond belief. Everyone laughing at me, not just behind my back but to my face too. That's why I pulled out of the performance and why since then I'd always been happy to be in the background. I should have stayed in my lane. Stuck with what I knew I was good at. And the thing that I did best was to be behind the scenes.

I held my head up high and had a little word with myself out loud.

Right, lady! You've had your pity party. You've got through worse and you'll get through this. You have a responsibility to put on a bloody good panto and that's exactly what you'll do. Tom and Melanie are welcome to each other. Let them get on with it. Let them do them. And you do you. You've got this.

I rummaged through the pantry and found a packet of biscuits which I kept in for visitors. I opened the packet and dunked the first two in a cup of tea, and then before I knew it promptly ate the rest of the packet.

29

Jo's lounge was one of my favourite places in the world. It was the place I sat and fell in love with this little part of the village. That morning, while she was in the kitchen with Michelle, and I could hear them whispering, probably about me, I sat and gazed at the turquoise sea glittering beyond the dunes. I had been up since six, drinking tea, and then went out for a run on the beach as soon as it was light enough, thankfully not bumping into a soul.

Jo brought a tea tray in with a plateful of pastries on one side. Normally I wouldn't have touched anything like this, but today I felt like I deserved it. Michelle and Jo both looked at me with expectant eyes.

Jo broke the silence.

'We just want you to be OK, Em.'

I sighed. 'I know. I feel a bit battered and bruised but I'll be fine. Tough times like this come along to test us and see how strong we are.'

'You're one of the strongest people I know,' Michelle added. 'You've been through so much over the last few years and I hate that Tom made you feel that way. For what it's worth, I'm not sure there's even anything going on between him and Melanie. He really doesn't seem the type to be stringing two women along.'

'I've said to you before not to fall for his charms. It's like history repeating itself. I think that's why I felt so upset last night. When I had counselling after Ben died, she said that sometimes one trauma on top of another is the thing that tips people over the edge. It's not the thing that's happened at the time; it's the combination and the not dealing with everything in between. I suppose my self-esteem just took another big knock.'

'What surprises me most though is that no one would ever know that you feel that way. You're very good at putting on a show to others. You appear to always be confident and in control.' Jo put her hand on my arm. 'It's only your friends that see the real you.'

'Yeah. I'm very good at wearing a mask. I've been doing it for years. It's a habit that I got into when I was with Ben. When he criticised me, which he did quite a lot I've come to realise, he did it with a smile on his face, so it didn't seem like it was something that would hurt me.'

'Gosh, that's quite calculating. Not wanting to speak bad of the dead, of course.' Jo looked upwards and whispered *sorry*. 'How did you react to that when it happened?'

'I never wanted to show him how hurt I was. He wasn't a fan of crying. I learnt that in the early days of our marriage. I'd go and hide myself away, mainly in the bathroom. Have a shower most of the time, then even if he came in, he wouldn't see my tears and I could cover up by saying that I'd got soap in my eyes.'

It was hard to decipher what the expressions in Jo and Michelle's eyes were. I wasn't entirely sure whether it was that they felt sorry for me, or thought I was an absolute idiot.

'Don't get me wrong. He wasn't a cruel man. He was lovely. In most cases he was doing it for my own good, to make me a better person.'

I saw a glance exchanged between them. It was very well to judge both me and Ben, but they didn't know him like I did. Didn't love him like I did. No one really knows what goes on in a relationship and so shouldn't really comment. They'd never even met him and I wouldn't let them poison my memories of him. I swigged the last dregs of my drink.

'Anyway, I will be fine and I do appreciate your concern for me. I've got lots to get on with today that'll keep me busy and my mind off things. I need to work on some plans for the Lonely Hearts Club today. I've got a bit behind because I've been concentrating on the panto instead. Talking of which, you are both coming to rehearsals later, aren't you?'

And just like that my mask was back on.

30

The next afternoon, I gave a deep breath, held my head high and walked into the church hall. I knew I was going to be the first there. One of my defences in life was to turn up early. That way you can always be a little ahead of the game and that was exactly what I needed to be on this particular evening.

Graham and Tina had entrusted me with the key; a privilege not offered to everyone and one that I held dear to my heart. I wandered into the room and stood before the stage. When I closed my eyes, I saw Tom and me there on stage as teenagers before everything went wrong.

Laughing voices made me look up and a group of people entered the room, Tom and Melanie part of it. Tom immediately came over to me and before I knew it was enveloping me in a hug. I closed my eyes and breathed in the scent of him. The musky tones of his aftershave hit my senses and I had a momentary blip where I melted into his arms. He bent to kiss me, but in a split second as my eyes connected with Melanie's over his shoulder, I quickly came to my senses and turned my head. He ended up kissing my cheek before I pulled away. His puzzled expression made me realise that he had absolutely no clue why I was being cool with him. Maybe it was better that way; then I wouldn't have to admit the truth. I would just keep my distance where I could.

'Are you feeling better, Em? I have texted you a few times.'

'Yes, thanks. Much. My phone is playing up so I've not been getting messages.'

At that exact moment, the text tone on my phone pinged.

'It seems to be fixed now though.' The rising inflection at the end of his statement, made it more of a question.

'Yep. Let's hope so. Damned nuisance it's been.' I gathered my wits about me and headed towards the kitchen. 'Must get on. Lots to do.' I turned to my desk, picked up and shuffled some paperwork, pretending to skim-read the words until he walked away.

Stephanie had just arrived and was heading my way. I loved that she saw me as someone she could talk to. It was always good to have multi-generational friends and in the absence of a maternal figure, it would be good for her to have someone of a similar age to her mother around. I could only imagine that the time ahead was going to be tough for her without her mother. This should be one of the most exciting times of her life and probably one where she would have really appreciated some love and support and, more than that, advice from her mum. Bittersweet, I would have thought. Same for Tom. If nothing else, I could be a friend to them both and that thought made me ponder, as she approached.

'What are you smiling at?' she asked as she kissed my cheek.

'Just thinking how lovely you look today.' I stepped back and looked her up and down. 'Pregnancy suits you.'

'Ah, thank you, but I feel like a beached whale. My ankles are swelling up, but that's not too bad because I can't bloody see them any more past this bump.' She rubbed her hand protectively on her belly.

I had never known how it felt to have another person growing inside of you. The whole process was a literal miracle happening inside a body and it never ceased to amaze me.

'I can't sleep. I've got constant heartburn and need to pee *all the bloody time*! And what I really could do with right now is a bloody great big hug from my mum.' She blew out an almighty huff as her eyes filled with tears. 'Also, I could cry at the drop of a hat. Honestly, poor Martin is having to put up with all this shit and it's not very pleasant for him at all.'

'Listen, Stephanie. I hope you don't mind me saying this. Obviously, I'm not your mum, love, but I am a good hugger if that counts for anything. My friend Bev always said that it was because I have squishy boobs. I think it was meant as a compliment.' I smiled. 'Want to test them out?' I held my arms out and thank goodness she walked into them. I'd have felt a complete fool if she hadn't.

I took her in my arms and held her close against my chest and I could feel the tension leaving her body and start to relax as she sighed out loud. Sometimes a silent hug can say so many things. It felt good to be able to help her in this way. After around thirty seconds, we rocked gently from side to side, almost a sign that it was ending before we broke apart.

'God, I miss hugs. And that was a blooming fabulous one. They are great boobs. Bev was right. Thank you, Emma.'

'Anytime, lovely!'

She nodded over at Melanie and her dad, who were as thick as thieves, laughing in the corner. Tom was painting some huge MDF panels which were part of the scenery set which he'd put wheels on, to make it easy for people to get them on and off the stage. One side was the interior of Cindy's house and the other was the inside of the palace. He was clearly a very talented artist.

'What do you think about all this then? Reckon she's trying to get her claws into Dad?'

'Ah, I'm not sure, love. I don't know either of them very well to be honest. Don't really want to comment. It's not my place.'

'It's funny, isn't it? If I wondered what Mum would say about it, I reckon she'd say that despite their long and happy marriage Dad still has his life left to live and she would want him to find someone wonderful to spend it with. She always told me that life was too short to be unhappy and you never know what's round the corner.'

It was interesting that she thought her mum would say this, particularly because Tom said she wasn't aware there were problems in their marriage. A sudden thought hit me. What if Tom had lied? What if their marriage was as perfect as Stephanie thought it was and he was just saying that so that I thought it was OK for him to move on quickly? Maybe he was full of shit and really had charmed me all over again and I'd fallen for it hook, line and sinker.

'Maybe it's just Melanie I don't want him to be with.' She paused and her eyes locked onto mine. 'I did think the other day that there was a possibility that you and he would become more than friends.'

I could feel heat rise up through my chest and into my face. I hoped she didn't see me blushing.

'What? Me?' My tinkling laugh sounded alien even to me.

'Yeah, you. You and Dad are far more suited to each other than Mum and Dad were. You would never have put them together. And you're definitely more his type than that bloody Melanie.' She nodded over her shoulder towards them huddling in the corner, allegedly learning their lines.

'But then I decided that I don't think I want him to be with anyone right now. I know I'm probably being totally selfish. I think Mum deserves the respect that he is grieving her and the life they had. He needs to leave a respectable amount of time before he can let himself forget about her. Maybe in time I'll be ready for him to move on. Just not right now.'

'You do know that he'll never forget her, don't you, Stephanie?'

'Do you think?'

'I'm sure of it. She was the mother of his child and probably the love of his life.' I took a deep breath. 'Grief doesn't just disappear. It just becomes easier to deal with – at times. She will always be in his life because of you. You look so much like her, Stephanie.'

'I forget that you knew her. Did you like her?'

I remembered the pain and the hurt that Julie had caused me with her cruelness when we were younger. The way she laughed at me and called me fat. She mocked that I thought there was a possibility Tom might really like me, and I cried for days over the humiliation she caused. I know she wasn't responsible for the way I felt, but she was responsible for causing what upset me.

I looked into Stephanie's eyes. There was no need for me to shatter the great memories she had of her mum.

'She was great. She was fun and she was popular and had so many friends. I was always really envious of her. And she was beautiful. Just like you.'

'That is so nice to hear, Emma. Dad said she could be a right proper bitch at times.'

I laughed. 'Julie? No, never. Although I suppose I wasn't married to her.' I winked and instinctively moved closer, taking the liberty to reach out and tuck a stray strand of hair behind her ear. Realising how intimate a gesture this was, I stepped back.

'You'll be OK, you know. You'll get through this. I'm sure you have lots of friends around to help. And I hope you know that I'm right here to help you in any way that I can too.'

She reached over and gave me another hug, squeezing me tightly. 'That means the world to me. Thank you.'

'You're most welcome, sweetheart. Although don't be ringing me in the middle of the night because your baby is crying. At my age I need as much beauty sleep as I can get.'

We both laughed. I had always been good at diverting sadness with a quip, and laughter was always good to keep the tears at bay.

'Get off with you. You're gorgeous. Right, I need to go and compose myself and have a pee *again*. Baby is lying right on my bladder at the moment. Thanks again for the hugs and the kind words, Emma. I needed that.'

Little did Stephanie know that not only was I doing her a good deed by giving her a hug, she was doing me a huge one in return. When she said that she missed hugs, it made me realise how much I missed that bodily contact with someone. I'd never been much of a hugger through my life. Mum and Dad weren't. I suppose it was their military background. But I missed hugs so much in that moment that I could have cried.

31

For the first time in what felt like forever, that evening rehearsals went well. The cast were starting to gel, and people knew their words more which meant that a lot of them were not always looking down at the words in their hands but were starting to think of the acting side of things too.

Despite my feelings towards Melanie and Tom, it would appear that their 'rehearsing' was paying off. They seemed to be having a great deal of fun and the dynamic between them was fundamental for the scenes they were performing. They were a wonderful standard for the rest of the cast to aim for and everyone was trying to raise their game. It was a great encouragement for me to see how it was all starting to come together.

Mary from the supermarket played a brilliant, wicked stepmother, I think she was secretly getting all the negativity out of her body by throwing herself into the role wholeheartedly.

Melanie headed my way and I sighed, wondering what today's revelation from her would be. I had tried so hard to like her, but I just didn't. She wasn't my type of person.

'I'd like to ask your advice about something, Emma, if you

don't mind?' The surprise must have shown on my face as she continued, 'Don't faint at me asking.' She gave a little tinkling laugh.

I pasted on a sweet smile.

'How can I help?'

'Do you think we could ask Mary to,' she used air quotes around the words, 'tone it down a little. Her character bullying Cindy is one thing; but I do feel like it's running over into real life. She's been quite rude to me a couple of times today and I don't want to cause a scene, pardon the pun,' we both smiled at her choice of words, 'but I do feel quite violated. If this was in a workplace, I'd be taking this to an HR manager. Oh. Hang on!' She tapped her lip with her index finger. 'Tom's an HR consultant, isn't he?'

'Well, yes, he might have some advice on how to handle it. Shall I ask him?'

'Oh, that's a great idea. Maybe the three of us could grab a coffee together or a glass of wine in the pub later to discuss the best way to handle it.'

A feeling of dread washed over my body. I wasn't sure I wanted to play gooseberry again to Tom and Melanie.

'Not sure I can do that to be honest. I've... er... I already have plans.'

She squinted her eyes at me. I opened my mouth but no words came out.

'Sounds fun. What are you up to?'

As I racked my brains to think of something, she must have known it was a fib.

'I'd really appreciate it if we could find a time to do this, Emma. It's important to me that this behaviour doesn't continue.' She shouted to Tom. 'Tom, can we speak to you, please?'

For the second time today, I managed to find a fake smile from somewhere.

Tom arrived at our side.

'When would you be free to have a chat with Emma and me, darling?' She put her hand on his arm territorially and looked deeply into his eyes. His smile turned into a frown and he moved away from her and towards me.

'Is everything OK?' he asked.

'We do have a slight issue that we need some help with,' I answered.

'Why don't you all go off to the coffee shop now?' Tina piped up from where she was sitting beside us. She'd evidently been listening to the whole conversation. 'I can hold the fort here as long as you won't be longer than an hour tops.'

I wasn't sure whether to hug her because she'd intervened and saved me from a night of sitting in the pub with these two or be annoyed because she was forcing me into a situation where I had to go now. She seemed to feel my uncomfortable reluctance to spend more time with them than absolutely necessary though, so considering my options, I agreed that there was no time like the present.

As we left the church hall, Melanie linked arms with Tom and again, I felt like the spare wheel.

Melanie didn't seem to want to leave me alone with Tom, so I offered to go to the counter to order our drinks, and when I got back to the table, found them talking in hushed voices.

'So, what's this all about then?' Tom asked.

Melanie explained the situation to him.

'Do you think you're being a little bit oversensitive at all?' he asked gently.

She pouted. 'I do not.'

'Are you sure, Mel?'

She seemed to consider his question, turning her face away, deep in thought.

Tom patted her hand and a sudden pang of jealousy shot through me. I forced myself to push it away. I had no right to feel like this and more than that, it was a feeling that I didn't want to experience.

'Possibly.' She shrugged.

I had absolutely no idea what was going on and must have looked completely puzzled because Tom looked at me.

'Tell Emma. She's a wonderful listener.'

She nodded before taking in a huge breath and breathing out again. And then, looking down at the table while speaking, she poured out her heart.

'My husband and I have recently separated, as you know. I think I probably already shared that with you. What I didn't tell you was that our marriage wasn't all that it appeared to be to people on the outside.'

A tear trickled slowly down her cheek and she seemed quite embarrassed to be sharing this, still not making eye contact with me as she spoke.

'I discovered early on in our marriage that Rob was a complete and utter narcissist. A control freak who only wanted things done one way and that was his way. Nothing was ever good enough for him despite how hard I tried. He made out that he was doing it for my own good, and that he only had my best interests at heart. The worst thing was that I never even saw it until one day I bumped into an old friend who I hadn't seen for ages and she told me that he'd told her to stay away from me because she was a bad influence.'

I don't think I'd ever been so surprised by something. Melanie always seemed so in control. So forthright and stoic.

'I didn't realise that he'd been controlling everything in my life until she pointed it out. He stopped me seeing my friends, controlled what I ate, what I did, what I wore. At the time I just saw it as love, but when I met this friend, it made me look at things differently.'

Poor Melanie. There was me thinking that *she* was opinionated and controlling but maybe that was her way of dealing with this behaviour.

'So, what happened?'

'I broached the subject with him, and he said he was doing the best for me that he could, for my own good. Even then, I began to doubt myself. But then I researched it more and finally admitted to myself that it was something called coercive control. I plucked up the courage to call a women's refuge and talked to one of their helpline staff and I began to make a plan to get away from him. Thank goodness we never had children.' She broke into a quiet sob and I noticed that she even cried like a princess. Little diamanté tears coursed down her cheeks and Tom offered her a tissue from his pocket. If that was me, they would have been great big snivelling gasps.

This was not what I thought we'd be discussing on our coffee break and I started to wonder why we were discussing this, but then it hit me like a ton of bricks. The way that Mary in her role as the wicked stepmother was talking to Melanie was triggering her. Now I understood.

'And this with Mary is bringing it all back for you, I'm guessing?'

She nodded in response.

This time it was my turn to reach across the table for her hand.

'I'm so sorry you went through this, Melanie. I'll speak to Mary as soon as we get back.'

'Thank you. I appreciate it. I'm sorry to be a trouble.' She squeezed my hand back. 'Tom has been a great help to me. A sympathetic listener when I needed a friend.' She smiled at him and he held her gaze for a moment before looking away. Having Tom in her life as a friend, or whatever else he might be, was clearly helping her work through her issues. Maybe she wasn't as bad as I had previously thought. We all have baggage and this seemed like a huge weight she was carrying around.

'No trouble at all, Melanie,' I said. 'I can't have my leading lady upset now, can I?'

Her breath shuddered with emotion now her tears were coming to an end. She smiled at me and her next words were the ones that finally confirmed what I'd already been thinking in my mind: that my marriage had been far from the perfect memories that I shared with everyone else.

'I mean, Emma. Can you just imagine being married to someone like that?'

32

The rest of the day went by in a blur. The impending rain rendered the clouds a dark grey and we managed to get back from the café just before the heavens opened. After an hour or so I feigned a blinding headache due to the change in weather. I told Tom that I'd rearrange meeting up and asked Tina if she would mind finishing off and locking up. I could see the concern in her eyes, as I gathered my belongings.

'Are you OK, love? Do you want me to give you a lift back?'

'I'll be fine. Thank you. I just need to lie down in a dark room.'

'OK, but pop this on to keep you warm. The rain might have stopped but the temperature has dropped out there and the last thing we want is a panto producer with pleurisy if you get caught in the rain again.' She wrapped her scarf around my neck and tied it loosely before sending me on my way.

'Bit dramatic there, Tina?' I smiled but could feel that it hadn't reached my eyes.

'Yeah, but it was beautiful alliteration, wasn't it? Wouldn't have sounded the same if I said a cold. And it turned your frown upside down for a moment.'

I decided to walk the beach route back, despite the possibility of the rain returning. The waves had grown larger, more agitated, picking up pace as they bounced onto the shore instead of their normal gentle lapping. The rumble of thunder in the far distance made me quicken my pace and when I finally arrived home, I slammed the door behind me, shutting out the world.

I didn't have to imagine being married to someone like Melanie's husband, because I'd been married to someone with some of the same characteristics. And I'd only just realised.

33

I reached up to a cupboard to get down the box where we always kept things like antihistamines, plasters and painkillers, and took two headache tablets. Out of a longstanding habit I neatened the items in the box, ensuring that they all lined up and closed the cupboard. I then went to the fridge to grab some orange juice to swig the tablets down with. When I saw the bottles and jars all lined up, something within me snapped and I shoved one of them the opposite way round before pushing the door shut.

Entering the bedroom, it felt like my bed was calling out to me and I lay down, resting my head on the pillow, staring at the ceiling. When had I become this person who did as she was told? After school I became someone independent, I had my own views and opinions but when I met Ben, slowly all those things began to merge. I had become someone else but the worst part of all that was that I hadn't even noticed.

I closed my eyes, realising that sleep would only take this feeling away temporarily but it was what I needed right then.

When I woke, I noticed that I'd only been asleep for forty

minutes but as I sat up, I felt a little lighter. Maybe it was the realisation of my situation.

Across the room I could see all my items on the dressing table opposite and again, they were all turned round to face me so I could see what was on the labels. Yes, it was useful and it looked neat, but I didn't need them to be that way. I knew what they were from the jar, bottle or can. It had taken me until I heard the words that Melanie said to realise that I had also lived this way without even realising it and while Ben was nowhere near as bad as her husband had been, I could see how certain patterns of behaviour gained such momentum that they eventually reached a crisis point. I was grateful that it hadn't gone that far for me.

Melanie had done really well to get away. Her soul was clearly crushed and I probably hadn't helped by fighting her every step of the way because of my own insecurities.

I sprang up from my bed and swiped all the pots and potions into the drawer below. That felt good. Without delay, I headed for the lounge and pulled one of the throws off the back of the sofa which I straightened before bed every night, and scrunched it up, throwing it onto the sofa.

As I punched one of the cushions that I so meticulously neatened before bed, I laughed out loud to myself. When I caught myself in the mirror above the fireplace, I realised that I looked totally demented. A rage started to build within me as I went into the kitchen and started randomly opening cupboard doors. A rage towards Ben for making me feel this way but also towards myself. I became furious that I had allowed this to happen. I was even angry that it was Melanie of all people who had been the one that had shone a light on this.

There was a knock at the door. I didn't really want anyone to see me like this but I also realised that the lights were on and whoever it was would know I was in. I couldn't hide much as I wanted to, and had no alternative but to open it, to Michelle and Jo, though I did stand in the doorway to block it, hoping they'd realised that they weren't being invited in.

Michelle was the first to speak.

'Hey! Are you OK? We tried calling but it kept going to voice-mail. Tom has been trying to get hold of you too.'

'I turned my phone off. I've been asleep.' The rampant rage was still coursing through my body and I hardly trusted myself to speak.

Jo reached out to touch my arm.

'Em, what's wrong?'

'Nothing. I'm fine. I need to be alone. I'll call you tomorrow.'

She tried to reach out to me again but I took a step back and immediately shut her down.

Michelle tried next.

'Don't push us away, Emma, we're your friends. You're doing so well.'

I took a deep breath and tried to convey my thoughts but my words were all jumbled.

'Emma. We know how hard it's been for you since you lost your husband but...'

That was the final straw for me and my rage just wouldn't stop.

'How do you know how *I* feel?' I thrust my hands on my hips, waiting for a response. 'What do you know about husbands?' I snapped at them both and they stood and stared at me, totally startled by my out-of-character behaviour.

'*You*,' I aimed at Michelle, 'have never even had one.' I turned to Jo at that point. 'And you couldn't even hang on to yours, so please don't stand there telling me that you know how I feel about the fact that mine died. You have no idea. So don't preach to me. You know nothing about what's going on in my head. I've only known you for a short while. I knew him for over half of my lifetime and you never even met him but made an opinion.'

I wanted them to argue back with me. I needed an argument so this rage would dissipate but as soon as I said the words – which I knew I'd never be able to take back – the fire inside me started to snuff out. I knew that I was sabotaging my relationship with them but couldn't seem to stop myself. I mumbled back, 'Just go. Please,' and went to shut the door in their faces but Michelle put her foot in the way.

'I'm sorry you feel that way. We love you and care about you very much. And so does Tom, despite what you think of him. We know you are still grieving Ben and that this business with Tom has unsettled you. We're your friends but we won't stand here and be spoken to like this, whatever you are going through. We're going. But before we do, Stephanie asked me to give you this.' She pushed something through the gap and into my hands.

'Goodnight, Emma.'

34

Looking down at the object in my hand, I couldn't imagine why Stephanie had sent me a DVD. I closed the door behind my friends, annoyed with myself for treating them this way but unable to deal with that right now. I had disappointed myself so much. Another thing to beat myself up over. I would think of a way to make it up to them both. My words were spiteful and terribly uncalled for and that wasn't usual for me. I grabbed my laptop from the breakfast bar and opened it up, sliding the DVD into the media player.

I was confused as to why I was seeing myself and Tom on stage from years ago until it clicked. This was the day of the dress rehearsal performance of *Romeo and Juliet*. It was being filmed from behind the scenes. How on earth did Stephanie get a copy of this? My eyes hardly left the screen as I grabbed a glass from the draining board and poured myself a glass of wine from the bottle next to my computer.

Tom had taken both of my hands in his and had bent his head towards me. He and I were about to kiss when Julie walked into the scene. She scoffed out loud.

'You don't have to pretend any more, Tom.' She sneered at me. 'Honestly, Emma, you don't think Tom really likes you, do you? He told me the other day that you were just the chubby army brat who has no friends and he felt sorry for you.'

It was bizarre to watch this scene that I was a part of unfold before me, like I was watching a film on Netflix. I had wondered from time to time whether I'd remembered correctly or whether my memory had changed something along the way. If my mind had played tricks on me and I'd exaggerated the truth. However, it was now playing out exactly as I remembered; the words that had been in my head all along were the same. I hadn't imagined it at all.

'That's not true. Tom and me. We... love each other. Don't we, Tom? He would never say anything like that. Would you?' My younger self searched his face, willing him to speak up and agree. Tom went to speak as I dropped his hands and stepped away from him. 'Did you say that about me, Tom?'

'Well...'

I raised my voice.

'Did you say those words? Yes, or no?'

'I may have said something that...'

'I hate you!'

'Emma. I didn't mean...'

I knew at the time I didn't stick around to hear any more and whoever was filming watched as I fled down the stage steps towards the audience seating. Even now, many years later, I vividly remembered exactly how it felt in that moment as tears streamed down my cheeks, and Julie cackled behind me and gathered her friends around. Their hateful group laughing was all I could hear from the stage as I ran down the aisle and straight out of the double doors at the rear of the room. I recalled that I kept on running until I could run no more and when I reached home, I flung myself on the bed and cried till I fell asleep.

What I hadn't seen was that Julie then turned to Tom and put her hands on his chest. He gently pushed her away and shouted after me to no avail.

He swung round to face Julie.

'You, Julie Cartwright, are a total cow. Why did you do that? You knew very well that I really like Emma. Why would you tell her that?'

Now this got my attention. This was now unfolding in front of my very eyes. Gripped and trance-like, I couldn't wait to see what happened next.

'You don't know anything about her, Tom. You're not the only boy she's been fluttering her eyes at, you know. She's a bit of an old slapper if you really want to know. Puts it about a lot, I hear. In fact, I heard that she might even be pregnant.'

My hand flew to my chest; I couldn't believe the lies I was hearing from this girl's mouth.

Tom stood with his hands on his hips. 'I don't believe you.'

'It's true. Isn't it, girls?' She looked around at her huddle of friends who stood around her, nodding. She'd clearly poisoned them all. 'Well, when you've finished mooning after Emma, and you want a real woman,' she ran her hands over her body in a seductive manner and then made the sign of a phone with her hand, 'call me.' The mean girls all marched off together, a sight to see and I probably would have laughed if I hadn't been in the middle of this shitshow.

Tom sank to the edge of the stage and his friend Lee came over and sat beside him.

'You never said that about Emma, did you, mate?'

Tom loudly blew out a stream of air.

'Well... Not in that context.' He raked a hand over his face.

Lee shook his head.

'How can something like that be taken out of context?'

The shot panned out, the screen wobbling a little, as if the person filming was removing themselves from the immediate scene. Even though the view was a little blurry, and the two young men more shadows in the distance, the microphones must still have been switched on, as the audio was crystal clear.

'I was talking to Julie the other day by the lockers. We were friends. She said that she'd heard I'd been hanging out with Emma a lot. I answered her and said yes, I was. That when I first met her, everyone said that she was the chubby army brat with no friends.' He held his hands up. 'It was never me who said that, I was just repeating what the gossip was.'

Lee listened intently and I realised that I was still holding my breath.

'But then I went on to say that Emma meant the world to me and that I thought I was in love with her. At that point Julie said she really liked me and asked me if there was any point in her asking me out on a date and I said no; told her that Emma and I were together. I confided in Julie, because I thought she was my friend, that I was in love with Emma.'

'Well, clearly Julie wasn't your friend and you pissed her off big time.'

'And now I've managed to piss Emma off big time too.' He buried his head in his hands and then started smacking his head with the pads of his hands.

Lee pulled his hands away presumably before Tom could do any damage to himself and then tried to haul him up.

'Come on, mate. Let's go and try and sort this mess out. You are supposed to be the lead roles in the play.'

'And I've managed to make my leading lady hate me.' He

stared into a mirror at the side of the stage and spoke to his reflection. 'You are a frigging idiot.'

He and Lee went to walk away but Julie returned on the other side of the stage.

'Could I have a word, please, Tom?'

'I'll be there in a minute, Lee. What do you want, Julie? Don't you think you've done enough damage already?'

'I'm sorry but I just wanted to let you know that my mate Mandy has just seen Emma with the boy who was supposed to have got her pregnant. They were walking hand in hand together and Emma shouted out to Mandy to say that she was going to be moving into a flat with the dad and they were to tell you to put that in your pipe and smoke it.' She touched Tom's arm. 'I'm so sorry, Tom. But she's clearly in love with someone else. Not you. You just need to get over her. Forget she ever existed. She's a fraud. I'll help you. I'm your friend.'

Tom lowered his head and sniffed. Julie put her arms around him and muttered.

'It's OK, Tom. I've got you.'

In all of this vision playing out before me, my stage director radar was telling me what a fantastic actor Julie was.

They both walked off to the left of the stage and down the stairs at the back and left the theatre through the back door. And whoever had been filming the whole thing stopped the camera.

I waited to see if anything else came on afterwards but there was just nothing.

I stared at the darkness on the screen.

My brain was trying to compute all that it had just seen.

So, I'd got it all wrong? What a fool I'd been.

Tom hadn't been with Julie. He had loved me after all. And why hadn't we discussed it at the time? Behaved like adults. Because we were still kids I suppose.

Huge miscommunication between us, and each of us being stubborn in not speaking about what had happened had completely changed the course of our lives. I was annoyed with Tom for not giving me a chance to explain but more than that I was annoyed with myself.

First thing tomorrow, I knew that after I'd apologised profusely to Jo and Michelle for the unkind things I'd said, the next person I would need to speak to was Tom.

35

The first text I sent off the next day was a joint one to the girls.

> I know I was a vile, horrible, spiteful cow to you both last night but I'd love the opportunity to apologise with coffee this morning x

> PS. I have YumYums!

> PPS. If you say no, I'll have to eat them all on my own and I know that you probably both hate me right now but even so, that would be very wrong of you to allow me to eat a whole pack of 4 to myself because that will equate to a weight gain of at least six pounds in one go.

> PPPS. You two are the best thing that has happened to me for a long time and I'd hate to think that you wouldn't let me grovel effectively to make up for what a bitch I was.

Jo was the first to reply, pretty much immediately.

> It's a good job you added the first PS or my answer would most definitely be no. However, you redeemed yourself with the promise of YYs and if you grovel really well and because I'm such a nosy cow and I'm dying to get the goss on why you turned into a raving psychopath, I'm in. Let me know what time. I'm free all morning x

Michelle's answer was short and sharp.

> You are a badass blackmailing bitch but as I love you, I will also agree, as long as we get one each and share the final one three ways. Could we do 10am please as, well you know, I do have other friends too ;-)

Smiling at the fact that they clearly didn't hate me enough to shun my explanation, I put the kettle on. Nervously, I went into the lounge and went to plump up the cushions and then gave a hollow laugh at myself and left them as they were.

The next text I sent was to Tom.

> Hi Tom. Any chance you could spare me some time today? I really hope you'll give me the chance to do some explaining x

Those three little dots that you get while waiting for someone's text back is one of the worst inventions in technology ever. I wasn't sure if he was deliberately dithering over what to put or whether he was just getting interrupted but it was doing nothing for my nerves which were already in tatters.

After just over ten minutes, there was a response.

> Sure. Can you meet on the beach at the end of the path through the dunes at 12?

The fact that he hadn't put a kiss on the end sent me into a bit of a tailspin. Maybe I had ruined things after all. I sent a thumbs up emoji back as my response, trying not to overanalyse.

The knock at the door made me jump a little even though I was expecting it and I took a deep breath before opening the door. Thank goodness these ladies didn't bear a grudge because Michelle yelled, 'Group hug!' and they threw themselves at me, squeezing me tight.

I could see tears glistening in Jo's big brown eyes as they met mine. 'I can't believe you used YumYums to entice us here. You know we'd have come anyway, right?'

'I do, but I always think an apology is best served with a sweet treat. Come through. I've just made a fresh pot.'

* * *

They both listened intently and without interruption as I explained everything. From how, when I heard Melanie describing her husband, it made me realise that maybe my marriage wasn't all I thought it was, to how the video I had watched had stunned me. That when I thought Tom had pulled the wool over my eyes and made a fool out of me years ago, he hadn't.

'So what happened then?' Jo asked, eager for the next instalment. 'After you'd run away from the school?'

'Nothing really. The next morning Mrs Dawes rang the house because I told Mum and Dad I was ill and they let me have a day off sick. I told her I didn't want the lead role any more, and when I got back to school the next day Julie had stepped into my shoes. Then at some point, Tom and Julie became a public couple and that was it really.'

'The cow!'

'Don't speak ill of the dead, please, Michelle.'

'Well, she was. Did you speak to Tom again?'

'Not really. We used to pass each other in the corridors when we were in sixth form but we were never alone again and never had the opportunity to talk about what happened. We went about our lives as if it had never happened. I directed the play. It was a huge success and Julie and Tom were the stars of the show. When we left school, I never saw them again although about five years ago I did bump into that girl Mandy – she told me that they'd got married, had a daughter and they were living in Australia.'

'Wow. That's quite a story, you know,' Michelle remarked and Emma nodded sagely.

'It is. So what are you going to say to Tom?'

'I have no bloody idea but I'm going to meet him on the beach at lunchtime.' I looked at my watch. 'In fact, I should probably think about making a move.'

I stood and the others followed suit.

'I just want to say how sorry I am again that I said those cruel nasty things last night. I never even meant them. I was just lashing out at you both because you were the nearest to me. It was a lot to deal with, the realisation that my marriage hadn't been anywhere near perfect – that was just a lie I'd been telling myself. It was myself I was angry with. Not you two. I should never have taken it out on you. I've never been anything but grateful for your friendship. Thank you for listening to me explain. And I *will* make it up to you.'

'Hey, we love you. It's OK. However, you might have to keep us supplied with YumYums every Saturday morning for the rest of our lives to redeem yourself.' Michelle shook her head, reached forward and hugged me. 'You silly arse.'

'Thank you kindly. It's a deal.' I smiled gratefully at her.

Jo stepped into the space that Michelle had moved out of and pulled me towards her, squeezing gently.

'Maybe you could mix it up with a doughnut occasionally. Custard filled, obviously.'

'Obviously,' I replied.

'Now, go see that gorgeous man and we want to hear all about it later.'

As I waved them off as they walked up the garden path, I knew that the next chat was going to be equally as uncomfortable, but I had no idea whether the outcome would be as positive as this one.

36

When I noticed him down by the water's edge, Tom was kicking at something in the sand with the tip of his trainer. The sea had calmed somewhat since yesterday's unexpected weather, the smell of sea salt more pungent from the rain but the sea was still quite feisty. For the few moments before he noticed me, I stood and watched him; his stature hadn't changed much since he was a teenage boy, those familiar emotions within me evoking deep-rooted feelings of nostalgia.

As if he sensed me watching, he turned and raised a hand and I approached him. He went to kiss my cheek at the same time as me leaning towards him to go in for a hug, resulting in an awkward situation but we both smiled and it seemed to break the intensity of the moment.

'Feeling better?' he asked.

'Much, thank you.' I turned, indicating that we should start walking. 'Shall we?'

Neither of us spoke for a while and it was starting to feel slightly uncomfortable.

Tom broke the silence. 'So, you wanted to talk?'

I passed him the DVD.

'Oh, my goodness.' His brows furrowed and there was a mixture of confusion and questioning on his face. 'How on earth did you get that? Oh, wait! Did Stephanie give it to you?'

'Well, she gave it to Michelle to pass on.'

'Ah! I see.' Tom combed his fingers through his hair and as I took a sneaky peek at him, I could see he was biting his lip.

We continued to walk, neither of us wanting to be the first to speak. The silence clearly bothered me more because I started to talk.

'I watched it last night.'

'Ah.' He put his hands in his pockets.

I laughed. 'You're saying ah a lot.'

'Mmmm,' he replied and as I glanced over at him again, he smirked. He stopped and reached out to my arm, so that I did the same. 'So you know what happened then?'

I nodded, looking him straight in the eyes, which began to twinkle and his face broke into a broad grin. The butterflies were back.

'Emma, do you remember how we used to hold hands and run into the sea together and we'd laugh and squeal when we hit the cold water?'

'Well, you squealed. I didn't.' I winked at him.

His grin got wider. 'OK, so I was a wuss.'

'Yes, you were,' I agreed, grinning back.

'Let's do it again now,' he suggested.

'What, now as in right now?'

'Yes, or are you too chicken?' His raised eyebrows mocked me.

I reached down and slipped off my trainers then my socks, without taking my eyes from his. I only broke our stare when I flung them up the beach and away from the water.

'Who are you calling chicken?' I asked as I rolled up my trouser legs and walked nearer the shoreline.

'Oh, so we're really doing this, are we?' he asked as he followed suit, wrapping his phone and keys in one of his socks and tucking the rolled parcel into one of his trainers, before throwing them further up the beach where they landed next to mine. He held out his hand and my small hand fitted perfectly into his large one, exactly as it used to.

As our feet hit the cold waves, the temperature of the sea made me gasp out loud. I realised what fools we were that we were running through the cold shallow waters well into the autumn season and noticed that the sea got even more icy-cold as we waded further in. I laughed. Tom did not as a bigger wave swept the water higher up his trousers. A high-pitched wail escaped him.

'Oh my God, Tom Sullivan! You're *still* a squealer.' I laughed out loud. It felt good after a heavy day or so. 'Good to see some things don't change.'

'Well, there's a huge difference to the Aussie waters I'm used to paddling in on a November day, you know.'

'Would you ever consider going back?' I asked, a little apprehensive to know the answer.

'Not on your nelly.'

I didn't realise how relieved my heart would feel when I heard those words. We still had a lot to talk about, but I couldn't bear the thought of Tom not being in my life again. He'd brought sunshine back into my days and hopes and dreams of a future came alive again. Since he'd been back, I had started to accept that yes, I did still have a life and it was up to me to make the most of it. At that moment, I had no clue whether we'd be linked romantically, but just having Tom around in any way felt incredibly good.

'So, how far are we going in then?' he asked. 'You nutter!'

'Up to my knees and then I'm done. Let's go.'

I pulled at his hand and he stumbled, wobbled uneasily and then fell headfirst into the sea. I roared with laughter and he started to get up but fell back down again. This time as I threw my head back and laughed, he caught me off guard and grabbed my hand, and I landed next to him in the water.

'You rotter!' I yelled at him, still laughing.

Our eyes locked and instinctively we moved closer. He tucked a wayward strand of hair behind my ear and I shivered. I wasn't sure if it was the temperature of the water or the touch of his cold hand against my skin. His eyes flickered to my lips and then back again and his head bent towards mine. Just as his lips were about to touch mine, a massive wave swept over us both, knocking us over into the sea and we burst back into laughter again.

Coughing, spluttering, laughing and wringing wet through, we both dragged ourselves back to the beach and retrieved our footwear.

'Shall we go back to mine to warm up?' I asked, walking backwards up the beach path.

He raised one eyebrow.

'Now there's an offer you don't get every day,' he responded.

'No, I really do mean get warmed up.'

'Well, if that's the best you can offer, I suppose it'll have to do.'

I batted his arm. I loved and had always loved this playful banter between us. After the big gloomy grey cloud that had been following me around for the last two years, Tom made me feel lighter and like a teenager again. Even if we just stayed friends, I loved that he was in my life. There was still a lot that remained unsaid. Some mysteries to solve in order to finish the puzzle of our lives.

'We still need to talk, you know,' I said.

'Yeah, I know.' He held my hand and we walked back to my lovely little home in silence. And I knew that we had all the time in the world.

37

After I'd got changed and given Tom an old dressing gown of mine, I threw his clothes in the tumble dryer. The thought of him being totally naked underneath it was quite honestly getting me in a bit of a tizzy and I made sure I sat as far away from him as I could. He should have looked ridiculous in my lounge in my flowery dressing gown but he looked like he belonged there. It was nice in a way that this was my new home, and it wasn't like he was sitting in Ben's place. I was glad that I'd made the decision to move from our together home and start to make new memories of my own. Ironic really that my new memories now contained one of my oldest ones.

We both sipped our hot chocolates in silence, staring out at the sea. It had become even calmer now and seemed to be at peace again.

We both spoke at the same time.

'So...'

'So...'

I gave a forced laugh. 'May I?'

He nodded his affirmation.

'So, I watched the DVD.'

'And...'

'It's not true, you know. What Julie said. There was never anyone else for me. It was only ever you, Tom. Just you.'

He moved from the chair he was sitting on and sat beside me on the sofa. 'That's nice to hear. I knew I shouldn't have believed a word she said.'

'Why *did* you believe her and not me?'

Tom raked his hand through his hair.

'I'm struggling to understand it myself now let alone explain it to you. It all seems so obvious all these years later. I should have believed in you more. In *us* more. I'm *so* sorry, Emma. I let you down big time. You and I never really got the opportunity to speak about it again. It seems like Julie manipulated the whole situation. She told me further down the line that you had lost the baby but were still with the boy, who was older than us, and had left school and I think I was just so gutted at the time, and felt so insecure, and just presumed that you'd moved on. I suppose the more time Julie and I spent together, we just drifted together as a couple and then when we found out a few years later that she was pregnant, I did what I thought was the right thing and suggested we get married.'

'And it seemed to work out OK in the end?' I said, the inflection in my tone indicating that it was a question rather than a statement.

'Yeah, I suppose it did. We had our good times and our bad but mainly we muddled along and we were OK. Stephanie was our focus and it wasn't until she left home that we realised we didn't have anything in common any more. If we hadn't had her, I don't think we'd have talked about it. As I told you before, I finally plucked up the courage to tell Julie I wanted us to separate and that I was going to come back to the UK. On the same day, she got her diagnosis and I couldn't be that cruel. And you know the rest really. Apart from one thing which I haven't told you yet.'

I moved closer to the edge of the sofa.

'A few days before Julie passed away, she gave me the DVD and told me to promise to bring it to England with me when I returned and apologise to you from her. She wanted you to know that she'd changed so much since that girl at college, since becoming a mum really. Having Stephanie made her a better person. She'd never really forgotten or forgiven herself for how she treated you and she felt that she owed it to you to apologise.'

I tried to take in all that he was saying. It was a lot.

'She'd had a tough upbringing herself, not my story to tell and it's no excuse but it is a reason why she felt that if she didn't become a bully, she'd be bullied herself. She told me that she wanted me to find love again and be happy and that if that meant finding you again, then I should.'

I couldn't believe what I was hearing.

'But why has this video just come to light?' I asked, trying to piece everything together and make sense of it all.

'There was so much going on at the time and I hadn't even seen the box again myself until last week when Stephanie was sorting through some stuff and came upon it. It was just marked up *Romeo and Juliet*. Stephanie and I sat together watching it. If I had known what was on it, I wouldn't have let her see it because she saw her mum as that mean girl in college.'

'But why did Stephanie give it to me? I don't understand that part.'

'I told her the full story about what happened all those years ago and she sat and cried and said she was really disappointed in her mum. I told her that she shouldn't sully her memories of her lovely mum by something she did years ago when she was young and daft. She hadn't been that person for a very long time.'

I couldn't help but feel for Stephanie. The poor girl couldn't even talk to her mum about this and that must have been really hard for her.

'When she thought there might be a possibility of Melanie and I getting together, she said she wasn't ready for me to have a relationship. Also, totally daft because it was never even on my radar to want to be with Melanie. But then she quickly realised that maybe it wasn't the idea of me being with anyone again, it was the fact that it might be Melanie. She does, however, really like you and said that if I was going to be with anyone, she could see us together. She wants me to be happy and said that if you were the person to make me happy then I should give it a go. See if you felt the same.'

This was such a lot to take in. After I heard Stephanie talking about Melanie, and being quite vocal about the fact that she wasn't ready for her dad to have a new relationship, this was the last thing I expected to hear.

He moved towards me, closing the gap, but we were interrupted by a high bleeping sound going off in the kitchen. I stood hastily.

'I'm sorry but I'm struggling to have a sensible conversation with you while you are sitting in my dressing gown and it's gaped open around the...' I waved my finger around in the air above his crotch, 'you know, erm... there. It's quite distracting. I'll go and get your clothes out of the tumble dryer.'

As I got up, he stood to face me, and my heart did a little hop, skip and jump. And this time there was no crashing wave to stop us kissing as he raked his hands through my hair and steered me gently towards him. I melted into his body as his lips tenderly locked onto mine.

38

Breaking away from Tom, I went to retrieve his clothes. I needed a moment to gather my thoughts. I gave them a good shake out so that the creases dropped out and handed them back to him. When he went into the bathroom to get dressed, I put the kettle on, needing to keep myself busy. I gazed out of the kitchen window at the dunes and the beach beyond, my mind in turmoil. After many years of marriage, I was finding it hard to believe that I had now, for the second time, kissed another man.

In the heat of the kiss, thank goodness, I hadn't thought about Ben at all, but now it was all I could think of. The guilt I was feeling was in danger of becoming completely overwhelming. My mind was at risk of being totally confused and I wasn't sure how I was meant to feel.

The sound of gentle footsteps coming into the room pulled me back to the present and I turned to face Tom. I knew I was frowning but couldn't seem to stop myself. He stood awkwardly beside me, leaning up against one of the kitchen cupboards, and nudged my shoulder with his.

'Feels a bit weird, doesn't it?'

I nodded sagely, unable to find any other appropriate words.

'When I say weird, I don't mean that the kiss was weird. The kiss was totally bloody wonderful.' He smiled at me, his blue eyes twinkling, and I noticed his laughter lines more than I had before. 'But I think that's what makes it weird. Don't know about you but I can't help feeling like I'm being unfaithful to Julie.'

Another nod from me and then I turned away, busying myself with pouring tea into the pot and setting up the tray with two china mugs.

'Here, let me.' Tom grabbed the tray and carried it through to the lounge where he placed it on the coffee table and then took the seat opposite the sofa, purposefully putting some distance between us.

'I've never kissed another woman until I kissed you recently, Emma. Julie and I have been married for years and the only other woman in my life that I have kissed is you.' I smiled at him. 'Have you? Kissed another man, I mean, obviously, not woman. Well, you never know.'

'Never say never is my motto,' I replied and grinned. Despite what he was saying, it did break the tension a little. 'The answer is not many. I hope that doesn't make me sound like an old slapper.' He laughed. I loved that we still managed to have this really relaxed relationship even at a time like this. 'The people were not even worth mentioning. I had a mad fortnight when Ben and I split up in the early days but then we got back together. So, including you, which is quite nice as you only count as one, because I'd kissed you before, just four. Do you feel guilty that we just kissed?'

'I do and I don't. I'm not sure whether to beat myself up because I kissed you and felt like I was being unfaithful to Julie, or because I kissed you and enjoyed it so much and want to do it all over again.' He smiled and then raised his eyebrows. 'Does that sound mad?' He moved closer to me, sitting next to me on the sofa and took my hands in his. 'Tell me how you feel, Emma. I'm feeling a little bit out of my comfort zone here. Am I alone?'

I smiled and shook my head.

'You're not alone, Tom.'

He raked his hands through his hair and dragged them down his face, sighing loudly before whispering, 'Thank God.'

I honestly don't know what came over me right then, but as he turned to face me and I looked into his eyes which were searching mine, I felt a desire flash through me that I'd never felt before in my life.

'Maybe we should...'

'Put things on hold? Give ourselves a bit more time? Work out how we feel?' He looked a little sad and I didn't know whether to go ahead or not. I looked across at the photo of Ben and me together on the mantlepiece. He wasn't here any longer and the girls were right. Life was short and we all deserved happiness for the time that we were here on earth.

'I was going to say, do it again and see how we feel. Just to test out whether...'

I didn't get chance to finish my sentence before Tom's lips were on mine, gentle at first then turning more passionate. His arms pulled me closer and we fell further back on the sofa, and that little flash of desire that I had experienced a few moments ago now whooshed through my entire body. I knew that for me it was now time to grab happiness with both hands.

39

Because I'd been neglecting the Lonely Hearts Club in favour of the panto, I had spontaneously decided that I was going to put on an event for them too so had put the word about for the next afternoon. There was still a couple of weeks before the big performance and so I could afford to take some time away. When I suggested it, I hadn't known how many people would be interested in a five-mile hike along the coastal path and then lunch in The Smuggler's Rest but when Michelle shared the social media post I was staggered by how many people signed up.

On the beach, when I turned around and saw the group behind me, it really lifted my heart to see the group of around twenty or so, mostly women but there were a few men too, including Tom, who was walking by my side, and Scott, Aggie's husband, who was chatting along with another man who I recognised from the pub. I was glad to see that she'd persuaded him to come along.

Surprisingly Melanie had also joined the walk. She started in the small group behind us and caught us up quite quickly, linking her arm through Tom's. When he looked at me to gauge my reaction, I just shook my head at him and smiled to show that it was fine. He seemed to visibly relax, his shoulders less tense.

Neither Tom nor I wanted to give this *thing* that we had going on between us a name right now, we both just knew that we thoroughly enjoyed each other's company, laughed a lot when we were together and he gave me butterflies in my tummy. We wanted it to be just us, before we were ready to share it with anyone else.

What did shock me was that Melanie tucked her other arm through mine so the three of us were strolling along the beach together.

'This has been great, you know, Emma. Thanks so much for letting me tag along. I honestly never came along before because I thought it would be full of losers.'

'Gee, thanks, Melanie!' I responded, laughing at her back-handed compliment.

'But that's what I'm trying to say. I've spent time today chatting to people that I would never have connected with if it wasn't for this group. What a lovely bunch of people too. And the thing that really surprised me is that they're people just like us. I'd really like to come along to some other events too if you'll have me.'

'Of course we will. The more the merrier.' I smiled across at her and squeezed her arm. Maybe we could be friends after all.

'In fact, I've been thinking...' she started and I tried not to roll my eyes. 'Have you ever thought about doing things like theatre and cinema trips?'

'Yes, we already do those,' I replied.

'Oh, well, how about bowling trips? And I know you do coffee mornings but what if you did them with a bit of a difference and got an inspirational speaker to come along. You could charge a little bit for everyone to come and then you could pay the speaker. What do you think?'

I actually thought it was a cracking idea but still couldn't help but feel that when she made suggestions like this it was as if she was criticising me and thought that my ideas weren't good enough. I knew that she was genuinely trying to help though. Some people were made this way and couldn't help themselves from making suggestions to make things better. Taking Tina's earlier advice of not taking it personally, I smiled at her and said those were great ideas. They could be really beneficial for the group and it gave me lots to think about. Maybe I didn't need to take on everything myself and some help would only improve on our already fabulous community that we were building.

When we reached a narrow stretch of coastal path, we could only walk single file and couldn't come back together again as a threesome until the path widened into open countryside.

My heart lifted with joy when we reached the clifftop, seeing the sight of the bay below. The sea glistened in the winter sunshine; the vast golden sand deserted on this fresh autumn day.

As I removed my gilet, I smiled to myself, thinking that I'd been dithering for ages about what to wear for the walk. It was always a tricky time of year because you knew that when you started a walk wrapped up against the cold, it would lead to a gradual strip off of various layers. Similarly, a small rucksack that started off feeling quite light with the bare minimum ended up feeling that you were carrying a sack full of rocks.

When I took off my final layer which was a thin fleecy jacket, leaving just a long-sleeved t-shirt on my top half, Tom helped me to put it in my backpack.

'Thank you. It's hard to know what to wear for a walk, isn't it?'

'Put it all on and then take it all off, that's what I say?' He lowered his voice and raised an eyebrow. 'Preferably take it all off.' He winked, and grinned before he sidled away and my insides melted as I remembered the evening before. Things between us got very heated and we'd stopped ourselves before we did something that one of us, or both of us, might regret. If we were going to do this, we wanted to make sure it was something that we both felt was at the right time.

I smiled to myself and watched Tom walk away. He still walked in exactly the same way as he did as a boy and as he looked over his shoulder and gave me a cheeky wink it made my heart beat just a little bit faster.

As if by magic, Melanie appeared by my side, making me jump.

'You did this,' she announced.

'Did what?' I frowned, once again thinking the worst.

'Brought all these folk together. Forming friendships. Look at everyone in high spirits. Most of these people would have been sat home alone today without this in their calendars. I mean, look at you. A widow at your age and probably won't be looking for another man for a long time if at all. You need time to get over what's happened to you. And look how much fun you're having while you are adjusting. All these other women too going through similar things. Even me, trying to get through the breakdown of my marriage. And you're helping us all. You should be very proud of what you've done for these people.'

She was taking away with one hand what she was giving with the other, but regardless, it was true. I took in the group before me: there were people deep in conversation, others laughing, some arm in arm, helping each other along, but everyone had a smile on their face and rosy cheeks. There were people in the group that I know had been through life-changing situations.

One had lost her husband through suicide; another had lost a child and then her husband left her. One of the men had been on his own for years and lived with his mother, another had a terminal illness. Everyone had their own stuff going on and the thing that brought us all together was our lonely hearts and the need for friendship and support.

After we'd all hydrated, a huge cheer went around the group when I suggested we walk back and go for lunch in the pub. As the group gathered once more to begin the ascent, I watched from the rear of the group, feeling incredibly pleased with what I'd achieved.

I had been tolerating Melanie most of the time. I knew from the moment I met her that she'd be good for the lead role in the panto and she was. I had helped her with her lines when she was struggling to learn them. We had gone over and over them until she got them all off by heart, and I could recite them verbatim. She wasn't, however, someone I would have chosen as a friend, even though everyone else seemed to love her. She was cutesy and feminine, giggly and girly, wanting to be the centre of attention all the time. I was the sort who was happier just standing on the sidelines. However, I suppose that's one of the nice things about life. It surprises us at the most unexpected of times.

I was incredibly surprised when she tugged gently on my arm to stop me walking, pulled me into an embrace and whispered in my ear, 'Thank you for everything you do to help others. You're wonderful and I'm so glad you are my friend.' She then caught up with the group in front and left me to walk alone.

For the rest of the way back to the pub, I was mentally beating myself up. I felt quite mean for not taking to Melanie straight away when she was now being so nice to me. When Tom lagged behind and let me catch him up I was quiet and contemplative. However, when he gave my hand a gentle squeeze and those crinkly blue eyes locked onto mine, I wished that instead of going back to the pub with the others, I had him all to myself. I was beginning to want to spend more and more time with him and while on one hand, I loved the feeling that it was giving me – excitement, something to look forward to for the first time in ages – it scared the living daylights out of me too. And that's why I wanted to keep it to ourselves. Just for a little longer until we both knew we were 100 per cent sure it was what we wanted.

40

Friday evening soon rolled around and we were all wrapped up in blankets, huddled together on the terrace around the firepit.

'I wonder at what temperature we'll decide to have Friday nights indoors instead of out,' Michelle said.

'I was just thinking that we'll be needing hot chocolate with a big slug of brandy in it soon instead of these summer cocktails.' I pulled the furry throw around me even tighter, imagining my hands wrapped around a warm mug.

'Isn't that called a La Mumba? I'm sure that's what the barman in Spain called it when I had it there a few years ago,' Jo responded. 'It was lush.'

'Or even Tia Maria in coffee. Maybe we need to think about what hot cocks on Friday we can have instead.'

Seamus appeared at that very moment, walking up towards our little terrace with his dog Theo weaving in and out of his ankles.

'Talking about hot cocks...' Michelle shout-whispered. 'Sorry, I know he's yours but he is a mighty fine specimen of a man, you know.'

Jo grinned. 'That he is, my friend. That he is.'

He bent down and kissed Jo firmly, his lips lingering for a while on hers and a little moan escaped her own mouth. She was blissfully happy with him and it was wonderful to see.

'Are you staying for a tipple, Seamus?' Michelle asked.

'Are you kidding? You think I'd crash your Friday night ritual? Wouldn't dare.' He laughed. 'I was just walking along the beach. I couldn't see you but I could definitely hear you.'

'Ah, was it the dulcet tones of cackling witches that alerted you to us?' Michelle asked.

He grinned.

'No, just the sounds of friendship. It was lovely so I thought I'd come and kiss my woman and then head off again. That's all.'

'You got a brother, Seamus?' Michelle asked.

He quick-wittedly replied, 'You know I haven't, but there's always my dad. He's quite sprightly for an eighty-year-old, you know.'

Jo laughed. 'Oh my God. Poor Bill. She'd wear him out. And anyway, Chelle, you have Dr Hottie. Why are you looking around?'

'Ah, you know,' she responded. 'Just keeping my options open in case it doesn't work out and Demetri gets bored with me. Or vice versa.'

'And... I think that's my cue to leave. See you tomorrow, love. Bye, ladies.' Seamus scuttled off down the garden with Theo at his heels. When I turned to Jo, she was watching him walk away and had a dreamy expression on her face. She inspired me so much. If Jo could find love when she wasn't expecting it, maybe I could too.

'So, anyway,' Michelle said. 'That little distraction isn't going to put me off asking you whether that was Tom Sullivan I saw leaving your house late last night?'

I thought that Tom and I had been quite discreet but clearly not as Michelle had obviously spied us together.

'I wonder if this land of Jo's has got some kind of magical properties. Making everyone rampant.'

'Speak for yourself, sugar tits! We're not all raving nympho-maniacs, you know,' Michelle piped up and I grinned at her expression.

'I'll just remind you that I've seen Demetri's car at yours a couple of times this week, Michelle,' Jo added.

'I've been meaning to ask if Aggie helped you with those final bits on your costume by the way.' I winked at Jo, thanking her via eye contacting for diverting the attention from me but whip-smart Michelle wasn't missing a trick.

'Not so fast, lady! Dish the dirt. What's occurring?'

The big breath of air that came out of my mouth could have been my biggest ever.

'Oh!' Jo said as she realised what was unfolding. 'You really like Tom, don't you?'

I nodded slowly and chewed my lip.

Michelle bounced down next to me on the sofa and my drink splashed everywhere. We all laughed. 'I think maybe we might need to ease off on the cocktails. So what's the problem, Em?'

'What will people think of me? My husband has only just died and I'm moving on already? That I have forgotten all about him?'

'Or maybe they'll think good for you; you deserve happiness after all you've been through and they'll be really happy. Trouble is we all overthink things so much and worry about things that haven't even happened.' Jo was the most level-headed of us all and what she was saying did make some sense. 'We stress about other people's opinions, imagining things that probably haven't even crossed their minds. We should never assume to know what other people are thinking.'

'True that.' Michelle spoke up next, the alcohol loosening her tongue a little – a fact which could probably be said for the rest of us too. Either that, or we were just really comfortable in each other's company and valued what each other thought. 'It's like me and Dr Hottie. In my head I'm already thinking that he's going to dump me because I'm not as clever as all the gorgeous doctors and nurses he has around him all day long.'

'What? Michelle. You are gorgeous and he's clearly besotted with you. Have you not seen the way he moons around after you? Like your little lap dog,' Jo grinned.

'Do you think so?' She looked at us both for our answer.

'Abso-bloody-lutely. But be careful, Chelle, because if you do push him away, thinking he'll find someone better, then you might manifest that. Just take it as it comes. Don't ruin this chance. And I'll say the same to you too, Emma. We all deserve to be loved. We are all fabulous and these men in our lives are bloody lucky to have us. Ladies, please raise your glasses. To us, and all who have us.'

We all repeated Jo's toast. Her words meant a lot. Now I just had to believe them.

41

It was a week before the panto and we had a catch-up meeting scheduled in the church hall. There was a huge agenda to get through. First on the list was ticket sales which Tina gave us an update on.

'Going really well, guys. We do need to do a final push but at the moment, we've sold 150 tickets and we have fifty left.'

'That's amazing. Michelle, could you do an extra push on social media for the last week and see if we can sell them that way? And is the live stream coming along OK, Sarah?' I was in my efficient, assertive, no-messing-with-me mood that day.

'Yep, my brother has assured me that all the sound, lighting and video streaming is all sorted so nothing to worry about there.'

I ticked that off my list and moved on to the next item.

'Wonderful news, thank you so much for arranging all of that. So, next. Costumes. Aggie? Do you have an update?'

Aggie stood. 'I do. I think everyone is nearly done. The only people who are flatly refusing to tell us what they're wearing are

Graham and Bill, but they know what we need and they want to surprise us at the dress rehearsal.'

I glanced Tina's way.

'Don't look at me. That man is a law unto himself. He hasn't even shown me, so only the Lord himself knows what monstrosity he'll turn up in. He's very resourceful though so I wouldn't worry. He said he's got Bill sorted too, so we don't have to worry about either of them.'

'Aggie, maybe you could just ask him if he's good to go?' I suggested. 'And I was thinking that maybe we could run a session one evening where people can come and see you if they need any help with anything?'

'Yes, that's a great idea.' Aggie got her diary out. 'Tuesday from 5 p.m. OK? Can we use the little side room in the church hall, Tina?'

'You can use as much as you want. I've cancelled all our other groups this week and explained that we need the space. I did give a couple of tickets away to the people who moaned. Everyone else was fine.'

'That's fantastic and will be a huge help. We can leave stuff around in that case if that's OK.' A thumbs up from Tina was perfect.

'Next on the list is the final rehearsal. So, if we could do that on Thursday night, the dress rehearsal on Friday night and then it's the main show on Saturday night. Are we all good to go? Everyone learnt their words?'

Mel stood up. 'Can I just say that if anyone is struggling to learn their words, Emma has been an absolute angel and has really helped me. So just give her a shout if you need any more help.'

What I hoped was a smile might have been more of a grimace. With a week to go I really didn't have time to help people with their lines. There was still such a lot to sort out but I guess if someone was desperate, I'd have to make the time. I might not be able to remember what I'd had for tea the night before, but I had a great memory for words in the format of a play and knew the whole panto off by heart.

'Refreshments on the evening. I've got five volunteers from the Lonely Hearts Club who have offered their services in the kitchen. We're going to be serving mulled wine, soft drinks, mince pies, stollen and Christmas cake. Do we think that'll be enough choice for people?'

'Maybe some chocolate rolls or something for the kids. I don't know many children who would eat any of the food otherwise,' Melanie suggested. 'Ooh, what about some warm sausage rolls? They might be nice on a cold night too maybe?'

I pointed my pen at her.

'Great idea, Melanie. Thank you.' She visibly preened at my praise. 'OK, so I think that's it. Have I forgotten anything? I could do with Graham being here to be honest, to check everything is OK from his side.'

Graham rushed in at that point and, in a hilariously booming voice, declared, 'I'm be-*hind* you!'

Everyone laughed and he took a mock bow. He was such a showman. I shook my head while still laughing. He was going to be an absolute knock-out on stage.

'Sorry I'm late. Bloody parishioners.' He winked at me. 'Only joking, folks. I love you all. Has anyone talked about the car parking?'

'We haven't. Is there a problem?'

'Not a major problem but if we could encourage those who are coming from the village to walk to the venue it would leave the spaces that we have in the church car park for people coming from further afield.'

'Good thinking, Batman. Michelle, could you also put that on the social media posts please and we can put something on the church hall notice board?' Michelle nodded and tapped a note into her phone.

Another idea popped into my head. My brain was having its own mind map party.

'I wonder if maybe a couple of teenagers from the boy scouts group might help with car park duties on the night?'

'I can ask them if you like, dear. I'm seeing the scout leader tomorrow morning,' Tina said.

'Sorted.' I scribbled in my notebook.

Aggie took the opportunity to approach Graham. 'Do you need any help from me with your outfit, Vicar?'

'Oh, no, thank you, dear. I'm going to knock it out of the park with my outfit. Bill too. Has Tina told you that I won't even show her?' He slid into the chair beside his wife.

'She has but I just wanted to check that it's in keeping with what everyone else is going to be wearing,' she suggested gently.

'Oh, Agatha dear. That's the whole point. You must stand out in life, not blend in. Life would be very dull if we all looked the same. So no, I'm perfectly fine, thank you.'

Tina rolled her eyes and then gave him a little peck on the cheek. 'Don't worry, darling, no one will ever accuse you of blending in.'

Since Graham had mentioned his illness that night in the pub many weeks ago now, he seemed to look better. Not as stressed as he normally did. I hoped he was finally taking the advice of his doctors and looking after himself a little better than he did. It must be hard to take on everyone else's worries and woes when you have your own. He patted Tina's hand gently.

'So, I think we're there then. Anything else from anyone else? Tina?'

'No, just that we have a schedule of rehearsals going on through the week for the songs. The choir will sing Christmas carols while everyone is coming in and getting drinks, etc. and the cast are getting ready. And if, at any point, anyone wants to come and do some singing practice, I'll be free most of the week so please do give me a shout. I think I've finally cracked the Taylor Swift number for our little fairy assistant. So, we're all good to go.'

I heaved a huge sigh of relief. I sincerely hoped that I hadn't missed anything major but I supposed that only time would tell.

42

There was so much going on in the week before the panto that Tom and I hadn't made any plans so it was a lovely surprise when a text arrived from him on Monday morning.

> Morning beautiful. Do you have an hour to spare me today? We could go for a walk along the beach, go for lunch out of town, or I could just bring you a sandwich. All work and no play will get to you if you're not careful. What do you think? x

While I was so busy I didn't know what to do with myself, it might actually do me good to get away and have a break for an hour or two.

> I'd really love that Tom. Here's an idea if you have a little more than an hour. How about you pick me up at 12.30, we drive to Driftwood Bay, have lunch in the 5 O'clock Somewhere bistro and a walk on the beach and then be back for 3 p.m. I think it would do me good to get out of Sandpiper Shore for a while. Let me know if that sounds good to you x

It was a good ten minutes before he responded and in that time I'd whipped myself up into a bit of a frenzy again and convinced myself that he wanted to meet me to tell me he didn't want to see me any more, had met someone more interesting than me, or was going to tell me that he was going back to Australia. Why did I do this to myself?

> Sounds perfect! See you at 12.30 sharp. I've missed you and can't wait to spend time with you x

OK, so maybe I'd made all of that up in my head. The pressure of the panto and a new relationship when I'd not been expecting one was getting to me. I knew that I had to relax a little bit more and like the girls said on Friday night, you can't spoil something before it's happened. It's just daft. I *was* trying to look forwards instead of backwards and was trying to put my trust into another human. I'd done it with Jo and Michelle and now felt like they were my soul sisters. Now I just had to put my faith in Tom.

Because I knew I didn't have an awful lot of time, I decided to write myself a priority to-do list for that morning. I always found that it helped me to write things down before I got overwhelmed. A middle-aged woman trying to remember everything in her head was a recipe for disaster. I worked my way solidly through my list and was pleasantly surprised when I ticked off the last one at noon.

That gave me just enough time to jump in the shower, apply some concealer, blusher, mascara and lip-gloss. I didn't want to overdo the make-up as it was only lunch. Temperatures had dropped even more over the last week or so and the change of the seasons was definitely upon us so I chose jeans and a jumper and slipped my feet into a pair of trainers as we'd planned to have a walk along the beach too. I'd been so busy over the last few days, I hadn't even been out for my morning run and I was looking forward to filling my lungs with fresh sea air. I promised myself I would make more time for this.

When I heard the beep of a horn outside, I grabbed my Barbour jacket from the back of the kitchen chair along with a flowery scarf to add some colour. My heart skipped a beat when I saw Tom, who was standing next to his sporty Jaguar holding the door open for me.

'Your carriage awaits, my dear.' As he bent to gently kiss my lips, I closed my eyes and breathed in Hugo Boss aftershave. He smelt and looked absolutely gorgeous, dressed from head to toe in navy apart from his coat. We both laughed at the fact that we were wearing matching olive-green coats.

'Thank you, kind sir.' I slid into the car as gracefully as I could, which wasn't very graceful at all, and he closed the door. I took a deep breath as he walked around to the driver's side.

Once in, he leaned across to me and kissed me again and a little moan escaped his mouth. 'That's better.' He winked at me and started the engine. I felt like a little schoolgirl with a crush. It wasn't an awful feeling. I rather liked it, feeling light and happy. After the heaviness of the last couple of years it felt like some of the clouds around me were finally starting to lift.

When we arrived in Driftwood Bay, we parked up in one of the side streets around the harbour and headed for the beach. There wasn't another soul around and Tom took my hand in his. We were alone, apart from the gulls swooping and diving, and the noise of them squawking, the only sound apart from the gentle lapping of the waves.

'At least here we don't have to keep each other a secret.' I grinned.

'Yeah, well, I've been thinking about that. I think that maybe we should start to let people know that we are seeing each other. I don't want to be lurking around, hoping that no one sees us. I want to be able to hold your hand in public. Give you a kiss when I want to. Squeeze your gorgeous butt when I feel like it.'

I laughed. 'Squeeze away.' He parted my coat and put his hands inside, pulled me close to him and wrapped his arms around me. His hands started to drift from my waist and landed on my backside, where he squeezed gently and I heard that little moan escape his lips once more.

'Lovely day!' We both shot round to where the voice came from. It was a lady dressed head to toe in clashing animal prints, walking an English Setter. 'Come on, Hobson. Let's leave these lovebirds to it. Sorry to disturb you.' She grinned at us both and we couldn't help but smile back. She walked along the beach in the opposite direction to us and we joined hands again as we continued on our walk.

'What do you think about telling people then, Em?'

I chewed the inside of my lip. 'What will people say, do you think?'

'Well, I don't know about you, but I don't care what they think or say. This is our life, not theirs. We deserve this. Also, I let you go once in my life and I'm not letting you go again.'

My heart swelled at this man before me. A man that I'd known for over thirty-five years. I loved him when we were teenagers and I loved him now. But this was different; more grown up; more serious.

'Let's get the panto out of the way and then we'll talk about it some more. That OK?'

He smiled. 'That'll do for me. Now shall we go and grab some lunch from that little bistro? I'm famished.'

43

Lunch flew by but as I thought, a few hours away did me the world of good. When Tom dropped me off just before 3 p.m., I felt even more focused on the jobs I had left on my list for the rest of the day. Michelle was popping round after tea so we could look at the schedule for social media posts and Jo said she'd join us to help with anything else that was needed. We also said that after that we might pop to the church hall for the rehearsal.

During the afternoon, I didn't really have time to think about what Tom had suggested about us not hiding our relationship, but I did raise it with the girls when they arrived.

'Yes, absolutely. Christmas is just around the corner and there'll be lots of socialising going on. You don't want to be hiding away from everyone, do you?' Jo said.

I shook my head. 'I suppose not.'

Michelle jumped up and held her hands to her face.

'Oh, God, I completely forgot. Tomorrow afternoon the county magazine wants to come along and do a last-minute interview for the panto. I'm so sorry, my head is all over the place. They only called this afternoon and their supplement is going to print on Wednesday. It'll be in shops on Thursday so in perfect time for the last-minute promo before the event. It was Fliss who called and she told me to remind you about the Lonely Hearts column too. Said that she was going to start hassling you about it as soon as the panto is over. Are you going to do it, Em?'

I groaned at the thought. I'd already told her I didn't think it was my thing.

'Probably not.' I dismissed it with a sweeping gesture of my hand.

'Well, it's not every day you get an offer like that, you know, and Fliss knows her stuff. If she thinks you can do it, then you can. Just consider it, that's all. And remember, you are now the new Emma who is supposed to be grabbing life with both hands. Taking opportunities that are offered to her. Just saying!'

'I'll park it till after the panto. I haven't got the brain capacity to consider it now and to be honest I'd forgotten all about it until you mentioned it just now.'

Once we'd discussed all that we needed to, we wrapped up warm and headed to the church hall for the dress rehearsal. As we approached, we could hear the choir singing 'Silent Night', the voices of majestic angels filling the air. The contrast between their dulcet tones and our tuneless little fairy assistant Ruby would be huge on the night, but it didn't matter. We were making her dream come true and there was no better feeling.

Tina ushered us in, shaking her head and wiping her eyes. She did look like she'd been crying but her eyes were bright and she didn't look sad. It was puzzling me.

'Is everything OK, Tina?'

Her mouth twitched and those eyes brightened even more.

'Let's just say that my darling husband, your parish vicar, is ready and waiting at home for a text from me to say that everyone is here. I can only apologise for what you are about to see and issue a warning. This image will be forever burned upon your eyelids. Let me know when everyone else is here.'

Michelle gave her the all-clear and, not quite knowing what to expect, I could not believe my eyes when Graham crashed through the door and made his way to the stage, truly embracing his new persona. From the moment he entered the building, he exuded sass, charisma and style. Heavy and dramatic but stunningly applied make-up, with a costume consisting of more sequins and feathers than you could expect to see on the *Strictly Come Dancing* finale and boobs like Dolly Parton. He wouldn't have looked out of place on *Ru Paul's Drag Race*.

'Oh, my goodness, Graham, is that really you?' I asked.

'No, darling. I'm Anastasia. Graham is my little brother. He's such a dull boy!' I laughed out loud. He looked spectacular. He adjusted his fake boobs and ran his hands over his backside as he winked at Tom. 'Oh, hello, big boy! What's your name?'

There were laughs all round and I knew that despite the fact that Melanie was supposed to be the star of the show, Graham had just stolen her limelight. Luckily Melanie also found him totally hilarious or we'd have been in for a bit of a showdown.

'Do you have a sister too?' she asked playfully.

'Yes, she'll be here any minute. She wanted me to text her when I'd arrived and settled in.'

Seamus had joined us and laughed, knowing that his dad was the other half of the ugly sisters, but his eyes popped out of his head when the next person who came stomping through the door was Bill, also dressed up to the nines – in a red rubber catsuit and a long blonde wig. Because he was tall, the catsuit only came down to his calves and his hairy legs poked out from the bottom.

'Dad, what the f...'

'I'm not your father, young man. I am Dakota.' He addressed

the room. 'And because you're going to get to know us so well, you can all call us Ant and Dak.' A group giggle went around the room. 'And we...' he went over to Graham and they stood side by side with their hands on their hips, 'are looking for Prince Charming. Anyone seen him?'

A huge roar of laughter went around the room.

Seamus stood on my right, shaking his head and laughing.

'Is that really my quiet and reserved dad? You've created a monster, Vicar. But I've never seen him smile so much.'

Graham tottered on his high heels to the edge of the stage.

'He said, has anyone seen Prince Charming?'

Tom, who was standing at the back of the stage, meekly came forward, grinning widely. The church hall had come to a standstill and nearly everyone there took Graham's cue and in a loud voice answered his question.

'*He's behind you.*'

Bill crept closer to Graham. 'He's where?' He cupped his ear to their audience.

'*He's behind you,*' we all yelled as loud as we could.

They both fake jumped and turned to find Tom standing a few steps away.

Graham put the back of his hand to his forehead and fake swooned.

'Phwoar! He's a bit of a grey-haired old fox, isn't he?'

'I would,' Bill responded, winking at his crowd.

Tina shouted up, 'Family show, ladies!'

Bill and Graham tittered behind their hands.

My sides hurt from laughing and there were tears streaming down my cheeks. This was honestly the most unexpected thing I think I had ever seen. Bill was normally one of the quietest, most lovely people around. His alter ego was just hilarious. Seamus was so stunned that he could hardly speak, Tom couldn't stop laughing and Tina was just shaking her head at her husband.

'You see that skinny waist? That's because he's got my Spanx bodysuit on.' I looked at her in horror. 'And yes, I will be burning it when the panto is over. At least he'll know what to buy me for Christmas. Some replacement ones!'

'No one can accuse him of not getting into the Christmas spirit now, can they?' I was still wiping the tears from my eyes.

'I just hope the bishop hasn't bought tickets for the panto. Can you imagine?' She flicked an imaginary hair off Graham's green off-the-shoulder sequinned evening dress, which had a huge split up the left-hand side.

'Right! Much as I'd love to stand around admiring Ant and Dak's fashion sense, we have a show to get on the road. Shall we make a start?'

44

Tom waited behind for me as Tina and I locked up. She pulled me into a hug and looked me directly in the eye. 'He's a good man, Emma. And you need to stop thinking about everyone else and enjoy yourself.' She winked at me. 'If you know what I mean.' I was glad that it was dark so that she couldn't see my blushes. 'We all have sex, you know, love. Even vic...'

'Night, Tina.' There were some things that I didn't want to think about, especially after seeing Graham in that outfit. Who knew what went on behind closed doors? And what did go on at the vicarage was certainly not my business.

Tom walked me home, and while I desperately wanted to walk hand in hand with him, we were conscious of other people around us, so managed to keep our hands to ourselves. That was until we got into my kitchen.

As soon as I had shut the door behind us, Tom closed the gap and rested his forehead against mine.

'Hello, you!' he whispered.

Those two small words turned my legs to jelly.

He bent his head to mine, gently kissing me.

'God, I've wanted to do that all night, Em. I don't want to wish my life away but there's a little bit of me that just wants this panto over and done with so that we can tell the world about us.'

I freed myself and held up the kettle. 'Tea? Or something stronger?'

'Could murder a cuppa. How times change, eh?' We both smiled and I took a deep breath before raising an important question.

'How do you want to tell Stephanie about us? Do you want to tell her alone, or together? What do you think is best?'

'I'll sound her out over the next day or so. She's in a really grumpy mood at the moment. She's coming towards the end of her pregnancy and said she feels fat and frumpy, and has had enough of being kicked from the inside out. Said it's probably a footballer.'

'Talking of footballers, have you seen anything of Scott Foster since the walk we did?' I asked.

'We had a beer together last night actually. Nice bloke. I was quite starstruck, to be honest. Me, sat in the pub with an ex-premiership footballer. The team I used to follow too. We had quite a chat.'

'I love that. Aggie was saying that he needs a friend right now and is struggling to adjust to life as a normal person and needs some male company.'

'Well, I'm sure we're going to be best pals.' He closed the gap between us again and once more those eyes flicked down to my lips and back again. 'Now, where were we?'

* * *

I'd made sure Tom hadn't stopped too late. I couldn't even contemplate what we had between us going further just yet.

When I did, it scared me to think of someone seeing me without my clothes on or sleeping next to someone new. What if I dribbled in my sleep? What if I snored? Or worse! In fact, I knew I snored because I woke myself up sometimes.

I knew that us having sex was something that I couldn't put off forever and I didn't want to. I did, however, need to get my head around it and build up to it. In anticipation of him asking, I told him that I still had lots to do, with the performance night looming ever closer and I was pretty sure he believed me. Jo and Emma had said it was probably as big a thing for him too and he was probably also feeling quite nervous. Especially as Julie had been his only partner.

I was in danger of becoming overwhelmed if I thought about it too much so I tried to push these thoughts aside. This dating lark in mid-life sure did take some getting used to.

45

The actual dress rehearsal evening had finally come round. I think the Christmas fairies had been hard at work during the day because the church hall looked like it had been sprinkled by a Christmas glitter bomb.

I was reminded that as soon as the panto was over, I needed to bring the festive season into my new home as well. This would be my first Christmas there and I hadn't really had much chance to even think about it, let alone put any decorations up.

The rehearsal went absolutely perfectly and as the last words were spoken the cast gave a rousing round of applause. There were tears in my eyes. I was so proud of every single one of this amazing group of people. What they had achieved was incredible.

When Tom came round the corner carrying a tray of tea, my heart did that little skip again and he winked. I didn't think anyone had noticed, but the beady eyes of Jo and Michelle didn't miss a trick and Michelle shoulder bumped me and grinned. He walked back towards the kitchen and spoke over his shoulder.

'Emma, don't suppose you can give me a hand for a minute,

can you?' I could feel the blush on my face and hoped that nobody else could see it.

'Yeah, sure. Just coming,' I replied.

'You'd best go and see what you can help Loverboy with, Em.' I scurried into the kitchen before they could embarrass me any further.

'Hello, you!' Tom was leaning up against one of the cupboards.

'Hello, yourself.' I walked over, and stood beside him, mirroring his position. He turned to face me and leant in close. I felt a whoosh of desire through my body when he couldn't take his eyes off me. He made me feel like a million dollars; like he couldn't get enough of me. It was intoxicating.

'There's no one around at the moment and I think I might need to kiss you, Em.'

I looked over my shoulder at the open doorway and made a split-second decision to close it behind me. The hatch to the main room was locked and the only voices we could hear were from over by the stage.

'Well, in that case, don't let me stop you.'

His eyes flickered from mine to my lips and back again. He cupped my face and I leaned my cheek into his hand. This man made me feel a way I'd only ever felt when I was a teenager. Yes, I'd been intimate with Ben. Obviously, we'd been married for years, but that was a grown-up relationship, one that we dove straight into. We didn't seem to have any of this flirtatious, delicious, playful skirting around each other.

Ben slipped from my mind again as Tom's lips touched mine. My hands naturally wrapped around his waist and I pulled him closer to me. Both his hands were weaving through my hair, and I melted into his kiss.

Suddenly, the door flung open, crashing into the wall, at the exact same time that Melanie's voice made us pull apart. Melanie stood before us, her mouth gaping open and her eyes wide.

'Shame on you, Emma. Your husband is hardly cold in his grave and you're cavorting around with Tom. He's a widower too. He's vulnerable and you're just downright selfish. You're taking advantage of his good nature. There are no words for this, right now. *No. Words.*'

She darted from the room as quickly as she'd entered it and Tom and I stared at each other, aghast. When we gathered ourselves, we both walked out into the main church hall to see Melanie grabbing her coat, her car keys and her handbag and she slammed out of the door. I went to follow her but Tom pulled me back.

'Leave her. It's nothing to do with her what we do.' It wasn't but Melanie had just confirmed everything that I thought people would say. I wanted to explain so I followed her out to the car park but was too late as the wheels of her car spun round, leaving a cloud of dust behind her.

46

Melanie's outburst had put a dampener on such a wonderful evening and when Tom asked if he could walk me home I insisted I was fine and would walk back with Jo and Michelle. I felt dreadful and couldn't shake off the feeling that something awful was going to happen.

The other thing that was lingering in my mind was why Melanie was so upset when she saw Tom and me together, and why she'd blamed it on me only, Tom escaping the tirade of abuse.

At 7 a.m. on the dot the following morning, my phone started to ring, waking me. Tom's name flashed up on my screen. I lay looking at the ceiling until it rang off, deciding I'd call him back once I'd made myself a drink. Ten seconds later, the ringing started again. I picked up the phone.

'Morning, Tom.' I rubbed sleep from my eyes.

'Emma, I'm outside. It's Melanie. She's had an accident and is in A&E. I had a call fifteen minutes ago and they've asked if I can go. Will you come with me, please?'

'Of course. Let me just get dressed. Give me two minutes.'

I had so many questions running through my head as I grabbed the jeans and a jumper I'd worn the night before, giving them a sniff before I put them on to make sure they'd be OK. Wiping under my eyes in case I had panda eyes from last night's mascara, I grabbed my handbag and stuffed my feet into trainers as I walked out the door towards Tom's car. As I clocked my own reflection in the passenger window, I realised what a state I looked; I hadn't even brushed my hair before rushing out. I hoped that I'd left my make-up bag and a hair clip in my handbag.

Tom smiled at me as I got in, but the smile didn't reach his eyes. He handed me a travel mug. 'I know you need a coffee in the morning to wake you up. I'm sorry to alarm you in that way, but I didn't want to go alone and I rather hoped you'd want to come with me.'

'Of course.' I patted his hand. It didn't seem the appropriate time to ask why the hospital had called him of all people and I was still wondering why Melanie wasn't annoyed at him last night, directing all her venom at me. Her words had really hit home. They were everything I'd been expecting from people. I felt hurt but more than anything I'd felt shame. That I had no right to the happiness that my friends told me that I should have. That what she'd said to me must have been what everyone was thinking every time they looked at me.

We hardly spoke on the half-hour journey. Every time I glanced at Tom, he had a frown on his face and was clearly concentrating on his driving, judging by the force with which he was gripping the steering wheel. When we pulled up at the hospital, with it being a Saturday morning, the car park was reasonably empty.

Tom gave me a pinched smile. One of the very few things he had said in the car was that Melanie had asked the hospital staff to call him, because she had no one else and he was her best friend. But he also said that they wouldn't give him any other details about her injuries apart from the fact there'd been an incident the night before.

We checked into the hospital reception and were told to take a seat and when I glanced up I saw Demetri across the room. I practically ran over to him and explained what had happened and he said he would find out what the situation was. He soon returned and asked us to follow him. Tom and I looked at each other and he shrugged. He knew as little as I did.

He led us out of the reception area, and down a long, brightly lit corridor where he finally stopped and pulled back the curtain of a large cubicle. 'Here you go. I've quickly checked her notes, she's got a broken arm, a broken leg and concussion. She's had some painkillers so is sleeping it off. She'll have a banging headache when she wakes up but it'll be nice for her to have someone here.'

'Do you know what happened to her?' I asked. 'Did she have a fall? A car accident? Was she attacked?'

'Let me go and see what else I can find out. I want to make sure that I'm giving you the correct information.' He wandered over to the nurses' station and sat down behind a computer and began tapping away.

Melanie looked awful. Her face was full of cuts and bruises and even though she was sleeping, you could see that she was in pain as when she tried to move, even in her sleep-induced state, she winced. We still had no idea as to why she was here and in this state. Hopefully when Demetri returned, he'd have found out more details. Tom and I sat in silence either side of her bed. My heart was beating ten to the dozen and despite wanting to obviously make sure that she was OK and wanting to be here for her, it suddenly struck me that we'd probably have to cancel the panto. We couldn't go on without our leading lady.

Suddenly a loud, piercing scream from down the corridor cut into my thoughts and I looked at Tom, whose face was totally startled.

'Calm down, you mad cow! And breathe.' The male voice sounded incredibly panicky and stressed.

Tom's face had gone deathly white.

That scream cut through me like a knife.

A venomous woman's voice could be heard above the hubbub of the busy A&E department.

'Get away from me, you sex maniac impregnator. It's all your fault. It can't come yet. It's way too early. Argh!'

Tom jumped up. 'I'd know that voice anywhere.'

The penny dropped and we both spoke at the same time.

'Stephanie!'

He looked back towards me and then at Melanie who was somehow sleeping through all the commotion. I smiled at him.

'Go to Stephanie. I'll stay here. I'll be here when she wakes up. Go and meet your grandchild.'

47

'My head.' A croaking voice no louder than a whisper from the bed next to me stopped me scrolling on my phone.

I moved closer and took her hand.

'It's OK, Melanie. It's Emma. I'm here.'

A tear rolled down her cheek.

'Oh, Emma. What are you doing here? Where's Tom?'

'Well, there's a story. While we were waiting for you to wake up, Stephanie was rushed in. Not sure what's happening, to be honest, but Tom is with her.'

'Oh no, I hope everything is OK with the baby.'

'Yeah, me too,' I replied. 'Only time will tell.'

'You're the last person I expected to be seeing by my beside after last night.' The tears continued to fall down Melanie's cheeks.

'Well, I can go if you like. If me being here is bothering you, let me know.' I started to pull my hand away but she gave a tug and squeezed it tightly.

'Please stay.'

I sat back down again.

'Thank you,' she whispered.

'Do you remember what happened?' I asked.

'Vividly, sadly.' She squeezed her eyes shut and then winced. The left side of her face was badly bruised and she had an egg-shaped lump which was getting bigger by the second just under her eye.

'Do you want to talk about it?'

She gave an exaggerated sigh.

'When I left the church hall, I went to see my ex-husband.' My own eyes widened at that point. After what she'd confessed to me that day in the café, I didn't think she'd ever go near him again. 'I was all fired up and thought I'd go round and give him a piece of my mind. When I arrived, I let myself into the house. He hadn't got the sense to change the locks. What I hadn't noticed was there were two cars on the drive and when I walked into the lounge, there he was, all cuddled up on the sofa with a girl young enough to be his daughter. I was fucking furious, Emma.'

'I'm not surprised.' Melanie must have been beside herself with anger.

'I started picking things up and throwing them at him. Anything I could. Vases, glasses, plates.' She grinned slightly and then grimaced at the pain. 'Then as quickly as the rage entered my body, it seemed to leave again. I looked at him cowering on the floor and was glad that I'd picked up the courage to leave him. I felt satisfied that I'd had my revenge. That finally he feared me in the way that I used to be scared of him. And it was then that I realised that it was a horrible feeling. Why would any human being want another to fear them? So, I left.'

Poor Melanie. I looked at her with fresh eyes now. She was just a woman trying to get through life in the best way that she knew how – like all of us. We could only ever do what we thought was right. It might be right, it might be wrong, but it was what it was. However, I was confused. How had she ended up in the state she was in? Surely he hadn't come after her? I wanted her to tell me in her own time. Didn't want to push her, so tried really hard not to jump in with questions of my own.

'I drove away from the house, my mind full of what could have been and what might have been. My phone started ringing in my handbag and I only glanced over to see if I could see it and I never saw the lorry that was on the wrong side of the road, not until it was right in front of me. I swerved to miss it and the last thing I remember was seeing a tree in front of me in the headlights.'

The trauma in her eyes was totally obvious and the tears flowed more freely.

'Thank God I blacked out at that point and the next thing I knew it was 5 a.m. and I was waking up in here. When they asked me who they could contact, I realised that the only person I could call was Tom.'

At that point Demetri walked back into the cubicle, picking up on our conversation.

'All that matters now is that you are OK. I know you have broken bones and cuts and bruises but they'll heal. The lorry driver hardly has a scratch on him. And he'd love to apologise to you at some point but I've sent him home and told him to stay away. Emma, are you OK to stay with Melanie for a while?'

'Of course.' He swiped the cubicle curtain closed behind him.

'I'm so sorry, Emma, for everything. I've let you down.'

'How have you let me down, Melanie?' Suddenly it dawned on me. The panto was that night.

'You have no Cindy for the panto?' Hearing it aloud gave me a sharp shooting pain in my head.

At that point, Tom poked his head through a gap in the curtain.

'Oh, great, you're awake. I thought I heard voices. How are you? What happened?'

'Oh, don't worry about me. I'll explain later, or Emma can. How is Stephanie?' she asked. She was struggling to keep her eyes open, still bearing the after-effects of some quite heavy painkillers, I presumed.

'We're just waiting for the doctor now. I hope the baby isn't in distress,' he explained.

'It's probably important that you stay calm, Tom, she's going to be feeling quite anxious, I would think.' I put my hand on his arm to try to ease his own anxiety.

'But what if they end up doing an emergency C-section?'

I felt a little dizzy, the events of the morning catching up with me.

'I'm sorry, Emma, but not only do you not have a leading lady, it doesn't look like you have a leading man either. She's made me promise not to leave her.'

'Don't worry, Tom, just go and be with your daughter. She needs you.' He leaned through and kissed my lips.

'Thank you. Oh, and hi, Melanie. It's good to see you awake. I'll be back as soon as I can.'

It was then that I fainted.

48

The next thing I knew, I came to and was slumped in my chair and Demetri was checking my pulse.

'Welcome back, Emma. Don't worry. You just passed out for a second or two. Just sit still and get your strength back. I'm going to run a few tests to get you checked over thoroughly.'

'I'm fine, honestly. I just came out in a rush and then the stress of everything got to me. Please don't fuss.'

'I'm a doctor, Emma. It's literally my job to fuss over you. Your heart rate has come down significantly. I'll go and get you some water.'

'Blimey, he's rather nice. Well, from what I can see out of my squinty eye.' Melanie's right eye was now really starting to swell and turn an unusual shade of reddy-purple.

'He's lovely. He's Michelle's boyfriend. Well, I think that's what he is. Not sure they've named it. Such a nice man.' I smiled at him when he returned and thanked him for passing me a cup of water. 'Honestly, Demetri, I feel so much better now. It's just been one hell of a morning. I've got no leading lady and no leading man. We're going to have to cancel the panto.'

'Surely there's another way, Emma. The baby could come at any time now and Tom could still make it. But we do need to think of a backup plan.'

'We'd better come up with something bloody quickly because this panto is supposed to be happening in less than twelve hours.'

I closed my eyes, pondering how we were ever going to get out of this situation. I looked over at Melanie as I heard her let out a little giggle. I wasn't sure what she had to laugh about in the circumstances. She looked dreadful; it's a good job that there wasn't a mirror. She'd have been mortified.

'Who'd have thought this would happen? What a palaver.'

'A bloody great mess,' I replied.

We both started to laugh and before long there were tears streaming down both of our faces. Neither of us was sure why, but I think it might have been our similar states of hysteria.

As I wiped my tears away, I got my notebook out of my handbag.

Making lists was my way of making sense of everything and I needed to write my thoughts down now in a mind map. All the things we'd have to do if we cancelled.

'I might have to leave you soon, Melanie, but I'll come back later. There's a lot that needs to be sorted out.'

'Emma, I know that you and I have never seen eye to eye... but...'

I shifted in my seat. This was not a conversation I felt comfortable having.

'I admire you so much.' Now that was a sentence I wasn't expecting to hear from Melanie. She could clearly see the shock on my face. 'I really do. Look at everything you've achieved. You have an idea and you put it into action. Look at all the people you've helped in the Lonely Hearts Club.'

'That's not hard though. It's just about sorting out some venues and arranging for people to meet up,' I explained.

'It might not be hard to you, Emma, but the thing that sets you apart from other people is that you actually get off your backside and do stuff. Lots of other people sit moaning that there's nothing for them to do, but you don't. You get on with it and you've had so much success. On that walk the other day everyone was talking about how amazing you were.'

'Well, that's very nice of them to say. But I'm really nothing special.'

'But that's the bit that I'm trying to say. You *are* something special. But you just don't see it. I wish I could be more like you.'

I couldn't believe that Melanie was praising me like this. It didn't seem real.

'You know, Emma, the panto could still go ahead.'

I frowned at her. That concussion must be making her delirious.

'There's no one else that knows the lines of every character in the play off by heart like you do. You must have some sort of photographic memory.' I laughed, aware of the fact that most days I couldn't even remember what I'd had for dinner the night before. 'You just need to play the part of Cindy.'

My head spun round to face her. 'I can't!'

'Why ever not? You know every word. We've been through it tons of times. You're word perfect. And I'm sure the dress will fit you, albeit a bit long. But we're a similar size.'

I did think that Melanie was being overly kind. She was way slimmer than me.

'I'm a size fourteen,' I replied.

'Excellent, so am I!'

She was such a liar!

'I'm still not doing it,' I insisted. 'I don't do front of stage. I'm firmly behind the scenes.'

'But you're perfect, Emma. You'll make a brilliant Cindy and a fabulous princess at the end. You're beautiful. And who better to play alongside than your lovely Tom?'

'Why are you suddenly being so nice to me? Last night you were telling me I was selfish and taking advantage of Tom. What's changed?'

She looked down at her hands, one of which was at the end of a cast.

'I have to confess that I'm a complete and utter jealous idiot.'

I rubbed at my forehead. All this talk was making me uneasy.

'I was just feeling bitter and twisted and I took it out on you. Tom and I have spent a lot of time together over the last few weeks and at first I thought maybe something might happen between us. He is such a lovely man and everything that my husband wasn't, but all he could ever talk about was you. Emma this. Emma that.' She said that last bit in a whiny high-pitched voice and bobbed her head from side to side for extra dramatic effect. However, it clearly hurt her to do that as she grimaced at the pain.

'Did he say it just like that too?' I asked. We both laughed again. A little bit of me couldn't believe that I was sitting here once more in A&E, this time with Melanie and we were in a terrible mess, with no solution and we were both finding it funny.

'I owe you the hugest apology, Emma. What I said last night was not only untrue but also completely out of line and I hope that one day you can forgive me for saying it. When I was driving over to my ex-husband's I was thinking about you both. You're such a lovely person, always doing things for others, the least selfish person I know, despite my little outburst. And Tom is also just as lovely. He's been a really good friend to me and I mistook that for something it wasn't. He stopped me right at the start and said he only had eyes for you and that he'd been in love with you for the whole of his life.'

'Oh.' It was the only word that I could think of.

'Life is short, Emma. You and Tom are perfect for each other and I hope you do try to make a go of it. I can see it in the local paper or that county magazine. School sweethearts meeting up years later and all because of the Lonely Hearts Club. If you hadn't set the club up, Stephanie wouldn't have invited her dad along and you wouldn't have met up. It was meant to be.'

I hadn't even thought of it like that. I suppose when she said it out loud in that way, it *was* a great inspirational story. That life is messy and uncertain, you can be grieving over the loss of a loved one in one moment and then it can flip on a coin and become fabulous and full of love and joy the next. Maybe it's that unpredictability that makes life interesting and keeps us full of hope. Keeps our faith in humanity. No one knows what the future holds, but when it does offer something that fills you with joy, you should grasp it with both hands and never let it go. Live like it's your last day, as the saying goes.

Tom's head appeared around the cubicle curtain.

'Panic over. Very early and irregular contractions, apparently, but not dilated so they're sending her home. She's been checked over and all is fine with the baby. So she just has to go home and wait. Blimey. That was all a bit scary! Be back shortly; they'll be releasing her soon. Just doing the paperwork.'

What a morning it had been. My head was in overwhelm with the intensity of everything that had gone on.

'Err... Emma... Back in the room. Are you going to do it or not? There's a princess dress with your name on it, a Prince

Charming ready to sweep you off your feet and over two hundred people expecting a panto tonight. And it all depends on you. Go shine your big beautiful bright light over that audience. You will absolutely smash it out of the park. You don't deserve to stand in the shadows. You deserve the best. Go and be the leading lady of your own life.'

49

As I was waiting for Tom to take me back to Sandpiper Shore, I wrapped my coat tighter around me against the cold. The temperature seemed to have dropped quite dramatically again. My mind was all over the place, thinking about the morning.

Tom surprised me when he nudged into my side.

I rubbed his arm. 'Are you OK?'

He pulled me into a hug and squeezed me tightly, releasing a big breath. 'I am now.'

'So, what's the plan? Do you still need this Prince Charming or did you replace me?' He pushed out his bottom lip and fluttered his eyelashes.

'How could I ever replace you?' I replied. 'But are you sure you're up to it, Tom? You're going to be a grandfather pretty soon. I know at your age you have to be careful.'

He bumped my shoulder again. 'Cheeky. Come on, let's get you back.' He looked up at the sky. 'Don't know about you but that sky looks full of snow to me.'

As I stared out the window at the beautiful Cornish countryside, I wondered whether if it snowed we would have to cancel.

Sandpiper Shore was a nightmare in the winter, for some reason it was known for huge snow drifts and got completely cut off and people wouldn't be able to get in or out of the village. It could cause havoc for the panto. I looked upwards and gave a silent prayer for it not to snow until tomorrow.

'In all the excitement, I forgot to tell you that when you popped to the loo, I talked to Melanie and she told me that she'd suggested that you took the role of Cindy but you said you couldn't. Have you had any more thoughts about that? The show can't go ahead without the main character.'

I'd thought about nothing else since Melanie had suggested it. There were times in life when something scared the living daylights out of you and there wasn't a cat in hell's chance that you were going to take a risk. There were other times when you just had to tell yourself you can be your own superhero and go and be brave.

I took a deep breath before replying.

'Funny you should say that! I can assure you that Cindy *will* go to the ball.'

50

Tom dropped me at home and I had the quickest shower of my life. I left my hair to dry naturally and luckily for me, for once, it behaved beautifully and dried into perfectly formed waves. Perfect for me as at the start of the play, I would appear in a scene where I was scrubbing floors. When I looked out of the window, there were a few flakes of snow in the air. I checked the forecast and it said that there was definitely going to be snow but not until tomorrow. Thank goodness for that. The last thing we needed was bad weather to stop the performance going ahead. It seemed like the universe was throwing all it could at our event to challenge us.

As I walked down to the church hall, I pulled my coat closer and tied my scarf around my neck. The temperature had dropped dramatically and there were even more flakes drifting down. I couldn't help feeling a little like I was missing something vital, but I couldn't put my finger on what. Everything I needed was at the church hall already. I now just had to hope that Melanie's costumes would fit me, although we had tons of time and Aggie was meeting me there so that we could make any minor adjustments that would be needed.

'Emma! Emma!' Ruby's excited little voice greeted me as soon as I arrived. She was practically jumping up and down on the spot. 'How do I look?'

I stood up straight and put my finger to my lips. 'Mmm... now let me see...' As I circled her slowly, I connected eyes with her mother across the room and winked. She grinned widely. Next to her was a man in a wheelchair and a nurse stood at his other shoulder. As Ruby was the spitting image of this man, there was no way it could be anyone but her father. I was so glad that he'd got the opportunity to come along.

Sarah's brother, as promised, had arranged to have the whole event live streamed so friends and relatives of the cast from around the country would be able to watch online. The daily sign-up numbers were incredible and increasing by the minute, especially since Scott and a couple of his ex-teammates had posted about it on their social media.

'Come on, come on,' Ruby urged me.

'I'm sorry, Ruby, but a show producer can't be rushed. Now could you do something for me, please?'

'Anything.'

'Excellent. Could you wave your wand around and do a little twirl, do you think?'

'Bwilliant. I've been pwactising my twirls special like. Just watch me. Wheeeeeee!' She spun around and I kept my face serious despite wanting to break out in a smile.

'And one more thing. Who is this man in the wheelchair?' I asked.

'That's easy. That's my daddy. He's nearly better and he's not really allowed out but Mummy's friend is a nurse at the hospital he's in and she arranged for him to have a couple of hours out so he could come and watch me.'

'OK, so do you think your daddy would mind if he helped me judge your fairyness? I think I might need a second opinion.'

Ruby ran up to her father and flung her arms around him. I went and stood by their side.

'Careful, poppet. We still must be very careful around Daddy,' her mother explained.

'I know, I know, but I've just missed you so much, Daddy.' She squeezed his arm and leant forward and whispered in his ear. He kept a very straight face.

'So, Daddy,' I said. 'Can I call you Daddy?'

'You're silly, Emma, he's my daddy, not yours.'

'I'm so sorry, Ruby, I thought that was his actual name.'

She laughed.

'His name is Matt. That's what other adults call him.'

'OK, excellent. So, Matt, I wonder if you could help me. It would appear that Ruby, our fairy assistant for the evening, would like us to mark her ten out of ten for fairyness. Could I ask you what you think?'

'It's a ten from me,' he replied, grinning. She put her thumbs up to him and wrinkled her nose. 'Thanks, Daddy.'

'I'm sorry to say it's *not* a ten from me.' I bent down to her level. Her smile dropped and I thought she was going to burst into tears. I thought my little joke had gone on for long enough. 'I think you are a... let me see... nine...'

Her face dropped even further.

I held my finger up. 'Wait!' She took a big breath and held it in, eager eyes awaiting my next words. 'I was going to say nine hundred and ninety nine out of ten.'

Ruby punched the air and then threw her little arms around my neck, squeezing so hard I thought she might break a bone.

'Thank you, thank you, thank you. You've made all my dreams come true, Emma. I love you so much.'

My insides filled with little red hearts like those on a social media post that fly up the screen. What a very special little girl this was and how delighted I was that we were able to make a simple dream like this come true. As she looked over my shoulder through the window, she screamed right down my ear and made me jump.

'Yay, it's snowing like mad.'

I groaned. We did not need it to snow yet. I willed the universe to be kind.

* * *

As I looked out from behind the side curtain, my anxiety levels were at an all-time high. For the last half an hour, people had been arriving, shaking off snow from their coats and hanging them over the radiators to dry. The room was full and I did a double take when I saw three England players on the front row. They must have been there to support Scott. That was amazing. Ruby and the Fairy Godmother were selling raffle tickets and when they headed back from being in that row, Ruby waved three fifty-pound notes in the air at me and grinned widely before placing them in the bucket.

I looked at my watch and headed backstage and rang a bell.

'Five minutes till the curtains go up, folks. Everyone ready to take their places?'

There were nods, whispers and shuffling sounds all round.

Graham was heading my way. I couldn't take him seriously in that outfit but I had to try to when he asked if he could have a quick word.

'I just wanted to wish you luck, my love. You're wonderful

and we didn't really give you a choice in the matter but to do this for us. I just wanted to say thank you. From the bottom of my heart. Which is incidentally much better, by the way, according to my GP. He's sat somewhere on the front row, I think. Let me look.' He peered around the curtain to see if he could spot him.

When he closed the curtain, he turned to me. 'Yes, he's right there. Another one in the front row. Next to the bishop.' He put his head in his hands and I thought he was upset but when he pulled his hands away he was laughing. 'Oh, bollocks, don't let me laugh. My mascara will run.'

Little did I ever imagine those words to come from the mouth of the Sandpiper Shore vicar. I wasn't sure whether it was worse that he'd sworn or mentioned the fact that he might make a mess of his mascara.

I put my fingers under each of his eyes and told him to blink the tears away. They fell onto my fingers and I wiped them on my dress. It was meant to look grubby anyway.

'You, Emma, are a bloody marvel. Break a leg, darling.' He air-kissed me, saying that he didn't want to make a mess of his make-up, and he walked away to the dressing room, blinking his false eyelashes dramatically.

Those five minutes flew by and finally it was time. It was time for another deep breath and then it was all stations go.

51

Our Fairy Godmother, Michelle, and her fairy assistant, Ruby, entered the stage from the left, holding hands in front of the long red velvet curtains.

'Good evening, everyone. We'd like to say a huge thank you to everyone for coming along tonight to see Sandpiper Shore's first-ever pantomime.' There was a round of applause from the audience. 'And now I'd like to introduce you to Ruby, my beautiful fairy assistant.'

She looked to Ruby and nodded her head. Ruby threw back her shoulders, proudly pushed out her chest, took a massive and loud deep breath and nodded back at her.

'Good evening, Sandpiper Shore.' She took a little curtsey and then, seeing her mum and dad at the end of the front row, she gave them a toothy grin and waved.

'All the money waised this evening will go to the Cornish Air Ambwance. So please do donate lots and lots.' She circled her index finger and then pointed to the footballers in the front row. 'Specially you!'

The crowd roared with laughter, and we all heaved a sigh of

relief, knowing that we were off to a good start. We just had to keep it up.

Ruby and Michelle had the audience eating out of their hands as they introduced the story, giving some background to Cindy's situation and how awful her stepsisters were to her.

And when Michelle stepped away from Ruby and she sang 'Shake It Off', this time she got all the words right and was far more in tune than she had been before. She'd clearly been practising. She left the stage to rapturous applause.

I was so proud of this super little six-year-old girl who'd had the courage to ask to be part of something that she'd always dreamed of. I took my own deep breath and channelled my inner Ruby as the curtains opened. My own teenage dream of being an actress, even though I was now a middle-aged menopausal woman, was about to come true.

52

The crowd roared as the main characters held hands and took a bow. Then they roared twice as loud when Michelle and Ruby joined us. Ruby was beside herself with excitement and I don't think she'd ever sleep again. When I looked over at her parents, they were both shedding the proudest of tears.

We took one last bow and left the stage. Everyone was laughing and in such good spirits. There was half of me that was glad it was over and done with, yet the other half wanted to go and do it all over again. It was everything that I dreamed it would be.

I thought back to the best moments of the performance. There were laughs all round when the ugly sisters made me do all the housework, and I said it was just like being married.

When Tom, aka Prince Charming, found a sparkly trainer that Cindy had left behind and I explained to the audience, 'What middle-aged lady do you know who goes out without wearing a pair of trainers and a denim jacket even if it is with a ball gown?'

And when Prince Charming realised that the trainer fitted

Cindy, and he said he'd come to rescue her and asked her to marry him, I replied, 'I don't need a man to be happy. I'm a strong independent woman and I'm perfectly capable of rescuing myself, thank you very much.'

When Prince Charming proposed to Cindy, she also had an important question for him. 'And can I ask whether you'd mind signing a prenup before I agree to anything?' When the prince agreed, Cindy then asked if he was prepared to put the bins out on a Thursday night and mow the lawns to which he asked about equality and she responded that she only wanted equality when it suited her.

Graham and Bill got brilliant cheers for their performances as Ant and Dak and while everyone should have hated them, they collectively loved them instead.

It was just a fantastic experience all round and one that would stay with me till the end of my time on earth.

When a grey-haired old lady with a walking stick hobbled towards me, I narrowed my eyes. I thought I recognised her and was trying to place where from. It was only when she opened her mouth that I realised who she was, even though she only spoke two words.

'Hello, Emma.'

'Oh, my goodness. Mrs Dawes. It's been years since I've seen you. How are you? You are looking wonderful, by the way.'

'Emma, Emma, Emma. I hope you've been doing amateur dramatics all your life. You were absolutely made for this life. You were amazing.'

'Ah, sadly not. Since college I've never even dabbled. I'm better behind the scenes.'

'Well, I hope you realise now that that's totally untrue, my dear. When I was doing the filming of all our plays at college, I knew that you should have continued being an actress. You had huge potential, you know.'

'It was you who did the filming then? We watched it recently and saw all the shenanigans that followed. We wondered who was behind the camera.'

She tapped the side of her nose.

'Sometimes it's the things that you see from behind the camera that are the most significant. Powerful stuff when you see it all put together when you're not there, eh? I hoped that seeing yourself on stage might encourage you to continue. I can't actually believe that it took this many years for you to see it. I asked Julie to pass it on to you. I should have known better, really. She always was a little madam, that one.'

It was good to finally know who was behind the filming. The mystery had been solved.

'I knew you could do it, Emma. I always believed in you. I just wanted you to believe in yourself.' She reached across and gave me a hug. She smelled exactly how I remembered her. Lily of the Valley perfume and cigarettes. A heady mix.

Tom wandered over to us.

'Tom Sullivan. Still an idiot, are you?'

He grinned. 'Probably.'

'You will be if you let this one go.' She nodded at me. He came and stood next to me, taking my hand.

'I let her go once, Mrs Dawes. I am not going to let her get away a second time.'

She patted his arm. 'Glad to hear it, son. And don't ever let this woman hide in the shadows. She deserves to be the centre of attention. Always! Goodnight, you two. My son is going to take me home now. It's been so lovely to see you both.'

Tom turned to me and kissed me again, not caring who was

around. Mid-kiss we realised that someone was shouting his name.

When we broke apart, his son-in-law, Martin, stood before us.

'Tom. Stephanie's waters have just broken. We need to get her to hospital. But...'

Tom went into full on caring dad mode. 'I'll go and bring the car round. I'll drive you there myself. You can sit in the back with her.'

'Yeah, sorry, folks, but that's not looking likely, to be honest.' All three faces dropped to the floor at the words that came out of Graham's mouth. 'While we've been in here, it's been snowing like mad outside and we're snowed in. Nobody can leave the church hall.'

53

I jumped back up on the stage and started to bang a metal container. 'Is there a nurse or a doctor in the house?' I shouted. 'We have an issue that we need some help with.'

As if by magic, Demetri appeared with Michelle by his side. He'd only just arrived after missing the whole performance.

'Dr Hottie to the rescue,' she grinned.

'How can I help?' he asked.

'Have you ever delivered a baby?' Stephanie asked, holding her stomach and groaning loudly.

He rolled his sleeves up. 'I'm an A&E doctor. What do you think?' he grinned. 'Can someone call an ambulance, please, and tell them that I am with her. Also, in the meantime, just in case baby doesn't want to hang on, we'll need towels and hot water. Emma, Michelle; can you help me in the kitchen, please?' His calm demeanour gave me some relief from the panic I was feeling and I'm sure gave Stephanie and Martin some comfort too.

Once in the kitchen, Demetri started to open cupboard doors and pull towels out and run the taps at the sink before grabbing the hand soap and washing his hands. Michelle turned to him. 'So how many babies *have* you delivered?'

Demetri pursed his lips, probably trying to remember the exact number.

Michelle narrowed her eyes at him, trying to work out what he wasn't saying.

'None,' he replied. 'But I've watched all twenty series of *Grey's Anatomy*.' He winked at her as he dried his hands on a clean tea towel and carried an armful of towels through to the main hall. 'I mean, how hard can it be?'

'Shit the bed,' Michelle said as she fanned herself with her hand and followed him. 'How amazingly hot is that man right now?'

I laughed nervously, panic rising within me. 'I think we'd better hope that the ambulance has got a snow plough with it and they can get through.'

54

'This baby is in a bit of a rush to get out, Stephanie. I need you to stay calm and breathe, short sharp breaths.' Demetri was cool and exuded an air of confidence. You would never have thought that he'd not done this before. His phone rang and he answered it, with a few ums and ahs in the conversation.

'The road is closed into Sandpiper Shore. There's a tree down and the ambulance can't get through.' He locked eyes with Stephanie. 'So, it's you and me. We've got this. OK?'

She hesitated, then nodded. 'I really want to push.'

'OK, if you can, try not to push right now, Stephanie. Let's give this lady some privacy, folks. We have a baby to deliver. Mum and Dad only, thank you.'

Stephanie shouted out to Tom. 'Dad. Dad. Where are you? I want my mum.' A tear slid down her face.

He grabbed her hand and squeezed it tight. 'I'm here, love, and I know you do, darling.' He mouthed to me, 'I was kind of waiting for this to happen.'

'Will you stay with me, Dad? Please.'

Tom's face was an absolute picture but he clearly put his own thoughts to one side.

'Of course I will, darling, but do you mind if I stay up near your head? I don't fancy being down the business end.'

I laughed as I walked away.

Stephanie shouted again, 'Where do you think you're going?'

'Just off to help everyone clear up and give you some privacy. I won't be far away.'

'Get yourself back here, lady. If we're doing this, you're helping too.'

'Oh, great, so I have to stay down this end then, I suppose.'

All three of us laughed at the expression on Martin's face as he then screamed out. 'Oh! My! God! I can see something coming. That's disgusting.' He dry heaved.

'That's your baby, mate. I think you should probably be saying something nice maybe?' Demetri said to Martin, who had gone as white as a sheet.

'Thank you, Doctor. I'm going to name my baby after you to thank you for delivering him.'

Demetri smiled at Stephanie's words, as proud as punch at the thought.

'It's a boy?' Martin asked. 'Do you know for sure?' He squeezed his wife's hand.

'Just a feeling I have.'

At that moment, Kelly, my former neighbour, appeared shaking snow from her hair and removing her coat.

'I'd just got home from work and put the kettle on when there was a hammering at the door. One of the neighbours came and told me that Stephanie had gone into labour. It took me ages to get home so I've trudged through the snow to get here instead of trying to get the car back out. I've brought my midwifery bag of tricks. Can I help?'

The look of relief on Demetri's face was priceless and he stepped aside as she explained that she did this for a living.

'Midwives trump doctors any day. They're all yours.' He stood back and let Kelly step into the small group that had formed around Stephanie. Although he shouted over his shoulder, 'I hope that doesn't mean you've changed your mind about the name though,' before he wandered over to Michelle.

Kelly moved swiftly and efficiently to what Tom had called the business end and declared that this was quite common and that Stephanie had tipped into full, established labour, and was quickly fully dilated and would need to start pushing. Martin looked like he was going to throw up and Stephanie burst into tears.

* * *

We all stood around with bated breath, as we waited for some sort of noise from the bundle that Stephanie had delivered. Panic showed on everyone's faces except the midwife, who remained the epitome of calm and grace. After a second or two, a squawk filled the room, which would definitely give the local seagulls a run for their money.

After Kelly checked its heart, lungs and hips, she handed the baby to Stephanie. Martin's face was full of sheer awe, love and adoration for both his wife and his child.

'Aw, would you look at this bonny face,' Kelly cooed. 'Congratulations, you two. You have a beautiful baby daughter. Well done, Mum.' She winked at Stephanie. 'You did great.'

I hoped she hadn't heard Martin mutter to Demetri, 'I thought she said it was going to be a boy.'

Demetri shrugged. 'You can't argue with Mother Nature, mate.'

I noticed Tom wiping a tear from his face. This must be a really poignant time for him as well as the proud parents. I felt superfluous in that very personal intimate moment and didn't know whether to try to sneak away without being noticed.

'We need to keep baby warm so let's have some skin-to-skin contact with Mum.' Kelly's soft and melodious Irish lilt was the most calming influence on us all. Baby's mouth turned immediately to Stephanie's breast, the most natural instinct in the world kicking in on both sides. 'Ah, there she goes.'

Tom reached across and kissed his daughter on the top of her head.

'We'll leave you to it for a while, but we won't be far away. Well done, love. Your mum would be so proud of you.' His voice cracked on his final sentence and he turned away from his daughter.

I was struggling to process my own emotions so couldn't imagine how Tom must be feeling. We walked together towards the kitchen area and he closed the door behind us. I didn't know whether to speak or not, whether to reach out to him, or keep my hands by my side. His eyes found mine and I saw them fill with tears.

'I'll make some tea,' I said, not knowing what else to say or do. When I turned round, his lower lip was wobbling and he was clearly trying to hold himself back. I crossed the room and took him in my arms, as he sobbed.

55

A really good heart-to-heart session, which we had once we got back to mine that evening, was cathartic for Tom. He said that he'd been building up to it for a while. He still felt so incredibly sad that Julie wasn't there for this monumental moment but felt privileged that he was and was trying to enjoy it for what it was.

Kelly had done all her routine checks on Stephanie and the baby and said that they were both in fine shape and that as soon as the roads were clear enough to get the car out, she was very happy for them to go home, without a trip to hospital. The snow was turning to sleet as the temperatures lifted and she offered to go back with them to make sure they were settled and happy. We all laughed at Martin when he asked whether there was an instruction book that they got to take home.

Tom and I had sat up until the early hours and I tried hard to just listen and to let him share his emotions.

He pulled me close into his arms and snuggled up next to me.

'Thank you, Emma.' He breathed into my hair.

'What for? I haven't done anything,' I replied, puzzled.

'You've done so much, my love. You've been there to hold my hand through a really tough time. You've not put any pressure on me for anything at a time when I haven't really known what the pace should be. And more than anything, you've been a wonderful friend and you've listened to me when I needed to talk.'

I was a big believer that you shouldn't hold on to feelings like that in your body, otherwise they presented themselves in other ways, like illness. We both fell asleep on the sofa and when we woke up early the following day, the dastardly snow which had caused chaos for Sandpiper Shore had completely disappeared as if it had never happened.

* * *

The days in the lead-up to Christmas were lovely and such a contrast to my first year as a widow, when I felt sad and alone and had spent too much time wallowing in self-pity and my own miserable company.

There were a few outings we'd planned, from cinema trips in the evening, to garden centre visits in the daytimes. The carol service in the church was one of the most magical musical events I think I'd ever been to and Tina had even offered Ruby a solo performance of 'Silent Night' which went down a storm.

Tom and I spent Christmas Eve together at mine and I'd invited Jo and Seamus and Michelle and Demetri over for drinks and nibbles, although Demetri wasn't able to make it, as he was on shift at the hospital. Therefore, Jo and I spent the evening chatting to Michelle more than our own partners as we never wanted her to feel as if she was left out. We all knew how rubbish that could make you feel.

It was a sedate evening in the end, but lovely to be in the

company of true friends. They didn't stay late and Tom did stay over at mine.

As we sat on the floor under the fairy lights on the tree as they twinkled above us, we exchanged presents.

Tom smiled as he opened his parcel.

'Oh, Em. This is fabulous.' I'd bought him an easel, some paints, and a few different-sized canvases. He'd said a couple of times that he'd love to get back into painting for pleasure. The set design for the panto and his new-found lust for life had kick-started his long-lost passion again. 'No excuse now then. I honestly can't wait to use these.'

He handed his gift to me and I unwrapped the beautifully wrapped present, smiling as I realised what it was.

'*Romeo and Juliet.* My own copy.' I leaned across and kissed him tenderly before returning to the stunning edition of the play, running my fingers over the raised gold foil on the beautiful suedette cover. 'How thoughtful.'

He handed me an envelope too which, after frowning as he'd already given me one amazing present, I ripped open.

'Oh my God, Tom. This is incredible. Are you sure?'

He nodded, a smug expression on his face, clearly delighted with himself.

'I thought we could do with a long, romantic and maybe slightly dirty weekend away somewhere and where better than the place that *Romeo and Juliet* was set? We could even visit the Juliet balcony if you'd like to. There's a sunset food and wine tour too if you fancy that. Entirely up to you though.'

I was absolutely made up with the long weekend in Verona that he'd booked. It was thoughtful and romantic and I couldn't think of a present I could have loved more.

'I hope it's OK and not too presumptuous to book without asking you. I did confer with Michelle and Jo.'

'Obviously!' I laughed.

'They said you'd love it.'

I flung my arms around his neck and covered his face in tiny kisses.

'I do. And I love you.' The words were out before I could stop them and I gasped.

The grin that spread across Tom's face told me that there was no need.

'I didn't want to scare you off by telling you that I love you too. That was something I checked out with Michelle and Jo too.'

'Obviously!' we both said at the same time and as our bodies moved closer together, he lifted his hand to my face, his finger tracing the outline of my jaw and his eyes moved to my lips. When his lips met mine, we kissed passionately, and he lowered me to the floor, still snogging like a pair of teenagers. His hands were on my hips, and we both gasped when mine found the naked flesh of his ribcage under his shirt. Tom made me feel more alive than I'd ever felt in my life. Well, apart from thirty-five years ago when he made me feel exactly the same. I stifled the thought that this might have been the longest foreplay in history.

When he pulled back and questioned me with his eyes, my own nodded in approval and as we made love under the glow of the Christmas lights, it couldn't have been more perfect.

Maybe fate played a part in our lives. Maybe we were meant to be exactly where we were right then.

* * *

Tom spent Christmas Day with his family. We had both agreed that our plans would remain the same.

When they opened The Fisherman's Haunt, Stephanie and

Martin had decided that Christmas Day would be the one day of the year that they would close, to enable the staff to spend time with their families. They were back open again on Boxing Day and Tom and I had both said we would be on call for Stephanie if she needed us as Martin would be away from home for the majority of the day. Parental leave was a little shaky when it was your own business and Stephanie totally understood that. Tom said that she'd taken to motherhood like a duck to water, but like most new mums her hormones were all over the place. She swung between wanting to spend time with just her and the baby, and being totally overwhelmed with love, to not knowing what the hell to do when she wouldn't stop crying and needing some help.

We both felt that there was a fine line between interfering and being there to help and Tom was struggling a little to find the balance, especially when he loved seeing his daughter and granddaughter together. It was a work in progress for this family unit who were trying to find their way in a whole new world.

Michelle and I were invited to Jo's for Christmas day. Jo was already cooking when I arrived, with Seamus's support. Tessa and Bill had been picked up late morning and it was such a lovely, relaxed day spent with good friends. Michelle had been disappointed when Demetri told her he'd be working but was trying hard not to show that she missed him.

Tom joined us at seven thirty. Baby Demi had gone down peacefully for the first time in days, and Stephanie and Martin were nodding off on the sofa, so he covered them with a blanket and crept out to join us.

He came next to me on the sofa and whispered in my ear, making my spine tingle.

'God, I've missed you!' He sighed as he put his arm around my shoulder, pulling me close.

'You too, love. But you do realise that you've arrived just as the party games are about to start, don't you?' I smiled and melted when he looked deep into my eyes.

'I don't care what we do as long as I'm with you.'

It came out louder than he intended and Jo threw a dice at him and laughed.

'You might regret saying that, because you're up first and we're playing Twister.'

'Geriatric Twister, more like!' laughed Bill. 'I can get down but I might need some help to get up again. You playing, Tessa?'

Tessa shook her head.

'Not on your nelly, my friend. My old bones won't let me cavort around on the floor. I'll leave it for the young 'uns.' We all laughed, none of us in the room under fifty, so it was nice to be classed as younger. 'I'm saving myself for a good game of gin rummy later. Seamus, I don't suppose there's any more of that port and brandy left, is there? Nice little tipple that is.'

Bill had introduced Tessa to his favourite Christmas Day drink earlier in the day, citing that it was good for digestion and went well with cheese, biscuits and grapes after the Christmas pudding course, and her eyes lit up when she first sipped at the glass. She sat beside Jo on the sofa, their arms linked and her hand on top of Jo's like she never wanted to let go.

When it got to around eight o'clock, Seamus kept glancing at his phone a little mysteriously, frowning and starting to cough. It seemed a little fake and I wondered what he was up to. While Theo snuggled up against him, he asked Michelle to fetch him a glass of water from the kitchen. He claimed 'the law of the dog' which apparently meant that anyone who had a dog on their lap couldn't be disturbed.

We all jumped when an ear-piercing scream echoed from her in the next room but soon realised it was one of surprise and joy, when she returned hand in hand with Demetri, a huge grin on her face.

'I thought you were working,' she managed to stutter out, lost for words yet beaming all over her face. She then showered his face with kisses.

'Yeah, well, I was but it was really quiet so they let a few of us go home. I texted Seamus, wondering if he thought a surprise visit would be in order.'

Michelle mouthed thank you to Seamus from across the room, clinging onto Demetri's hand like her life depended on it.

'I am on call,' Demetri continued, 'so could get called back in for an emergency, so can't have a drink but... hey, I'm here and keep your fingers crossed that nothing major happens to call me back in.'

Michelle couldn't hide her excitement to have him beside her. It was lovely to see her finally giving in to her true emotions.

When Jo said that she'd go and put some food out, mainly to feed Demetri but also in case anyone was a bit peckish, there were groans all round from everyone else who said they were still full of a wonderful dinner. However, each and every one of us managed to polish off turkey, stuffing and cranberry sauce on thick crusty bread, with pigs in blankets and crispy roasties on the side. I mean, who could ever refuse leftover dinner on Christmas night?

When we fell into bed later, I curled up in the crook of Tom's arm and breathed a huge, contented sigh.

'OK there, love?' he asked. 'Had a nice day?'

'Perfect,' I replied.

He pressed a kiss against my hair.

'You?' I turned to face him. His eyes were closed and I heard a soft snore in response.

'Merry Christmas, darling,' I said and as I was falling asleep, I could feel that I had a smile on my face.

* * *

On Boxing Day morning, while Tom and I were strolling along the beach, hand in hand, we were stopped by Donna and Marnie, two of the ladies who came along to most of the Lonely Hearts Club meet ups. They'd got on like a house on fire since their first joint event and struck up a friendship, seeing each other outside of the group. It was lovely when this happened. As though a little bit of magical fairy dust had been sprinkled upon the members.

Marnie spoke first. 'I'm so glad we have run into you, Emma. I wanted to thank you on behalf of us all for everything that you had arranged recently but particularly for yesterday. You must have known there would be several of us that would be alone on Christmas Day. Organising lots of events so that people could pick and choose what they did was genius. I don't think there was anyone in the group who was alone.'

'That's so lovely to hear.'

Donna spoke next. 'With my family on the other side of the world, I thought it was going to be one of my loneliest days of the year. But we helped out at the soup kitchen after the Christmas morning service and then joined in the Christmas dinner at the church hall with Graham and Tina. We had such a wonderful day and there's lots to choose from over the next few days too. Thank you so much, Emma. If it wasn't for you, there'd be a lot of lonely people this Christmas. You are our own little Christmas angel.'

'You are so welcome, ladies. There's still lots more events to plan too, when I've had a bit of a rest. So, watch this space.'

Marnie grinned. 'Can't wait, and thanks again, Emma. You are a very special person and we're so glad we met you. Enjoy your day, both.'

'You too,' I whispered as they walked away in the opposite direction.

My heart filled with pride and delight. It was great to know that what I was doing made a difference to so many people. *That* was the purpose that I'd found over the last few months. Because I'd found Tom again, I was even more determined to help others. I was one of the lucky ones. There were still people who were alone, some happy to be, but still needing company. And I would continue to give them a little helping hand along the way to connect with like-minded people and form special friendships. After all, without friends, where would we be?

Tom slung his arm around my shoulders, pulling me close.

'I'm so proud of you.' He spoke into my hair.

'Do you know what, Tom? I'm pretty darn proud of myself right now.'

56

New Year's Eve had never been my favourite night of the year. I always felt like there was a lot of expectation surrounding it. People were always asking what you were doing. If you were doing nothing, because you were single, it made you feel even more sad and lonely than you already felt. Cementing the fact that you had no one to spend what some people classed as one of the most important dates in the calendar with.

Then there was the added pressure of people asking you what your resolutions are for the year ahead. To be honest, last year it was just getting through the year but it didn't seem right to admit that.

When Ben was alive, we spent the evening with his family mainly. He and his brother would drink a lot, I normally drove so remained sober. And our joint plans for the year ahead were always his ideas which I just went along with rather than jointly decided ones.

Last year I went to bed at 10 p.m. and shut the world outside. Jools Holland was getting on my nerves with his joviality and the party spirit of the presenters on the other channels wasn't floating my boat at all. I told myself that it was just another night and the sooner I went to bed, the sooner it would be over and I could start a new day; a new year.

This year, I was delighted to say, felt very different.

Graham and Tina had decided to have a grand party at the church hall and I'd been a little involved with the arrangements but not massively. After the intensity of being the organiser of the panto, and the Christmas events for the Lonely Hearts Club, I needed a bit of a break from it to ensure that I came back with some creativity and great ideas for the months ahead.

There was a knock at the door and I moved away from the breakfast bar to open it. Tom filled the doorway and just seeing his smile lit me from within. Whenever he said his signature, 'Hello, you,' my heart skipped a beat. When he reached across and kissed me tenderly, I took a deep breath, enjoying the moment. Kissing him had become one of my favourite pastimes.

We were in a really good place, still taking things slow, but life was good. I absolutely adored spending time with him. Tom had moved into his new home and I was helping him to decorate, what Stephanie called 'zhuzhing it up'. I stayed over there some nights, he stayed with me for some, and there were other nights that we stayed at our own places. We were both used to our own space and I was actually now really thriving in mine, continuing to get to know *me*. I'd come to realise that the most important relationship you had in life was the one you had with yourself.

Cocks on Friday nights with the girls were still going swimmingly, in fact this was the one concession of the year where the men were officially allowed to join us after we'd all spent the majority of the evening at the church hall. My friendship with Jo and Michelle was getting stronger each day.

Life was good.

'How are you getting on, love?' Tom asked, peering over my shoulder as I sat back down at the kitchen table.

I pulled the lid of my computer down slightly so he couldn't see what was on the screen.

'Nearly finished. Can you give me another ten minutes?'

'Sure. Mind if I put the TV on?'

I glanced at my watch. 'Not if you do that after you've made me one of your speciality G&Ts.' I don't know how he did it but he made the perfect drink. Maybe the magical element was love.

'You do realise that it's only just after 5 p.m., you big lush!' He laughed as he walked into the lounge.

When he returned, I saw him squint at my screen again. He had no chance of reading it anyway without his glasses but I didn't feel the need to point that out to him. He'd only recently had his first pair and was still a little self-conscious, getting used to being a wearer. If possible, I thought he looked even more handsome with them. With his short salt and pepper hair and his well-trimmed greying beard, he looked completely dashing.

He placed my drink beside me, gently kissed the top of my head and went into the lounge, plonking himself on the sofa, asking if there was anything in particular that I wanted to watch. I shook my head and smiled, not used to being asked. One of the other benefits of being alone, and yes, I was finally starting to think about benefits of being alone, was that you got to choose what you watched on the TV.

A few minutes later, I read through the words I'd typed one last time and when I didn't feel that I could do anything more to improve them, I emailed them off and closed the lid. I snuggled in next to Tom on the sofa and laid my head on his shoulder, smiling to myself at how comfortable I felt with this man.

'Are you going to let me read it?' he asked.

'Absolutely not. You can wait until it comes out like everyone else.'

He turned to face me and put his finger under my chin, tilting my head towards him.

'I'm so proud of you.'

My heart swelled. I wasn't sure in the past that that was a phrase I heard very often but Tom had said it to me on the night of the panto and again when I'd made my recent decision to take Fliss up on her offer of doing a column about loneliness. My first piece was due out in the New Year edition and I just hoped I'd got the tone and the topic on target. I was also due to host my first podcast in a few days' time. I was a little nervous but had the next few days to prepare myself as best as I could.

'Thank you. That means the world to me.'

He smiled. 'And you, Emma, mean the world to me.'

I don't think I'd ever, in my life, felt so *seen*. I couldn't stop smiling. Tom was a tonic for my soul. He bent to kiss my neck, and I could feel that he was smiling, knowing that he had discovered my weakness as I gave a little moan.

'I really should be getting ready,' I whispered.

'Yeah, I know, but I thought that maybe we could...'

Before he continued, I turned my head and kissed him.

'Well, maybe we have half an hour or so to spare.'

And right there in the glow of a million twinkling fairy lights, which we'd not only adorned the tree with but had strung up everywhere else we could, I showed him how much he meant to me too.

* * *

The church hall was rammed. The vicar was circulating between everyone while Tina was busy in the kitchen and we joined her as soon as we arrived, helping her to lay the food out which we'd prepared and taken down earlier that day. There was quite a lot of home-made stuff that folks had offered to take along and those who didn't have time to cook just bought something from the local mini market. May as well plough money back into the Sandpiper Shore economy.

Jo and Seamus had arrived a little later than us, as they went to collect Bill and Tessa and bring them to the party. Jo's relationship with her birth mother was thriving. They clearly adored each other despite a little bit of a rocky start and Jo wanted to spend as much time with her as possible to make up for all the time they'd missed out on over the years.

Michelle and Demetri walked in hand in hand, her eyes bright and sparkling, a big contrast to his which were dark and tired; this was his first night off in a nine-day continuous stint. When Michelle offered to stay in with him so that he could catch up on his sleep, he adamantly refused, claiming that this was his first New Year's Eve off in five years, and he was going to make the most of it.

Stephanie and Martin were next to arrive, pushing a pram containing their beautiful little girl Demi, who they'd still named after the doctor who very nearly delivered her. Her middle name was Kelly after the person who *actually* did. Demi was fast asleep and looked adorable wrapped up as snug as a bug in a rug.

Graham groaned loudly when he saw the bishop arrive.

'Oh, heck! When I invited him, I didn't think he'd come.'

I laughed as the bishop walked towards him.

'Good evening, Graham. I've not seen you since your performance in the pantomime. About that, by the way...'

'Evening, Bishop. I'm so sorry but I'm needed in the back

room.' Graham quickly excused himself. 'I'll catch up with you as soon as I can.'

I turned to the bishop and he smiled. Tina joined us.

'I think your husband is expecting me to tell him off when all I wanted to tell him was how fabulous I thought he was.'

'I'm sure he's not expecting you to say that but don't worry. It'll do him good to sweat a bit and think he's in trouble. Keep him on his toes.'

We all laughed and Tina took the bishop off towards the kitchen with the promise of some mulled wine.

The sound of a metal spoon clanking against the side of a glass quietened the excitable crowd and everyone turned to Graham, who was standing on the stage.

'Ladies and gentlemen. Welcome all and thank you for coming along this evening. Before we kick off the buffet, I'd just like to say a few words and a huge thank you.' He nodded at Tina, who materialised from the back of the kitchen with a huge bouquet of festive flowers.

'We have one very special lady to thank for our recent panto performance. To the lady who saved Sandpiper Shore – our very own Emma Montgomery. Emma, come on up here.'

I joined Graham and Tina on stage, where he continued with his words.

'I don't think Emma knows quite how amazing she is. In the space of eight weeks, she wrote, directed and oversaw our wonderful panto, *Cindy Rella*. She agreed under duress, but I think there was a little bit of her that thrived on the excitement, isn't that right, Emma?'

I laughed. 'Maybe...'

'Well, on behalf of the whole of Sandpiper Shore, I would like to say the hugest of thanks to you. I know that one of the reasons you agreed to do it was because the proceeds are going to the air ambulance.'

I nodded.

'We have a very special guest who has something that she'd like to give to you, for you to pass on to the charity.' He shaded his eyes with his hand, peering out to the audience, where little whirlwind Ruby was bouncing up and down at the front. 'Come on, poppet. Come and join us.'

Ruby thundered on stage waving a piece of paper around in her hand and flung herself at me, throwing her arms around my neck as I bent down to hug her.

'Thank you again, Emma, for making me a fairy assistant,' she whispered in my ear. 'I love you.'

My heart caught in my throat.

'So, Ruby, do you have something to give to Emma?'

She nodded and handed me piece of paper. It was a cheque made out to the air ambulance charity for fifty-five thousand pounds. I couldn't believe it and had to blink to make sure I was seeing the right amount.

'You can thank him for a lot of that.' She pointed to Scott, who was standing at the front with his arms around Aggie, their two children at their side. 'He made his friends cough up apparently. Said they earned shit-tons so could afford it.'

The whole crowd gasped and then laughed.

Scott shrugged his shoulders at me, laughing.

Ruby whispered. 'I started doing a sponsored sing and they told me if I stopped singing that they'd give me lots of money. How wude!'

I laughed.

'Your singing is... well... erm... legendary, Ruby. Well done.'

'Well, talking of which, the karaoke is about to start. Emma, will you come and sing with me?'

My heart started to thump. My brain started to pound. I didn't do karaoke. I'd even managed to wriggle out of singing in the lead role of Cindy by getting the whole cast involved in the number that Melanie was going to sing.

'Please, Emma.' She tugged at my hand. 'I'll sing anything you like.'

I took a deep breath, ready to refuse.

'Don't worry if you don't want to. Michelle and Jo said you'd say no.'

'Oh, they did, did they?'

Maybe it was time that, as well as surprising myself, I surprised my friends.

'Do you know any Take That, Rubes?' I laughed at her shocked face which then broke into a toothy grin.

'How about "Could It Be Magic"?'

'Perfect! Let's do this.'

I won't say it was the most confident I could be; my car singing sounded so much better, but I got through it. Nothing bad happened, nobody laughed, in fact the audience sang along, and it had actually been fun.

When Tom came over and asked me if I'd like to dance, and I took his hand, Michelle and Jo just stared at me, agog. I bobbed my tongue out at them both and Michelle laughed.

'Who are you and what have you done with our friend Emma?' Jo asked.

'Yeah, lady. I thought you didn't sing. Or dance,' Michelle piped up.

'Well, it appears that wonders will never cease. Now I do both,' I answered and they joined me in a group hug.

When 'Relight My Fire' came on, we screamed a little bit and Michelle ran off, yelling, 'I want to be Lulu!' leaving us all at the side of the dance floor, Tom laughing at her antics.

As I turned to him, his eyes softened and he mouthed, 'I love you.'

57

Even on a dark, cold and clear December night, with the glimmering stars above, the terrace at Jo's was still one of my favourite spots in the world. When we arrived, Seamus was just lighting the second of the two patio heaters and Demetri was mixing us a special drink to welcome in the new year.

As I meandered to the far end of the terrace, away from the others, I looked out to sea. I could see the lights of a boat on the horizon and stared hard at it, wondering who it might be, why they were out there at this time and what they were thinking.

Looking back at my friends, I knew that I was finally surrounded by people I loved and who loved me back for who I was, and my heart felt full.

I thought back to the final thing Mrs Dawes had said to me on the night of the panto. We chatted alone when Tom went off to the gents and she dished out words I'd never forget as long as I live.

'Emma, I hope you realise that your worth is not based on what you do for others. You have to love yourself for who you are. Only then are you truly free to let others love you too.'

I had held these words close to my heart since and always would.

* * *

I took a moment to collect my thoughts, lost in my own little world. Gazing out at the sailboat's lights twinkling away in the distance, I realised how much my life had changed over the last two years since Ben had gone. There had been times when I thought I'd never get out of bed. There were times when I never thought I'd recover; that the tears would never stop and my heart would never mend. But those moments had made me who I was today.

There were times when I'd felt sad that I'd never had children of my own and therefore thought that I'd never have the pleasure of grandchildren either. But when Stephanie told me that she was officially making me Demi's surrogate nana, my heart literally melted.

I'd learnt so much about myself over the last few months and for the first time in a very long time, I decided that instead of making resolutions, I would recognise these learnings and incorporate them into my everyday life.

The first would be *to be* myself and *to love* myself. Not everyone would like me, but I knew in my heart that I was a good, kind-hearted person, and if people didn't like me that was their business and not mine.

The second would be to trust myself to say no, when I really meant it. People would still like me. And if they didn't, again, that wasn't about me. I needed to protect myself and treat myself like I would treat a friend. I would spend time doing things I really wanted to do, things that made me happy. Stepping outside my comfort zone from time to time might just turn out to be great fun. I originally thought that I probably wouldn't ever sing again in public but when Graham announced that he would be holding Rock Choir every Tuesday evening, I thought what was the worst that could happen? Tom and I had also signed up to go to a Salsa class every Wednesday afternoon in the church hall starting in a couple of weeks. It seemed that I was still capable of surprising myself.

The third was to keep remembering those words of Mrs Dawes; that my worth is not based on what I do for others. If my friends think that it is, then they're not my real friends. Real friends are those who really understand and respect you. Who are there for you with no judgement. Friends just like Jo and Michelle.

The fourth was to realise that feelings are not facts. Emotions are deeply personal and incredibly powerful, but it is only when we rationalise these feelings that we can truly grow and move past them.

The fifth was to realise that you can be lonely at any point in your life and it doesn't always mean that's because you are alone. I was alone, however, and had been so desperately lonely since being widowed, and I could have wallowed endlessly, but I decided that it wasn't serving me to do that. Admitting my loneliness to others, since I'd been on my own, was life changing. Not just for me, but for the other people in the Lonely Hearts Club. I hadn't realised that there were so many lonely people in the world. So many wore masks to let others think they were OK. Through the group we had created a community of friends so that when people were feeling that way, there was always someone that they could do something with. Just looking at the Facebook group warmed my heart. Seeing conversations, invitations and photos of the group having fun made me feel so proud of all that we had achieved.

And the sixth was to remember that life is short and that it's here for living and loving. And no, the future can't be predicted but if you shut out love, then you'll miss out on so much pleasure in the meantime.

* * *

A hand on my shoulder brought me back to the present.

'It's time, darling.'

I stepped backwards and nestled against Tom, feeling his warmth not just in my body but in my heart too. Who would have thought that the first boy I ever fell in love with would be back in my life over thirty-five years later? Second chances don't come around often, and when they do, they are a true gift. We didn't know what the future held, but we were going to slowly explore it together and enjoy getting to know each other. We would help each other to heal. It wasn't all going to be sunshine and rainbows. There were going to be good times and possibly not so good times while we negotiated this new life. But I was now open to living life to the full.

Demetri handed me and Tom a glass as we joined our friends back at the seating area, then he slung his arm around Michelle's shoulders and pulled her in tight. She smiled up at him, totally besotted, and we knew that despite her trying to sabotage this relationship along the way, she had fallen totally and utterly under his spell.

'Are we all ready?' Seamus asked. He leant across and kissed Jo. I'd never seen a couple so comfortable in each other's presence. It was as if they were an extension of each other. Where one finished, the other began. It was such a pleasure to see her so happy.

I thought about these very special ladies and how recently

they'd come into my life, but felt like I'd known them for ever. It was true what they said, some friends were for a season, some for a reason and others for a lifetime. In Jo and Michelle, I had all three and I hoped that this would never change.

We counted down to a very significant year ahead for all of us.

'Five... four... three... two... one.'

Together, we clinked and raised our glasses, and in unison, six voices rang out into the cold clear night air as the stars twinkled above us, one shining brighter than all the others.

Tom's eyes found mine and he winked at me.

'Here's to us all and a fabulous New Year. Hip, hip, hooray!'

* * *

MORE FROM KIM NASH

The next book in the Sandpiper Shores series from Kim Nash is available to order now here:

https://mybook.to/SandpiperShores3BackAd

ACKNOWLEDGEMENTS

To Kelly Mottershead – thank you for being the best midwife I could have ever wanted when I was pregnant with Ollie. You literally changed my life and you know why! And for also giving me advice for this book when I needed Stephanie to go into labour and for certain things to happen at certain times to make the story work. You are an absolute gem Kelly!

To Michelle from Make New Friends. Thank you for being the inspiration behind me writing about friendship groups in the book. Thank you for all that you do for people who you don't even know. Not all angels have wings! You are definitely one of those! I hope you know how amazing you are. Your mum would be so proud of you and all that you have achieved. And I will come back to some events with you soon.

To my readers. You are the ones that keep me writing. Your wonderful messages spur me on, especially when I'm feeling that I'm the worst writer in the world. They mean the world. You will never know what impact you have when reaching out to an author to tell them how much you love their work. Thank you also for recommending my books. I'm so grateful to you for spreading the word to your book loving friends and within the reader community.

To the author friends who have supported and cheered me on over the years. To those who check in on me from time to time. You've been amazing.

To the Boldwood team. Thank you to each and every one of

you for all you do throughout the whole publishing process to bring my books into the hands and onto the electronic devices of readers.

To the freelancers who have also worked on my books. From the cover designer to the editors who pick up on all the things that I don't. And for reminding me that it's only people from the Midlands who say Mom! Thanks also to the audio narrators who bring my books to life.

A mahoosive thank you must go to my closest friends. I must be the luckiest person in the world to have the friends that I do. You make it easy for me to write about fabulous friendships in my books because you are my inspiration. I love you all.

To Bev and Steph. You've kept me (reasonably) sane over the last year or so. I appreciate all that you do for me so very much. Love you both to the moon and back.

To the Jenkins. We may be a tiny family, but we are mighty in strength when we work together. Here's to health and happiness for you all.

To Roni, my furry boy. I love you but if you could just stop bothering me when I'm writing, and barking at all and sundry that have the audacity to walk down our cul-de-sac, it would make it all happen so much quicker!

And last but never least, to my Ollie. I can't imagine my life when you weren't in it. You are, and will always be, my most favourite person in the world. Thank you for being you. Love you to the moon and back, and I'm so proud to call you my son.

ABOUT THE AUTHOR

Kim Nash is the author of uplifting, romantic fiction and an energetic blogger alongside her day job as Digital Publicity Director at Bookouture.

Download your exclusive bonus content from Kim Nash here:

Visit Kim's website: www.kimthebookworm.co.uk

Follow Kim on social media here:

facebook.com/KimTheBookWorm

x.com/KimTheBookworm

bookbub.com/authors/kim-nash

goodreads.com/kimnash

instagram.com/kimnashauthor

ALSO BY KIM NASH

The Cornish Cove Series

Hopeful Hearts at the Cornish Cove

Finding Family at the Cornish Cove

Making Memories at the Cornish Cove

The Bookshop at the Cornish Cove

Standalone

Amazing Grace

Escape to the Country

Sandpiper Shores

The Cornish Cottage by the Sea

Life Begins at the Cornish Cottage

BECOME A MEMBER OF

THE SHELF CARE CLUB

The home of Boldwood's book club reads.

Find uplifting reads, sunny escapes, cosy romances, family dramas and more!

Sign up to the newsletter
https://bit.ly/theshelfcareclub

Boldwood

Boldwood Books is an award-winning fiction publishing company seeking out the best stories from around the world.

Find out more at www.boldwoodbooks.com

Join our reader community for brilliant books, competitions and offers!

Follow us

@BoldwoodBooks

@TheBoldBookClub

Sign up to our weekly deals newsletter

https://bit.ly/BoldwoodBNewsletter

Printed in Dunstable, United Kingdom